PENGUIN CRIME FICTION

THE LONG DIVORCE

Edmund Crispin was born in 1921 and educated at Merchant Taylor's School and St. John's College, Oxford, where he read Modern Languages and where for two years he was organist and choirmaster. After a brief spell of teaching he became a full-time writer and composer (especially of film music). Among other variegated activities in the same departments, he has produced concert music, edited many science-fiction anthologies, and written for many periodicals and newspapers. For a number of years he was the regular crime-fiction reviewer for the London *Sunday Times*. Edmund Crispin (whose real name is Bruce Montgomery) once wrote of himself: 'He is of a sedentary habit – his chief recreations being music, reading, church-going and bridge. Like Rex Stout's Nero Wolfe he leaves his house as seldom as possible, in particular minimizing his visits to London, a rapidly decaying metropolis which since the war he has come to detest. He is married and lives in Devon, in a quiet corner whose exploitation and development he does his utmost to oppose.' Penguin Books also publishes Crispin's *The Moving Toyshop*.

Edmund Crispin

THE LONG DIVORCE

THE LONG DIVORCE OF STEEL

Henry VIII Act 2 Sc. 1

PENGUIN BOOKS

Penguin Books Ltd, Harmondsworth,
Middlesex, England
Penguin Books, 625 Madison Avenue,
New York, New York 10022, U.S.A.
Penguin Books Australia Ltd, Ringwood,
Victoria, Australia
Penguin Books Canada Limited, 2801 John Street,
Markham, Ontario, Canada L3R 1B4
Penguin Books (N.Z.) Ltd, 182–190 Wairau Road,
Auckland 10, New Zealand

First published in Great Britain by
Gollancz 1951
First published in the United States of America by
Dodd, Mead & Company 1951
Published in Penguin Books in Great Britain 1958
Reprinted 1961
Published in Penguin Books in the United States of America 1981

LIBRARY OF CONGRESS CATALOGING IN PUBLICATION DATA
Montgomery, Robert Bruce.
The long divorce.
Reprint of the 1951 ed. published by Dodd, Mead,
New York, in series: Red badge detective.
I. Title.
[PR6025.046L6   1981]   823′.912   80-24584
ISBN 0 14 00.1304 0

Printed in the United States of America by
George Banta Co., Inc., Harrisonburg, Virginia
Set in Times Roman

To Pat and Colin Strang

CHAPTER 1

ON the afternoon of Friday 2 June 1950, a Mr Datchery, having put his week-end bag on to a bus with the request that it be civilly ejected at an inn named 'The Marlborough Head', set out to walk the four miles which separate the market town of Twelford from the village of Cotten Abbas.

He was a tall and wiry man of between forty and fifty, with a lean, ruddy, clean-shaven face. His brown hair, ineffectually plastered down with water, stood up in mutinous spikes at the crown of his head. His manner was eupeptic and affable. From the town hall at Twelford, where the bus had relieved him of his bag, he strode westwards along the main street, and by three o'clock he was past the outlying estate of council houses and into open country.

The sun that Friday had risen in a blur of rain; but at breakfast time the clouds had cleared, and by mid-day all traces of the shower had been eliminated, and the earth was beginning to absorb and accumulate heat. To an obbligato of bird-song Mr Datchery marched beneath a bright sky towards Cotten Abbas. And he carolled lustily, to the distress of all animate nature, as he walked.

'I will make my kitchen,' sang Mr Datchery, 'and you shall keep your room, where white flows the river and bright blows the broom.' And the cattle, lifting their heads as he passed, lowed a mournful burden to the tune.

The directions given him at Twelford had been explicit. But since he believed himself to possess an infallible bump of locality, he was soon tempted to modify them with a variety of short cuts, and after about three miles he discovered, much to his indignation, that he was lost. We first distinctly see him, then, standing oppressed by this realization at the junction of four lanes, like a pilgrim in an allegory. The land lies flat and featureless on every side; the ancient wooden finger-post is indecipherable; and for the moment the only visible representative of organic life is a very small black kitten engaged

7

in pouncing on something at the exact centre of a very large green field.

The kitten, however, suggested that humanity must be somewhere in the offing – for kittens, even when avid for field-mice, seldom stray immoderate distances from their homes. Mr Datchery, selecting a lane at random, began to move energetically along it. And presently he was rewarded by coming within earshot of a combination of sounds which, though not readily explicable, were undoubtedly of human origin. Rounding a bend in the lane, Mr Datchery came upon a surprising and improbable sight.

What he saw first was a football ground – a football ground unaccountably isolated from mankind amidst fields of wheat and pasture. What he saw next was a diminutive, but evidently new, grandstand at its far side. And what he saw last was about a hundred schoolboys jumping up and down on the grandstand with a noise like houses falling.

This unlikely performance brought Mr Datchery temporarily to a halt. Schoolboys were apt, no doubt, to jump up and down on grandstands whenever an exciting game was being played – but in this instance there were no footballers on the field at all. Open-mouthed, Mr Datchery looked on while the boys leaped and cavorted and giggled and roared. Then, the first shock of amazement wearing away, he became aware that he was not alone in his admiration.

Close to the more distant extremity of the stand a man and a girl stood shouting at one another – shouting not in wrath, but because the noise made communication impossible on any other terms. The man was elderly, and a member of what used to be called the artisan class; the girl was about sixteen. Beyond them, and to the left, a younger man could be seen wandering about aimlessly behind the goal-posts – but it was towards the group of two that Mr Datchery made his way, for he knew from experience that a female, however young, can always be relied upon to give more sane and accurate directions for getting anywhere than a male.

'*One*, – TWO – *THREE!*' shrieked a spotty boy. And at the final word, two hundred stoutly-shod feet descended with shattering force on the tiers of the stand, so that it quivered as if at the impact of a typhoon. 'Ah,' the elderly man said smugly to the girl. 'She'll 'old. Yes, she'll 'old all right.' It was evidently he who had been responsible for the stand's erection.

Mr Datchery, joining them, was received incuriously. 'There's a sweet job for you, sir,' said the elderly man with inane satisfaction. 'Firm as a rock, that is. Them lads 'as got the afternoon off to try 'er out for safety, and if they can't knock 'er down, then no one can.'

'Where am I?' Mr Datchery bawled at him as the assault on the stand was renewed.

'Ah, you may well say so, sir,' the elderly man replied. 'You'll not find a better piece of work than that, not in the 'ole length and breadth of the land.'

'What I want to know,' shouted Mr Datchery irritably, 'is, where I am.'

'Costly, sir?' said the elderly man. 'Not a bit of it. Why, if they'd 'ave 'ad Phelps and Co. from Twelford, they'd 'ave 'ad to pay double my price.'

Mr Datchery stared coldly at the girl, who had lapsed into convulsions of laughter.

'You old fool,' he yelled, 'for the last time, where am I?'

A spark of enlightenment which now appeared in the elderly man's glazed eyes suggested that he had at last caught the drift of Mr Datchery's questions, but he was distracted from the use of this discovery by a sudden ominous noise of splintering wood.

''Ere, you damned boys,' he bellowed, 'you watch what you're doing, can't you?'

'Firm as a rock,' said Mr Datchery malignantly. But the elderly man had already departed on a punitive expedition. 'Is there no one,' said Mr Datchery in despair, 'who can tell me where I am?'

The girl was by now in such uncontrollable fits of laughter that she had to lie down on the ground. She was a thin, long-legged creature, Mr Datchery saw, with straight brown hair, acid-stained fingers, and clothes which, though good, were sloppily worn and little cared for. But for all that, she was pretty in a coltish sort of way, and it seemed to Mr Datchery not improbable that she was intelligent as well.

'You'll make yourself sick in a minute,' he said. 'For heaven's

9

sake pull yourself together and tell me how to get to Cotten Abbas.'

'Cotten Abbas?' The girl sat upright and spoke breathlessly through a residual attack of giggles. 'Where have you come from?'

'Twelford.'

'I don't know how you've managed to land up here, then.'

'What is this place?'

The girl relapsed into mirth. 'Ah,' she spluttered convulsively, 'sweet as a nut, that wood is. You wouldn't find a better, not if you was to search from Land's End to John o' Groats.'

'*For heaven's sake*,' said Mr Datchery.

The girl wiped her eyes with a rather grubby handkerchief.

'Oh, gosh,' she said in a choking voice. 'Laughing makes me so *weak* ... Help me up, will you? This is awful.'

Mr Datchery helped her up and stood waiting grimly while she recovered her equanimity.

'I say, I'm awfully sorry,' she said presently. 'But honestly, I've never heard anything so funny in my life ... What was it you were asking? Oh, I remember ... Well, this isn't any place, really, except a football ground. Cotten's the nearest place.' With a supreme effort, she gulped the last of the giggles into extinction. 'I tell you what: I'm walking back to Cotten myself in a minute, so you can come with me.'

'Is it far?'

'Only a couple of miles,' she said, hitching her skirt to a more comfortable position and brushing grass and earth from it with the palm of her hand. 'But if you're in a terrific hurry you can walk from here to the Twelford road and pick up a bus.'

Mr Datchery's enthusiasm for physical effort had never been of a very enduring kind. 'When is the next bus?' he inquired.

The girl considered. 'In about an hour,' she said.

'Then it's just as well,' said Mr Datchery rather coldly, 'that I'm not in a terrific hurry. Do you live at Cotten Abbas?'

But his questions to-day seemed all destined to be ignored, for at this point they were joined by the young man who had been wandering behind the goal-posts, and whom Mr Datchery supposed to be the master in hypothetical control of the schoolboys. He was a very clean, very thin young man of rather less than

10

average height, with small, sharply-cut features, myopic pale eyes behind angular shell-rimmed glasses, and straight yellow hair; and his shirt, neat and spotless like all his clothes, was open at the neck. Upon the boys in his charge, and upon the elderly man expostulating with them, he gazed with the tolerant air of one who has acquainted himself with progressive educational theories and found them good. And when he spoke, it was in the careful, pedantic English of the German intellectual.

'I say, Peter' – the girl turned eagerly to him as he strolled up – 'I'm afraid they've smashed something. The old man's frightfully cross.'

The newcomer showed no surprise at this intelligence – and in the circumstances it would have been remarkable if he had.

'It is good for the children,' he observed benevolently, 'to destroy things sometimes. If they are allowed to do that, they grow up to be saner people.' He looked politely to Mr Datchery for confirmation of this doubtful thesis. 'Is it not so, sir?'

'No,' said Mr Datchery briefly.

The young man smiled at him with great sweetness. 'The experiments of your Neill,' he pursued equably, 'they have proved it. And in Switzerland also we have such schools. But perhaps I am tedious for you?'

'No, *please* go on, Peter,' said the girl; and then flushed as she caught Mr Datchery's eye. 'After all,' she added defiantly, 'when you get an expert talking, you can –'

But the expert was not attending to her, and Mr Datchery saw her wince as she observed it. It was not, Mr Datchery thought, that the expert was being deliberately unkind; it was just that he was not in the least interested in young girls. Producing a card, he now handed it to Mr Datchery with a stiff little bow, and Mr Datchery read on it the neatly printed words:

Dr Phil. Peter Rubi
Zürich

with the written address 'Fiveways, Cotten Abbas, England' underneath.

'Rubi,' said the young man, shaking hands.

'Datchery,' said Mr Datchery.

'And I'rr Penelope Rolt,' said the girl.

'It is for the experience that I am teaching for two years in England,' Rubi explained. 'I like England very much. They are an interesting people.'

Mr Datchery, who happened to be familiar with the list of topics that appeal most readily to the foreign intelligentsia, perceived a discussion on National Character looming up over the conversational horizon.

'You might say I was a teacher, too,' he said hurriedly. 'University people are often mistakenly supposed to be that.'

'Ah,' said Rubi, 'you are a university person. And please what is the subject, your faculty?'

'English,' said Mr Datchery.

'I read many of your English writers,' said Rubi with marked self-approval. 'I think that of the moderns it is Evelyn Waugh I prefer, though your Graham Greene is spiritual also.'

'And a very sound preference too,' said Mr Datchery heartily, hoping by unqualified approval to gravel in advance the debate whose shoals and shallows he glimpsed ahead. 'A very sound preference,' he repeated with emphasis, 'too.'

It failed to work. 'Waugh is perhaps the greatest of your symbolical authors,' said Rubi, happily launched on a long-premeditated disquisition. 'The girl Runcible in *Vile Bodies*, she is the great contemporary symbol of dissociation in our modern world. She drives the car in the race; it swerves from the course; she dies ... I have written an article about this in the *Neue Züricher Beobachter* which has been praised by many of the best critics.'

But at this early stage in his remarks, and as much to his and the girl's annoyance as to Mr Datchery's relief, the elderly man elected to rejoin them. Though worsted in his unequal encounter with the citizens of to-morrow (who by now had tired of testing the stand's endurance and were divided into two gangs for the purpose of a bloody, crack-bone fight), the elderly man continued to be in a state of considerable dudgeon.

'Them young bastards,' he announced, breathing heavily in his exhaustion, ''as bust 'alf the fencing down the middle.' Then he swelled up with sudden beserk rage. 'Get 'em out of 'ere!' he

12

shrieked. 'Get 'em out of 'ere afore they knocks the 'ole blasted lot down!'

'You think the experiment has been sufficient?' said Rubi amiably. 'It will be proper now for me to take them back to their afternoon tea? Very well, I shall do that.'

'I'll have to be getting back, too,' said the girl rather hurriedly; and Mr Datchery suspected that she was not anxious to witness the admired Rubi's foredoomed attempts to exert his authority over the milling rout on the field and the stand. 'Shall I see you to-morrow, Peter?'

Rubi shook his head. 'To-morrow,' he stated firmly, 'I am to go alone for a long hiking, and I shall not be returned till very late.'

'Well, what about Monday? It's a whole holiday for you, isn't it?'

'Monday,' said Rubi with condescension, 'perhaps.'

'Will you call for me? We could see a film. There's *The Third Man* at the Regal, that isn't commercial a bit, you'd like it.'

'All right,' said Rubi ungraciously. 'But for the morning, I'll be busy, remember.'

'Yes, I'll remember,' she said earnestly. 'I promise I won't disturb you.' Then, after a moment's uncertain pause: 'Well, bye for now ... Are you coming with me, Mr Datchery?'

Mr Datchery was and it was patent that Rubi regretted the loss of him far more than the loss of the girl.

'You are staying in Cotten Abbas, sir?' he asked; and when Mr Datchery assented: 'Then we must meet again. I would wish to talk a long time about the man Waugh.'

Mr Datchery thought this very likely, and considered it, as an argument in favour of reopening the acquaintance, singularly lacking in force. But he managed to feign an enthusiasm for the project, and presently he and the girl departed together. They turned once to look back on the scene. Rubi, they saw, was at the centre of the field, feebly gesticulating with his arms and calling 'Boys! Boys!' while the outraged contractor stumped irascibly up and down behind him; and although the girl waved to him, he did not happen (as seemed to be common in their relationship) to be attending. She turned away, disappointed;

13

but later, when they had climbed a stile and were making their way towards a wood of beech and birch, she said defensively:

'He's very clever, you know.'

'Very,' said Mr Datchery without enthusiasm.

'I mean, he's got a terrific lot of degrees, and he's lived in all sorts of countries.'

'So I guessed.'

There was a pause; then: 'But you *didn't* think he was clever, did you?'

'My dear girl,' said Mr Datchery mildly, 'I'm no judge of whether a man's clever or not. But I did think he behaved rather uncivilly to you.'

'Oh, I don't matter,' she said in a flat voice. 'I expect he gets sick of having a – a child hanging about him all the time.'

'If you mean yourself, then I hardly think the word "child" applies.'

Penelope, who had been walking with her head bent, scuffing at the grass with her shoes, turned to look at Mr Datchery, for the first time, with real attention.

'You're rather nice, you know,' she said judicially.

'No, I'm not.' Mr Datchery seemed to find the compliment obscurely irritating.

'You are, though. That's why I wish you felt the way I do about Peter.'

'For the way you feel about him,' said Mr Datchery with candour, 'there's a sound biological reason from which I'm luckily exempt. You're a scientist, aren't you? Well then, be scientific about it.'

'A scientist ... ?' For a moment Penelope was startled; then she looked at her slim, discoloured fingers and smiled. 'Oh, I see. Sherlock Holmes stuff. But as to me being a scientist, that's all hooey. I muck about with chemicals, just for something to do, but I'm no good at it. Peter's far more of a scientist than me.'

'How is he a scientist?' Mr Datchery demanded fretfully.

'Psychology.'

'Psychology is a metaphysic.'

'I don't see why.'

14

'For one thing,' said Mr Datchery, 'it can never make a control experiment. For another – '

'Oh, all right,' said Penelope rather sulkily. 'I ought to have known better than to try and start an argument with you. But whatever you like to call it, Peter's jolly good at it ... I admit,' she said carefully, 'that some of his ideas about other subjects seem a bit odd. For instance, that book he was talking about – *Vile Bodies*. He told me I ought to read it, and I did, but the only thing about it I could see was that it was *funny*.' She shook her head, perplexed. 'Still, that's not the point. The point is that he's wizard about anything to do with people's minds.'

And at the fringe of the wood, Penelope, who had been walking and talking a little ahead of her companion, halted so that he might catch her up.

'For example,' she said, 'there's this business of the anonymous letters.'

CHAPTER 2

'ANONYMOUS letters?' said Mr Datchery. 'What anonymous letters?'

His tone betrayed no more than a civil interest such as any stranger, encountering a case of this sporadic affliction, might be expected to show; but if Penelope had been less preoccupied with justifying Rubi, she might have seen that his pale blue eyes narrowed at the words, and that he began to follow what she said with a new alertness. They pushed on – she still leading – along a bracken-bordered path into the wood, where rabbits thumped and rustled in the undergrowth and the sunlight was striated by a lace of boughs. And Penelope said:

'Oh, didn't you know about them? They've been going on for two or three weeks now.'

'What sort of letters are they?'

'Obscene,' said Penelope with a sort of abstract relish. 'At least, some of them are. But the obscene ones aren't the worst.'

'Why aren't they?'

'Because they're just nonsense. It's the other sort that's causing all the trouble.'

'And the other sort – ?'

'The other sort says things about people that are true.'

'An unpopular practice,' Mr Datchery remarked drily, 'I admit.'

'Oh dear, I'm afraid I'm not explaining it very well ... But – well, for example, there was Mr Mogridge.'

'Who is Mr Mogridge?'

'He's landlord of "The Marlborough Head". And he was carrying on, you see, with Cora.'

'I don't see at all,' complained Mr Datchery.

'Patience, patience!' The girl turned her head to grin at him. 'That's what Miss Bowlby always used to say at school when we didn't understand something ... Where was I?'

'You'd just conjured up someone called Cora.'

'Oh, yes. Well, Cora is – was, I should say – the chambermaid

16

at "The Marlborough Head". You know, the well-cushioned sort.' And Penelope glanced rather shyly back at Mr Datchery to see how this timid essay in worldliness would affect him; reassured by the complete blankness of his countenance, she went on: 'Anyway, Mr Mogridge had been – making love to her for, oh, years. Everyone knew about it, except, of course, *Mrs* Mogridge. But then about a fortnight ago she got one of these letters, and it told her where Mr Mogridge and Cora were meeting, and when, and of course then there was a terrific dust up.'

'I see.' Mr Datchery was pensive. 'Yes, I see. And have many of the letters been of this – this tale-bearing kind?'

Penelope nodded. 'Lots.'

'And the tales have been true?'

'Yes, almost always.'

'But isn't it rather odd that anyone should be acquainted with so many of the skeletons in other people's closets?'

'If you can say that,' Penelope answered sagely, 'then it's jolly obvious you've never lived in a village. In a village, everyone knows all the scandal about everyone else – but of course, people take terrific care it shan't get to the ears of anyone it'd hurt and upset.'

'I see,' said Mr Datchery again. And indeed he did see, for he knew that although small communities are bound to gossip, they develop by instinct a technique from preventing gossip from reaching the wrong ears, and realize perfectly well – though probably the knowledge is never consciously formulated – that any widespread breakdown of this technique would rapidly make life intolerable. 'But if,' he added, 'there are two sorts of letter – (*a*) the damaging and (*b*) the merely obscene – doesn't that suggest that there are two different people writing them?'

'Peter doesn't think so,' said Penelope, remounting her hobby-horse with alacrity. 'He says both sorts of letter show exactly the same kind of paranoia, and that it's not likely we'd have two people in Cotten who are potty like that. He says it'd be frightfully interesting to talk to this woman who's writing the letters, and find out about when she was a child and so forth.'

'Woman?' queried Mr Datchery.

'Peter says it's always a woman who writes foul letters,

17

because of being repressed and so on, and he says it's usually a middle-class spinster.'

Mr Datchery's enthusiasm for Rubi, which had never been excessive, waned still further. It was really unforgivable of him to have stuffed the girl's head with this muddled, inaccurate, prurient lore. Mr Datchery judged, however, that this sentiment had better be kept to himself for the time being, and all he said was:

'Interesting. I take it that you haven't been troubled with any of these letters?'

'No. Pa has – but then, so's everyone else who's anyone.' Penelope's face clouded. 'A bit of Pa's was about me and Peter. He was furious. He doesn't like Peter very much. He says it's *dangerous*' – this with great scorn – 'for me to go about with him.'

The which persuasion, Mr Datchery reflected, seemed distinctly a point in Mr Rolt's favour. It was true that, to judge from what Mr Datchery had seen of Rubi, a woman trapped naked with him on a desert island would run no more intimate risk from his company than the risk of death from boredom. But perhaps it was only his opinions that Mr Rolt thought dangerous – and in that case Mr Rolt had much reason on his side . . .

'And just what form,' Mr Datchery asked, 'do the letters take?'

'*Form* . . . ? Oh, I see what you mean. Well, I haven't actually seen one myself, but, of course, everyone's been gassing about them, so I know what they're like. They're made up of words and letters cut out of lots of different newspapers and stuck on to a bit of writing-paper. Oh, and the envelopes are addressed in capitals. That's all, I think.'

'Are they signed at all?'

'You mean *Pro Bono Publico*, or something like that. No, they're not.'

'And what is being done about them?'

'Well, the police are on to it, of course. And so they jolly well ought to be,' said Penelope censoriously, 'considering there's two of them actually living in the village. Colonel Babington got one of the letters himself. He was frightfully angry.'

'Who is Colonel Babington?'

18

'He's Chief Constable. And the other's Inspector Casby, who lives next door to Dr Downing. He belongs to the county C.I.D., so he's been in charge of the case.'

'And are there any clues?'

Penelope shrugged elaborately. 'Don't know. Shouldn't think so.'

'You consider the Inspector incompetent?'

'N-no, not exactly. He's all right. But if he hasn't succeeded in stopping the letters after three weeks, then it doesn't look as if he ever will, does it?'

'I think perhaps you're unduly pessimistic,' said Mr Datchery; and added, after a glance at the odd and unexpected expression on the girl's face: 'Or should I say, optimistic?'

'It all makes life a bit more interesting,' she answered slowly and warily.

'Really? But I can't imagine your enthusiasm is very widely shared. One way and another, the social life of the place must have been a good deal upset.'

Penelope laughed, shortly and unpleasantly.

'Upset?' she said. 'You're telling me.' And Mr Datchery, dismayed, saw that her eyes were alight with malicious pleasure. 'It's got so that they all suspect each other so much they can barely be polite.'

'And obviously,' said Mr Datchery, 'you yourself regard that as quite a desirable thing.'

They were out of the wood by now, and passing through a kissing-gate into a narrow, tree-lined lane. Penelope halted abruptly.

'It serves them all right,' she said. 'It'll teach them not to be so beastly superior in future.'

Mr Datchery, halting likewise, fished out a cigarette, put it in his mouth, and began groping for matches.

'I haven't the least idea what you're talking about,' he observed. 'But I'm afraid that like most people you over-estimate the refining powers of tribulation. Superiority, however beastly, often comes out of it quite unscathed.'

'Well then, it'll punish them.'

'No doubt.' Mr Datchery lit his cigarette, shielding the

19

match-flame with cupped hands from a mild breeze. 'Exactly what, in your opinion, do they have to be punished for?'

She turned away from his tranquil contemplation of her to stare pointlessly along the empty lane.

'It's Pa,' she said, and her voice shook a little. 'It's the way they treat Pa.'

'How do they treat him?'

'They – they're snobs, you see. They hate him because he's not cultured and educated, the way they are. Well, perhaps he isn't, but he's as good as them any day. And they say the mill spoils the – the village's amenities. And – and – well, I expect he is a bit rough and brusque sometimes, but he doesn't mean anything by it. I – I – ' Tears started into her eyes.

'Unpleasant,' said Mr Datchery, salutarily brisk. 'I'm very sorry to hear it.'

Penelope struggled stoically to regain control of herself.

'I – I don't know why I'm telling you all this. It must be very boring for you. And of course if people choose to be silly, it doesn't worry *us*.' Her pride was at once touching and admirable. 'I – I say, I've just remembered something.'

'Yes?'

'I said I'd be back by five sharp, and if I don't hurry I'm not going to be. D'you mind if I leave you and run on ahead? You can easily find your own way from here. You turn left at the next cross-roads and that takes you straight into Cotten.'

It was a justifiable pretence, Mr Datchery thought; like most people who have confided on an impulse, the girl was anxious to get away, as quickly as possible, from her confidant. He said, therefore:

'Please go ahead. It's very kind of you to have brought me as far as this.'

'Th-thanks.' She was already backing away. 'I'll be seeing you, I expect.' She paused, struggling with some emotion at which he could only guess. 'I'm not *really* glad about those rotten letters,' she blurted, 'but – but –'

And then she turned and ran.

Smoking pensively, Mr Datchery watched her thin figure until it was out of sight; and he gave her a long start before he himself

20

set off to stroll in the same direction. A lonely child, he thought, her loneliness complicated by the ostracizing of her father (though probably she had exaggerated that), by her devotion to the unconscionable Rubi, and by the normal worries and embarrassments – insignificant in retrospect, but sometimes looming formidably large at the time of their occurring – of adolescence. Her age, too, was the age at which children for the first time become objectively aware of their parents; at which, in consequence, they are apt for quite trivial reasons to become ashamed of those parents, and to be ashamed of that shame ... Mr Datchery sighed. If there was one thing about Penelope Rolt that was clearer than another, that thing was that she badly needed sympathy and guidance, and was not getting them.

The lane twisted between fields of maturing rye and barley. At the cross-roads Mr Datchery turned left into what he guessed to be a loop of the Twelford road. And presently, down a long and gentle slope, he came into the village of Cotten Abbas.

CHAPTER 3

COTTEN ABBAS is sixty or seventy miles from London, and obscurely conveys the impression of having strayed there out of a film set. As with most show-villages, you are apt to feel, when confronted with it, that some impalpable process of embalming or refrigeration is at work, some prophylactic against change and decay which while altogether creditable in itself has yet resulted in a certain degree of stagnation. But for all that, its charm is undeniable; and just past the alms-houses Mr Datchery halted, at gaze, in order to drink it in.

Cotten Abbas that afternoon was pranked out in sunlight like a woman dressed for a ball. Ahead of Mr Datchery, as he entered the village from the Twelford direction, was the gentle curve of the broad and airy main street; to his left was an irregular but graceful line of little Georgian and Queen Anne houses, broken halfway along by the façade of 'The Marlborough Head'; and to his right was a row of cottages, with a discreet and barely perceptible shop or two interspersed among them. This row was cut short by a right-angle turning; and just beyond the turning was the church – a large Perpendicular-style fabric which lay alongside the village street like a ship drawn up at a quay. Beyond that was the Vicarage; beyond that – recessed, and deducible only by its outthrust sign – a second inn; and finally, after a few scattered houses a little more modern than the rest, open country again.

It all had a prosperous look – but its prosperity, Mr Datchery thought, was less that of a working village than that of a village which has been settled by the well-to-do: in a population which could scarcely number more than a couple of hundred, it was obviously the invading middle class that ruled, badly weakened now by post-war conditions, but still hanging on. To them, no doubt, in their between-wars heyday, the preservation of the village's beauty must be ascribed. And their houses, eloquent of a time more prolific of servants than ours, were to be glimpsed through trees and past roof-tops, hemming the place in like an encircling force.

Lying placid under the June sky, Cotten Abbas at the moment was quiet and almost deserted. A baker's man whistled as he strode through a tradesman's entrance, his basket slung from his arm and his pouch fat with coppers. An infant, precocious in vandalism as in letters, was laboriously chalking the legend JANE LUVS BOB WATCHET on a convenient wall. The distant droning of a saw-mill was like the summer sound of bees . . . For perhaps a minute Mr Datchery stood accumulating and interpreting first impressions; then, squaring his shoulders with the resolute air of a man in transit from a steam room to a cold shower, he walked on along the street to the door of 'The Marlborough Head'.

'The Marlborough Head', he found, was an inn of low ceilings, uneven floors, and massive chimney-stacks, whose frontage of irregular beams and plaster, pierced by diminutive leaded windows, faced the Vicarage. Entering, you crossed a tiny golosh-littered vestibule and came immediately into the Lounge Bar – a long but rather cramped room, dark after the sunshine outside, and furnished in chintz and old oak. The hunting-prints on its walls, and in general its rather ostentatious rejection of modernity, gave it a vaguely self-conscious look; but it was nevertheless pleasing enough, and Mr Datchery, experienced in the astounding discomforts which the majority of rural inns provide, felt his spirits rise as he contemplated it.

It seemed that summer opening-time in Cotten Abbas was at five, for 'The Marlborough Head' already had a customer – a small, neat, energetic-looking elderly man with a clipped grey moustache, who was drinking Guinness in a window-seat and bullying the landlord over the top of his glass.

'You bore people, Mogridge,' he was saying as Mr Datchery entered, 'when you go on and on like that about your dreary conferences and resolutions and by-laws. No one in his senses cares twopence about the grievances of inn-keepers, except for wishing they were ten times worse. If you ask me, their putting you on that committee was nothing short of disastrous. It's got so that you're incapable of talking about anything else.'

Mogridge laughed feebly. He was a little, rounded person of indefinite age, whose slightly protruding eyes were moist as

23

though with appetite or secret sorrow; and he had something the air – as a result, possibly, of the domestic upheaval sketched by Penelope Rolt – of a man trapped without trousers in a crowded tube train.

'You will have your joke, Colonel Babington,' he said. 'Would you care for a packet of twenty Players? I've got a good stock in at the moment.'

Colonel Babington stiffened.

'Damn you, Mogridge,' he said with feeling, 'how dare you offer me cigarettes? You know perfectly well I've given up smoking.'

'Why, so you have, sir.' Clearly Mogridge was delighted with the success of his counter-thrust. 'I was forgetting. And how do you find yourself?'

'*Find* myself, Mogridge? *Find* myself?'

'I mean, sir, are you managing to keep it up?'

'Of course I am,' said Colonel Babington sharply. 'When I decide to do a thing, I do it.'

'They do say it's a bit unpleasant, sir, at first.'

'Tcha!' Colonel Babington waved this effete suggestion away into limbo. 'Will-power, that's all that's needed. Will-power.' He nodded emphatically. 'It's trying, of course, I don't deny that. But my view is that a man who lets a drug get control of him and then can't throw it off isn't a man at all. He's a mouse.'

'I never heard,' said Mogridge, 'that mice were much addicted –'

'A mouse, Mogridge!' snarled Colonel Babington in sudden rage. 'A mouse, a mouse, a mouse!' With some difficulty he managed to control himself. 'I've no use for these chaps who say they *can't* give up smoking. No use for *them*, at all.'

'Now, I've never smoked,' said Mogridge complacently, 'so I wouldn't know what it's like to give it up. But Will Watchet, he's been trying to do it, and he says it's hell.'

Colonel Babington snorted. 'Never heard such rubbish in my life ... It's a mild discomfort, that's all, a mild discomfort.'

'What's more,' Mogridge persisted, 'he says it plays the devil with a man's temper.'

'*Temper?*' Colonel Babington was convulsed with anger.

'Whatever next? You don't find *me* losing my temper just because I've stopped fouling my lungs with smoke.'

'Ah, but then, sir, you've not been at it long.'

'I've been at it nearly thirty-six hours, damn you, Mogridge. And the first two days are always the worst. It gets easier after that.'

'I once,' said Mogridge, staring reminiscently at the ceiling, 'met a man in a train who said he'd given up smoking five years ago, and still longed for one.'

Colonel Babington had no answer to this. He looked at Mr Datchery, who had moved to the bar and was lighting a cigarette in a sneaking, apologetic manner, and then looked hurriedly away again.

'But he was unusual, I dare say,' pronounced Mogridge in hot pursuit of his advantage. 'Most people lose the craving after' – he pretended to reflect – 'oh, *six months* or so.'

'Well, all I can say' – for the moment Colonel Babington was definitely subdued – 'is, that I feel better for it already. Appetite's improved. More energy. Mark my words, Mogridge, all this smoking enervates a man.' He gazed at Mr Datchery with hatred and groped automatically in his pocket for an absent cigarette-case; then, abruptly realizing the futility of this proceed ng, sighed heavily and desisted from it. 'Afternoon, sir,' he said to Mr Datchery with unexpected mildness.

Mr Datchery, having returned the greeting, inquired whether Mogridge could let him have a room for a few days.

'Can do, sir,' said Mogridge with watery affability. 'Would that be your bag, I wonder, that came in on the bus?'

Mr Datchery agreed that it probably would. 'But before I move from here,' he added, 'I want to drink a pint or two of beer.' He eyed Colonel Babington. 'What will you have, sir?'

'Very good of you,' said Colonel Babington gruffly. 'Mine's a Guinness. Don't feel I have to give that up, I'm glad to say.'

'Drink is sometimes more harmful than smoking,' said Mr Datchery unkindly. 'Of the two –'

'I dare say.' The Colonel was evidently not prepared to stand any further inroads on his self-confidence. 'I dare say.'

'A pint, then, of bitter,' said Mr Datchery, 'and a Guinness.

I've walked here from Twelford and I'm thirsty. This is a remarkably pretty village, isn't it?'

He exchanged remarks on this subject with Colonel Babington while Mogridge drew the beer; and subsequently, having conversed neutrally on neutral topics, was conducted to his room. Returning thence, ten minutes later, he met Mogridge at the foot of the stairs.

'All comfortable, sir?' asked Mogridge with offensively old-world hospitality. 'Got everything you need?'

Mr Datchery's room had reversed his earlier opinion of the inn's amenities. He had lain down experimentally on the bed and found it of a board-like rigidity.

'And there are spiders,' he complained, 'pelting about the walls like racehorses.'

'Ah,' said Mogridge unabashed, 'but you've not seen any flies, sir, I'll wager. One of my colleagues on the Regional Committee of the Innkeepers' Guild was saying only the other day that –'

But he had no chance to finish, for at this point a thin, pale, straggle-haired woman with an expression of settled malevolence popped out of a near-by door and cut off Mogridge's colleague's dictum in its uninteresting bud. 'Oliver!' she snapped.

'Coming at once, my love,' said Mogridge weakly. 'I was just making sure this gentleman had everything he wanted.'

'Spiders,' Mr Datchery reiterated testily. 'There are spiders.'

'Yes, yes, sir, I know.' Mogridge was petulant. 'There's no need to keep on about it.' Then his petulance faded as a possible pretext for eluding his wife occurred to him. 'I'd better go up straight away and deal with the trouble myself.'

But his wife punctured this feeble artifice without effort, and carried him off incontinently to whatever of marital purgatory she had hoarded up for him, and Mr Datchery went back to the bar, where Colonel Babington, glum and in solitude, was still ingesting stout. At Mr Datchery's entry he opened his mouth to speak; in the event, however, his utterance was obliterated, after a single incomprehensible vowel-sound, by a violent fit of coughing, and by the time he had recovered from this, circumstances, in the shape of a newcomer who entered the inn from the street, had effectively distracted his attention from whatever he had intended to say.

The newcomer was a man probably in his middle thirties. He was lean, dark, quiet, unobtrusive; and the most noticeable thing about him was a long white scar which traversed his left cheek from ear to mouth – the consequence, as Mr Datchery learned later, of a Japanese sabre-cut clumsily mended in the makeshift conditions of the Burmese jungle. But he was handsome in spite of it; and when he spoke, it was in the cadences of a warm Bucks accent which his education had minimized without ever quite abolishing. After a hurried, appraising glance at Mr Datchery, he addressed himself immediately to Colonel Babington.

'Ah, here you are, sir,' he said. 'I've been trying to get in touch with you all afternoon.'

'Been out walking,' Colonel Babington explained. 'What's up?'

The newcomer murmured something which Mr Datchery, to his great chagrin, failed to catch. But the impact on Colonel Babington was plain enough: he jerked and grew rigid like a man whipped.

'Beatrice?' he blurted incredulously. 'But that's impossible – I mean –' His voice tailed away as a new thought struck him. 'Not another of those damned letters?' he asked.

The man with the scar nodded. 'I think so. And if you wouldn't mind, sir, I'd like to have a word with you about it.' He moved his head fractionally in Mr Datchery's direction. 'Perhaps if we were to stroll up and down outside...'

'Yes, yes, of course.' The Colonel stood up. 'My God, what a ghastly business ... And if anyone had asked me, I'd have said Beatrice was the very *last* person to – to –' He gestured helplessly, and Mr Datchery saw that his normally vigorous complexion was now the colour and texture of grey sand.

'Are you feeling all right, sir?' The other man's question was matter-of-fact and agreeably free from impertinent solicitude. 'If you liked, we could –'

'No, no, I'm all right. Bit of a shock, that's all. Known her for years. Can't understand why a woman like her – No, this is no good: I'm maundering. Tell me about it.'

They went out into the village street, leaving Mr Datchery to solitary speculation. Since Colonel Babington was Chief Constable, it seemed reasonable to assume that the man with the scar was that Inspector Casby of whom Penelope Rolt had spoken; and what had happened was presumably a suicide – though naturally enough the name Beatrice conveyed nothing to Mr Datchery's mind. During the short interval prior to Mogridge's chastened reappearance, Mr Datchery meditated these questions in his habitual impatient way, and his thoughts were occupied with the supposed Casby to a greater extent than, from a dispassionate point of view, that individual might have seemed to have warranted. Presently, however, Mr Datchery abandoned these reflections for want of matter, and began catechizing Mogridge, who by now was once more in the offing, with a view to satisfying himself as to certain other problems which interested him.

'Who,' he demanded, 'is Rolt?'

Mogridge, polishing glasses in a comatose manner behind the bar, started at being thus abruptly addressed.

'Rolt?' he echoed. 'Would you be meaning Harry Rolt, sir?'

'I dare say I would. Tell me about him.'

'Well, sir, it's him that owns the saw-mill that's such a blot,' said Mogridge sanctimoniously, 'on our beautiful village.'

'I see. What sort of a man is he?'

'North-country,' Mogridge answered with irritating distaste. 'A pusher, if you know what I mean. With him, its money, money, money all the time.'

'You don't strike me, Mogridge, as being exactly unworldly yourself,' said Mr Datchery. 'And even if you were, you still seem to dislike the man more that mere money-grubbing would justify.'

'I'll tell you what it is, sir,' Mogridge ceased polishing, and held the cloth aloft in pursuance of some personal formula for imparting emphasis. 'Mr Rolt's not popular here. And when *no one* likes a man, then there's always good reason for it. I remember the Treasurer of our central committee, to whom I had the honour to be presented at a dinner at the Dorchester last year, saying to me "Mogridge," he said –'

'No, no, Mogridge,' said Mr Datchery kindly, 'you mustn't drift away from the point like that ... I'm assuming, of course, that there *is* a point, and that the people here aren't just common or garden snobs.'

'Snobs, sir?' The suggestion had plainly affronted some aspect of Mogridge's self-importance. 'Nothing of the kind. A nicer set of gentlefolk you couldn't hope to find. It's just that Mr Rolt – well, he's rude, to start with, and then –'

'And then?'

'Well, sir, there was a lot of trouble when he had the mill built, ten years ago. Our people – that's Colonel Babington and Miss Keats-Madderly and Sir Charles Wain and the rest of them – they wanted him to have it further up the stream, where it wouldn't spoil the amenities. But no, he wasn't having any of that, Mr Rolt wasn't. It'd got to be right on top of the village, or nothing.'

'But surely,' said Mr Datchery, 'there may have been technical reasons for that.'

'*Oh* no, sir. Not a bit of it. As a matter of fact, the site upstream would've actually been better than the one he's got, and Sir Charles, who owned it then and still does, was ready to sell it him at less than the market price, so as to save the village. But it wouldn't do for him, sir. He said he wasn't going to be stuck out in the wilderness because of what he called a lot of poppycock about unspoiled rural England, and if they didn't like it, they could lump it. They tried to stop him, of course, but there just didn't happen to be anything the lawyers could do about it.'

Mogridge's indignation was obviously second-hand; but in the persons he aped it would be real enough, no doubt, and Mr Datchery found that on this issue of the mill he was able to sympathize both with them and with the obstinate Rolt.

'But that,' he ventured, 'was ten years ago. Surely in ten years –'

'Indeed yes, sir. In ten years you'd expect the old grudges to have got glossed over a bit. And after the mill was built and the damage done, our people did make a bit of an effort to be friendly with Mr Rolt. But he wouldn't have it. It was just like their kind, he said, to come smarming up to a man they'd insulted and they weren't the sort of neighbours he wanted to be friendly with. So that was that – and that's *been* that, ever since.'

'I see.' Mr Datchery stared pensively out of the window near which he sat, noting that Casby and Babington were temporarily out of sight, their conversation having presumably impelled them down a side-turning. A nomadic chicken was pacing across the street, and by stretching his neck Mr Datchery could just make out a wheel, a mudguard, and a headlamp of the car in which, presumably, Casby had arrived. 'But all this' – he turned to Mogridge again – 'all this must be rather distressing for Rolt's family.'

'There's only his daughter.' A mere nothing, Mogridge's tone implied. 'His wife was dead, I've heard, before he ever came here.'

'But then, who looks after the daughter?'

'Looks after her, sir? Why, no one. She's sixteen or seventeen – just left school.'

'And is she as unwelcome here as her father?'

'Oh no, sir. Our people' – this proprietary phrase was beginning to jar on Mr Datchery's nerves – 'our people like her, because she's quite a different sort from her father. They'd do a lot for her if she'd let them. But she suffers, sir, from a sinful pride,' said Mogridge, shaking his head in hypocritical sorrow, 'so she gives them the cold shoulder half the time.'

'If you regard family loyalty as the equivalent of sinful pride, Mogridge,' said Mr Datchery severely, 'then it seems to me that you could do with a rather strenuous course in moral philosophy.'

Mogridge made no attempt to contest this thesis otherwise than by vacant mirth.

'Still, she's quite a pleasant young thing,' he said condescendingly. 'And I often think it a pity she should be tied to a father like that. Would it be him you've come here to see, sir?'

'No, it wouldn't.'

'Ah. Sir Charles, perhaps?'

'I am a Mass Observer,' said Mr Datchery at random, 'engaged in studying certain aspects of rural life.'

'Indeed, sir?' Mogridge was much interested. 'In that case you'll find –'

But just what Mr Datchery would find was destined to remain

for ever in the recesses of Mogridge's skull. In the last half-minute Mr Datchery had been aware of a car pulling up at the inn's door; and now, as Mogridge spoke, its owner entered the bar. She was perhaps thirty – tall and slender, with green eyes, a pink-and-white complexion, and hair whose undeniable mouse-colour was redeemed by its natural wave and its natural sheen. She wore a severely tailored brown coat and skirt which set off her admirable figure. And although she had the aspect of a professional or business woman, good nature and diffidence were both clearly legible in her face.

Inside the door she hesitated, looking a little dazedly about her. The fingers of her left hand, ringless, brushed her forehead as though she were shading her eyes.

'Has Colonel Babington been here, Mogridge?' she asked. 'I – I wanted to – I wanted to see him because –'

And then she fainted. Mr Datchery was just in time to prevent her crumpling up in a heap on the floor.

CHAPTER 4

HELEN DOWNING had woken that Friday morning before it was light.

It was several months now since she had started to sleep badly. At bed-time she was always tired – so tired that often she fell asleep over her book, leaving the light burning. But at one – or as near as made no matter – she was resigned to waking again, unrefreshed; to snatching vainly at the fleeting remnants of drowsiness; to getting up, eventually, and making tea. With any luck at all, she could doze off again at about two-thirty. But at four, or even earlier, she woke a second time, and there would be no more sleep for her then. As a doctor, she had remedies to hand – barbitone, nembutal, luminal; but she shrank from using them, knowing that in her position they were too easily got to be taken otherwise than as a last resort. In any case, their palliating the symptoms would not affect the cause. And Helen Downing knew well enough why she woke and why she worried.

So Friday's dawn, like many others, found her haggard, her body slightly aching, sitting up in bed with a tasteless cigarette in her mouth and the inevitable tea-tray at her side. As always, she had been taking stock, as she tossed and turned restlessly between the hot sheets, of her position and prospects – an exercise which, though doubtless salutary enough in itself, tends when indulged in on a burning pillow, at the turn of the night, to develop a pessimistic tinge. And certainly the conclusions which Helen Downing reached that dawning were too sombre for comfort.

It was now five years since, with the money realized by her father's life-insurance policy, she had bought her house and her practice in Cotten Abbas.

To state the transaction thus baldly is of course to oversimplify it. You did not, even before the introduction of the Health Act, buy a practice in the relatively casual manner of a housewife securing a cabbage at a shop. There were investigations to be made and a variety of contingencies to be anxiously assessed. There was the advice of knowledgeable friends to be weighed.

There was much heart-searching to be endured in the small hours of the night.

But general practice – in so many ways the most exacting career a doctor can undertake – had been Helen Downing's ambition all through the long and anxious years of her training. If she had any qualms as she put her name to the crucial papers, she kept them to herself. And when, in December of 1945, she moved into the friendly red-brick house at the back of the church, she felt able for the first time since her coming of age to face the future with reasonable confidence.

At this time, Helen was twenty-six. Alice Riddick, who had piloted her deftly through her Oxford career, told her that for a doctor she was much too good-looking, but Helen thought this judgement whimsical rather than impressive, for she was diffident to a fault.

'All the same, child, it's true,' Alice Riddick persisted. 'And if you imagine that looks are going to get you patients, you'd better think again. In my experience they're a hindrance, not a help.'

'But why?'

'Because people are stupid, child, that's why. They can't see a pretty girl without thinking of her in terms of lovers and flirtations and marriage. And that means that they'll never be able to regard you as the impersonal creature they idiotically imagine the ideal doctor to be. Of course, if you had a *husband*, now . . .'

But at twenty-six Helen was still unmarried, and her emotions had never been deeply stirred. A lonely life naturally makes for inexperience, and Helen's life had been nothing if not that. She was an only child; her mother had died not five months after bearing her; her father – a penurious, disappointed Essex parson – had lived (if you could call it that) withdrawn among his books; and since the social virtues cannot be exercised, even on a very limited scale, without a shilling or two to spare, the years of Helen's training had been almost as solitary as her childhood.

She had never complained. Complaint would have seemed to her an indignity, and in any case she was too grateful for the chance of pursuing her chosen career to imagine that she had anything serious to complain about But the scraping and saving which had so limited her youth made her look upon Cotten

Abbas as the gateway to something easier and better and more free; made her pin more hopes to her new life than it was destined, for a time anyway, to be capable of bearing. And if the subsequent bitter disillusion did not warp her, that was because she possessed a great deal more courage and tenacity than her rather confused good nature would have led an outsider to expect.

Of course, she had known all along that this practice which eventually she decided to buy would have its disadvantages.

'It's a prosperous bit of country, child,' said Alice Riddick. 'And that means it'll be relatively healthy. What's more, you'll find the farmers rather conservative-minded when it comes to having a woman prodding them and dosing them. You'd probably do better in an industrial town, because generally speaking it's the poorer people who take most kindly to women doctors. Still, I don't want to discourage you, and it certainly is cheap enough.'

This last consideration proved decisive. The resources left to Helen by her father (who had died, almost as imperceptibly as he had lived, a month before his daughter qualified) were far too scanty to cover the purchase of a really thriving practice, and the best she could hope for was to buy a more or less derelict one which looked capable of improvement. Cotten Abbas did fulfil this condition. There would be competition, of course – but since it seemed that this would take the form of a young man almost as raw and inexperienced as herself, Helen felt that she ought to be able to cope with it at least to the extent of being able to earn a modest living.

On the day she travelled to Cotten Abbas to embark on her new life there – an icy day with more than a hint of snow in the air – Helen Downing was troubled by all the wild misgivings of a small boy on his way to a new school. She believed, without conceit, that she would be able to do her job well enough. But in addition to this she longed to live more fully, to have more to do with people and parties and entertaining, than had been possible up to now, and she was horribly afraid of spoiling her chances by a false start – by over-eagerness, or by too much reserve, or by some unimaginable but conclusive *faux pas*. Such fears, as she well knew, were not a little absurd in a person of her age, but her circumstances had been uncommon, and had militated more than she could be aware against the growth of self-confidence in her. Staring from her compartment window at the bleak, flat country through which the train was moving, she experienced at certain moments on that crucial journey an emotion not far removed from panic.

She need not have worried. Whatever their other faults, the people of Cotten Abbas were certainly not stand-offish or un-friendly. During that first week they called on her in droves to drink her tea, talk amiable scandal about one another, issue satisfyingly specific invitations, recommend pig-keeping (a flourish-ing local hobby), laud or denigrate tradespeople, and proffer advice on the best disposition of her father's rather heavy and ecclesiastical furniture. In a word, they accepted her, without reservation or delay, as one of themselves. And since it never occurred to her that this excellent state of affairs might be due in any degree to her own personality and charm, Helen was deeply grateful. From the social point of view, she had been made magnificently welcome.

It soon became clear, however, that her professional welcome was likely to be of a rather less reassuring kind.

The prejudice against women doctors has in these days to some extent been overcome; but it would be foolish to pretend that its operation is not still powerful. Women, who on grounds of modesty alone might be expected to prefer being killed or cured by one of their own sex, prove as incalculable in this as in most other things; and as to men, it is rare, except among the poor, for a woman doctor to have more than a score or thirty of them among her patients. At the end of her first year in Cotten Abbas, Helen was already anxious. At the end of her third, her panel, far from increasing, had actually diminished, so that there were times when she was hard put to it to pay her modest bills. At the end of her fourth, she was very uncomfortably in debt.

Money troubles are seldom sudden. They accumulate, insid-iously, over quite long periods; and after a certain point they appear, to the dismayed observer, to proliferate and multiply – rather in the supernatural fashion by which wealth seems to beget wealth – without human intervention of any kind. It was in this disastrous situation that Helen found herself at the start of 1950. She had not been extravagant; she had not been idle; but just the same, she was in debt. And although her creditors were not pressing her, she could see, in her more pessimistic moments, no prospect of ever being out of debt again.

And the reason? Well, the main reason was Dr George Sims. Before as much as six months were out, Helen knew that where Dr George Sims was concerned her calculations and estimates had gone badly astray.

He had returned from the war, and taken over his father's practice, only a few weeks before Helen's arrival. It had been a good practice to start with, and he had soon, at Helen's expense, made it an even better one. A tall, stringy, vehement man of thirty-three, with an unruly mop of red hair and a humorously ugly face, Dr George Sims rattled about the roads and lanes in an ancient Morris, delighting his patients (and the women in particular) with uncomplimentary addresses on the subject of their appearance, tastes, habits, and mode of living.

'What the devil do you expect,' he would yell at them, 'if you stuff yourself with potatoes and chocolate from morning till night? Look at all this disgusting fat! Look at it! Your heart's labouring, your liver's defective, your thyroid's given up the ghost and you're developing flat feet. Ill? Of course you're ill! It's a wonder to me you aren't *dead!*'

And they loved it.

Even with women, Helen's gentleness proved to be no match for George Sims' cheerful violence. There was Beatrice Keat-Madderly, for instance. She had particularly befriended Helen – but when a doctor was wanted, it was George Sims she sent for.

'It's no use, love,' she said. 'I'm too old to change my ways now. I dare say you're a much better doctor than George, but I'd never get used to you, though you're a dear girl ... One of these days' – and here her eyes twinkled, as if at some secret joke – 'you'll forgive me, see if you don't.'

The inwardness of this cryptic prophecy was to be revealed soon enough. In the meantime, Helen went back to her bills.

And on Friday 26 May, 1950, she received, through the post, one of the first of the anonymous letters.

It came in a cheap envelope, addressed to her in round, illiterate capitals; and its matter consisted of certain brief and grossly obscene statements regarding the motives of women doctors who examine male patients.

Helen was not, of course, so innocent as to be unaware that such accusations are occasionally made; but at the same time she was not so sophisticated as to be immune from feeling sick and wretched when they were levelled at herself. Her fingers closed on the paper in readiness to crush it. Then she hesitated. Hadn't it better go to the police? The idea of anyone else's seeing such suggestions about herself was particularly disagreeable, but obviously she ought not to allow that sort of consideration to influence her. Other people might have received similar letters, and for all she knew, hers might be capable of providing the police with a clue which would enable them to expose the writer ... Sitting at her breakfast table, with a face as white as skimmed milk, Helen forced herself to read the thing again. It looked the work of an illiterate – but the illiteracy of anonymous letters, she remembered, was more commonly feigned than genuine.

Her indecision did not last long. Finishing her coffee, she put the letter and its envelope into her pocket and left the house. In another half minute she was knocking at her nearest neighbour's front door.

Helen would hardly have believed that it was possible to live for six months next door to a man, and yet to know as little about him as she knew about Inspector Edward Casby; conventional greetings, and the usual exchange of weather-lore, made up the whole of her relations with him hitherto. She knew he was unmarried, and suspected him of being temperamentally a solitary person. But neither her own observation, nor the resources of her friends in the village, had been able to supply her with any more substantial information about him, and she had sometimes vaguely wondered why she should feel so inquisitive concerning a man whom she glimpsed, and spoke to, so briefly and so seldom.

He opened the door to her himself, and from his raincoat and brief-case she saw that he was on the point of leaving for Twelford.

'I'm awfully sorry to bother you,' Helen said, 'and I don't

37

really know whether it's you I ought to be bothering anyway. But the fact is, I've just had rather a disgusting anonymous letter.'

'I see.' He smiled his involuntarily twisted smile. 'In that case it was very proper and sensible of you to bring it to me. Do come in.'

'You were just going out,' said Helen a little breathlessly. 'I mustn't delay you.'

'They don't make me clock in at Twelford,' he answered, still smiling. 'I'm much too exalted for that.'

'No, of course not.' For some reason Helen felt that she had spoken foolishly. 'I will come in, thank you, just for a moment.'

He took her into his sitting-room. Though austerely furnished, it was scrupulously clean – and knowing Mrs Flack, who 'did' for Casby, Helen felt tolerably certain that this latter circumstance could not plausibly be assigned to her efforts.

'Please sit down,' he said. 'And would you like a drop of brandy? It would probably do you good.'

Helen laughed rather shakily. 'Do I look as groggy as that?'

'You're a little pale,' he said matter-of-factly. 'I imagine this letter of yours has upset you – which isn't surprising.'

'Yes, it has.' Helen produced the letter and handed it to him. 'I'm over-sensitive, I expect.'

'Are you?' He unfolded the letter and glanced through it. 'But not morbidly, I should have said ... Yes, this is very much the usual thing. It's good of you to let me have it, because one does feel shy about nonsense of this sort.'

Without in the least knowing why, Helen was flattered and gratified. She said : 'You'll want to keep it, of course.'

'Yes, please. One or two experts will have to see it, but apart from them, no one need know anything about it. It came by this morning's post, I suppose?'

'Yes.'

He put the letter and envelope carefully into his brief-case. 'You're not the only victim,' he said. 'Two other letters like this have been brought to us, and I've no doubt there are some we haven't been told about.'

'Who else has had them?'

He smiled at her. 'I'm afraid I can't tell you that.'

'No, of course not,' said Helen, confused. 'It was very stupid of me to ask you.'

This seemed to surprise him. 'I don't see why,' he retorted. 'It's natural to be curious. I'm sorry to say that so far we haven't the ghost of a notion who's writing the things, but we're doing our best to pin him down.'

'It's usually a woman, isn't it?'

'In the past,' he said carefully, 'about seventy per cent of the writers of anonymous letters have turned out to be women. That's not counting blackmail letters ... By the way, if you get another of them – or something which looks from the outside as if it was another – will you bring it to me without opening it?'

'You mean because of fingerprints?'

'Partly that, and partly because almost all letters contain something in the way of hairs or dust. Laboratory analysis can sometimes show where the hairs and dust came from.'

'It sounds like Dr Thorndyke.'

'It's very like Dr Thorndyke, except that with us it doesn't come off quite as often as it did with him. Anyway, do you mind doing that?'

'Of course not,' Helen said. 'Would it be indiscreet to ask if there are any clues so far?'

'Well, we've got one or two rather anaemic specimens, but nothing at all decisive. Do you read many newspapers?'

The question took Helen unawares. 'Only one,' she said.

'Yes, it's the same with most people ... Thank you very much, Dr Downing. I wish everyone was as sensible as you are.'

'It isn't being sensible,' said Helen. 'It's reading detective stories.'

'Well, then, I wish everyone read detective stories. Are you feeling all right now?'

'Yes, thanks, perfectly.'

They left the house together, parting at the gate. And Helen, pensively clearing away her breakfast things, found that she was unable to make up her mind whether she liked Inspector Edward Casby or not. His cool common sense had, she knew, been precisely the right specific for the sick depression which the anonymous letter had engendered in her; but she thought that it had

been calculated rather than natural, and was inclined – most un-
reasonably, as she herself admitted – to consider this an affront.
Before setting off on her all-too-short round of patients, she
succeeded, with something of an effort, in dismissing him from
her mind. But he nevertheless showed an aggravating tendency to
return there uninvited throughout the remainder of the day ...

... And it hasn't stopped there, either, thought Helen wryly as
she swallowed, that Friday, the last of her very early morning tea.
But it can't be that I'm in love with the man, or any such nonsense as that, because although I keep thinking about him there
isn't a trace of affection in my attitude to him, or even of real
liking. Odd. I suppose the fact of the matter is that he's slightly
mysterious – which means that once I find out what makes him
tick I shall lose interest in him. Has he *got* any interests outside
his work? On the whole I imagine not: his room was about as
impersonal as a room can be ...

By now the full light had come. Slipping from her bed, Helen
went to the window and looked out. There was a mist, she saw:
but a gleam of weak gold on the angle of the church's high,
square tower suggested that the sun would soon disperse that.
Dew winked on the yellow roses in the garden. The untidy grave-
yard looked, as always, more friendly than sinister, and apart
from the birds Cotten Abbas was preternaturally quiet. Half past
five. Well, there was no question of sleeping now; better get
dressed and go for a stroll than sit moping in bed.

So that day claimed her, and the morning passed, and the sun
grew hot towards his zenith. There were letters to be dealt with,
surgery hours to be kept, a few patients to be visited in their
homes. Helen worked hard, working to keep reflection at bay. By
lunch-time she was almost cheerful.

And then, at shortly after two o'clock in the afternoon, the
first blow fell.

CHAPTER 5

LUNCH had been cleared. As Helen sat idly over coffee and a cigarette in her rather sombre little sitting-room, the telephone rang. Answering it, she missed the name and for a moment failed to recognize the voice.

'I'm sorry, but I didn't – Who is that, please?'

'Sims.' The word came thinly, a ghost at her ear. 'George Sims speaking.'

'Oh yes, of course. The line doesn't seem to be very good.'

'It's about Beatrice – Beatrice Keats-Madderly. There's been an accident, I'm afraid.'

'An accident?'

'At her house. I'm going there now. I thought you'd want to know.'

'But what exactly –'

'I only know it's bad, as bad as it could be.'

'She – she's not – not dead?'

There was a pause. Then:

'Yes . . . I'm sorry.'

'But how? How?'

'I can't be sure till I get there.' An obvious evasion. 'Shall I phone you again, or do you want to come yourself?'

'I'll come at once,' said Helen, and rang off.

By action you could keep your mind empty and your emotions in suspense, like dogs beyond a paper door. Helen got her car out, drove to the main street, turned into it with her usual precaution, accelerated past 'The Marlborough Head', came into open country. Half a mile along the Brankham road she swung the car into a narrow but well-kept lane – high grass banks, thorn hedges, nettles in flower. The small house she looked for stood alone against a straggling frieze of larches on the left.

It was compact, modern, well-built, uncompromisingly symmetrical: the front door mathematically central, the letter-box mathematically central in the front door. A large, tidy garden invested it squarely, lawns mown close and paths swept. The gate was freshly painted green, and across the lane from it a hedger had recently been at work. Leaving her car parked behind another, which she recognized, Helen half walked and half ran to where Burns, the village constable, stood sentry on the front step. He saluted her uneasily, his normally ruddy and amiable young face strained now, and pale. But before either of them could speak the door was opened and Casby looked out.

'I thought you were Sims,' he said.

'He's coming. He rang me up. He lives further away than I do, so of course I got here first.'

'Yes.'

'But he didn't make it clear what's happened. Some sort of accident...'

'You were close friends, weren't you?'

'Beatrice and I? Yes. Please tell me what's happened.'

He looked at her steadily before he answered, appraising her fortitude, gauging the expected reaction; and the knowledge of his doing this somehow strengthened her. 'What has happened,' he said levelly, 'is that Miss Keats-Madderly has hanged herself.'

Gravel crunched as Burns, who had stood aside at Casby's appearance, shifted his weight from one foot to the other. The hum of a third car sounded along the lane. 'I see,' said Helen in a flat voice; the paper barrier against emotion still held. 'May I come in?'

'Of course. But it's not pleasant.'

'I've seen a lot of deaths.'

'Yes,' he said. 'I was forgetting.'

Red hair glowing in the sunlight, a medical bag in his hand, Dr George Sims joined them. Beatrice Keats-Madderly had been his patient, not Helen's, and in any case he was the local police-surgeon. They entered the house together, in silence, to look at what hung from the banisters...

And then minutes later: 'Why?' said Helen urgently. 'For heaven's sake, *why?*'

They had finished what needed to be done and had adjourned to the sitting-room. Casby, his elbow on the mantelpiece and his foot on the fender, was staring into the grate. Helen paced restlessly up and down. And George Sims, his white face giving the lie to rumours of his callousness, sat slumped in a chair.

'As to why,' he said slowly, 'one just doesn't have a clue. There was no suicide-note, I suppose?' Casby shook his head. 'No. Of course, convalescents do sometimes get bad go's of depression, but I shouldn't have thought that that by itself ...' His voice tailed away.

'Convalescents?' Helen echoed vaguely; and then, a half second after saying it, remembered. A fortnight or three weeks ago Beatrice had succumbed to measles – an unromantic ailment, but one which in an adult is apt to be dangerous. For at least three days her temperature had hovered in the region of hundred and five, and it was said in the village that she had been intermittently delirious ... Imbecile to have forgotten that. And of course George Sims was right: Beatrice was only just over it. 'Tuesday was the last time I saw her,' Helen said. 'That was her first day up. She didn't seem in the least depressed then.'

Casby glanced at Sims. 'What was your impression?'

'Same thing. She was lively enough to disobey doctor's orders, anyway.'

'Oh? How?'

'Went off gallivanting somewhere or other this morning, after I'd told her she wasn't to go outside the garden before Monday. I came here this morning on my round, so that's how I know. The hedger chap working across the way, Harris or whatever his name is, condescended to tell me, after I'd been banging at the front door for about ten minutes, that she'd left soon after breakfast and hadn't come back yet. I was *not* pleased.'

Casby nodded. 'She went shopping in Twelford, I fancy. There's a shopping-basket in the kitchen with invoices in it, dated to-day, from various Twelford stores ... No, I doubt if her illness is to blame.' His gaze switched back to the grate. 'There's a likelier suspect here.'

Helen crossed the room to look. No fire was laid, but something – paper of some description – had recently been burned in the empty hearth. Helen stared at it blankly for a moment before the implication sank in. 'An anonymous letter,' she said.

'Very probably. Anyway, I can soon read it and find out.'

'*Read* it? But –'

He smiled faintly. 'Yes, it isn't too much broken up for that. A tricky job, but quite possible. Infra-red photography is what one uses.'

Helen said: 'Do you have to leave her? I mean, can't she be – be taken down?'

'The sooner the better. But I'm afraid that before that happens I must make absolutely sure this business is what it appears to be.'

'"Appears"?' Helen was startled. 'But what else could it –'

'It could be accident or murder. I don't as a matter of fact believe it's either, but I must be certain.' Casby went to the door, opened it. 'Moffatt! Harris!' he called. 'Come in here a moment, will you?'

Footsteps shuffled from the kitchen into the hall, and thence to the sitting-room door; Helen heard them pause, then scrape and quicken, as they came to the well of the stairs. Both of the men who now entered were known to Helen, but it was old Moffatt, Beatrice's gardener, that she knew best. His eyes met hers, flickered, looked away; and she could guess what he was thinking. Beatrice Keats-Madderly, large and formidable in her shapeless brogues and tweeds, with her kindness, her invincible prejudices, her close-cropped greying hair and her chain-smoking, had been a human landmark in Cotten Abbas for many years now; for her to leave, and go elsewhere, would have been comprehensible; but reason boggled at identifying Beatrice living with Beatrice dead, at equating a vivid personality with a black-faced dummy on a string, and the shock of that terrible alteration was like print on old Moffatt's wrinkled face.

However, his story, as elicited by Casby, was clear and level-headed enough. He had arrived that morning shortly after eight; had seen his employer leave for Twelford; had worked all morning in the garden behind the house, had eaten lunch there under a tree, and at about two o'clock had entered the house by the back door with a view to arguing his instructions about a herbaceous border. That was when he had found the body and telephoned to the police. Could there, unknown to him, have been anyone else in the house at that time? No, he was sure there couldn't. Could

44

anyone, during the morning, have entered or left by the bac̵.
No again. Certain? Certain.

Len Harris was coarser stuff; a youngish man, new to the village and not much liked, but a good worker. Yes, he'd been trimming the hedge out at the front. Yes, he'd seen her leave all right, about nine it'd have been, and she'd come back with her shopping towards one. No, no one had come to the house while she was away, except Dr Sims and the postwoman, he could swear to that. Nor between one and two, either, when he'd been having his bread and cheese. Helen mistrusted the gleam of unhealthy excitement in his eyes, but there could be no doubt that he was a completely reliable witness – as indeed was later proved. She herself was able to answer Casby's question about servants. There was only one, she told him, an elderly maid-of-all-work who two days ago had been taken to Twelford hospital to be treated for infective phlebitis; and Beatrice had refused to look for a substitute for her, insisting that she was quite well enough to see to her own needs till Elsie was better. Which meant –

But at this point they were interrupted by a knock on the front door. Towards the end of the interrogation Sims had wandered out of the room, and it was he who now put his head in to announce that the afternoon post had arrived, and that he presumed Casby would want to talk to the postwoman. Casby did want, and Helen, terrified of inaction, followed him out to the doorstep where Miss Pilkington waited. For over forty years now Miss Pilkington had delivered the mail in Cotten Abbas, and her small, bent, uncurious figure was as familiar there as the church tower itself, plodding on unexpectedly large feet from door to door in every sort of weather, never hurried, never late, never at fault. She waited now with the passive disinterest of a soul so long wedded to routine that nothing can rouse it; but her answers to Casby's questions were lucid and acute.

Five letters, she said, had come for Beatrice Keats-Madderly by the morning post that day. Could she describe them? – yes, certainly she could; since the anonymous letters started she'd been more than commonly interested in people's post, and if she was to be blamed for that, then all she could say was – Casby called a halt to this shadow-boxing and got her back to the point;

45

five letters, he reminded her ... Yes, well, one of them was a long envelope, address typewritten, penny stamp, obviously a circular; another, typewritten also, had looked like a bill; and the remaining three were all twopenny-halfpennies, addresses in writing, one of them in violet ink; no, none of them in block capitals. As to recognizing them again if they were shown to her, Miss Pilkington didn't think she'd have much difficulty in doing that.

A small, untidy heap of letters and envelopes, hitherto unexamined, lay on the hall table, and Casby now went inside to fetch them. Yes, said Miss Pilkington, that was them all right. Only four of them, though: the violet-ink one was gone ...

'And where?' said Casby as soon as Miss Pilkington had taken herself off. '*Where* has it gone? Anyone got any ideas?'

Helen was surprised. 'Burned, surely,' she said.

'The message, perhaps. But why burn the envelope it came in?'

'The other four letters are all right, then?'

'Perfectly harmless.'

'I see what you mean. If she – if Beatrice committed suicide because of an anonymous letter she'd destroy that, to stop people knowing what was in it. But there'd be no point in destroying the envelope as well ... unless ... oh well, you know, she may have done. I don't expect' – and Helen's voice shook a little – 'I don't expect she was feeling very calm and reasonable at the time.'

'The fact remains that the ashes in the grate are the ashes of a single sheet of paper, and nothing more. If that envelope's here I must find it. I don't like loose ends.'

'I'll help you look,' said Helen ....

But a quarter of an hour later they were still looking.

'It's no good,' said Casby at last. 'This isn't getting us anywhere. I'll have another go later on. In the meantime I must phone the mortuary for a van, and I suppose I'd better get in touch with the Chief Constable as well ... You don't know of any relatives, do you?'

Helen shook her head. 'She never spoke of any. There'll have to be an inquest, I suppose?'

'Yes. That certainly. And as to' – he hesitated – 'the other arrangements, if no relatives turn up, then I suppose ...'

'I'll see to all that.'

46

'Good. I hoped you might. By the way, who was her lawyer?'

'I'm not quite sure.' Helen frowned. 'Someone in Twelford, that much I can tell you, but I've forgotten the name.'

'We'll find him,' said Casby, and went to the telephone.

Helen might have left then; there was nothing for her to do, and she knew she was in the way. But it was somehow unthinkable that Beatrice should be taken away from the home where she had lived so long with no one but strangers to see her go, and Helen determined to remain at least until that had been done. She went out into the garden and sat down on a wooden seat which surrounded a sundial amid roses. By now, inside the house, they would be cutting through the scarlet sash of the house-coat, lowering the body, carrying it to – to the sitting-room sofa, Helen supposed: no point in putting it in the bedroom when it would so soon be gone ... Helen sat among the roses and cried quietly, easily, her shoulders hardly moving beneath her brown coat.

Half an hour later George Sims came out; evidently he had finished his examination and was leaving. He hesitated when he saw Helen, and for a moment seemed to contemplate speaking to her. But if he ever had the idea he soon dismissed it, raising his hand diffidently in lieu of good-bye, climbing into his car and driving off with much din and blue smoke. 'George Sims tells me you avoid him,' Beatrice had once said to Helen in her usual forthright way. 'Not been making unwelcome passes at you, has he?' And Helen had laughed. 'Good Lord, no – not but what I'd be the envy of every woman in the county if he had.' 'Well then, why?' Beatrice had persisted; and Helen had been hard put to it to adduce a satisfactory reason, even to herself. It was not, certainly, a question of personal dislike, for what little she had seen of George Sims had attracted her rather than the reverse. Nor – Helen was ready to swear it on her honour – could it be accounted for by professional pique. No, the only answer she had been able to find was that she had kept away from George Sims because she had obscurely felt that a distance between them would be – what was the word? – yes, *politic*, expedient. Beatrice, who was nothing if not practical, had been very little impressed by this halting and nebulous explanation; but then, Beatrice, as a well-to-do woman with an independent income, had never known what it was to be driven to the verge of insolvency by the legitimate rivalry of someone who was better at your job than you were ...

Helen sat on; and it seemed a long time before the front door opened and Casby reappeared. He scanned the garden, sighted her, and crossed the lawn to join her. 'Hello,' he said, 'I thought you'd gone long ago.'

'I was waiting for the van to come.'

'Yes, it's not exactly prompt, is it? I've got to get back now, but I'm leaving Burns to look after things. Will you be all right?'

'I shall, thank you. Is there anything –'

'Anything new? No, nothing. I think it was quite certainly suicide, if that's what you mean. The only oddity is the disappearance of that violet-ink envelope. She definitely didn't burn it with the letter, and yet it isn't anywhere to be found. Still, there's probably some obvious explanation I haven't thought of: I always was apt to be over-subtle about these things.'

'And you think you'll be able to read what's in the letter?'

'Probably. Why?'

'I was only wondering,' said Helen slowly, 'if whatever's in it will have to come out at the inquest. I suppose it's silly to think it matters now, whatever it is, but at the same time ...' She hesitated, and he said:

'At the same time, it'd be a pity. Yes, I agree. The trouble is that that depends on the coroner, not on me. But I'll see what I can manage.'

He nodded and went, and his car must have passed the mortuary van immediately after turning into Brankham road, for it seemed to Helen that she had hardly sat down again before the white-coated attendants appeared at the gate. She walked unselfconsciously beside the covered stretcher when they carried it from the house to the van, and with Moffatt the gardener watched from the gate as it was driven away. Then she went into the house and drew all the curtains. A meaningless piety, she knew – but to be always meaningful makes a cold world.

It was not until she was driving back into the village that the giddiness came, and the nausea. She felt her heart flutter, felt her skin go damp and cold, saw the village street blur and quiver before her eyes, pulled in frantically to the kerb outside 'The

Marlborough Head'. Helen hated physical weakness, and feared it; she fought it down, got out of the car and pushed open the door of the Lounge Bar: modern medicine disapproves of alcohol as a remedy, but Helen was in no mood for professional niceties, and in her present condition dared not, for the moment, go on driving. Inside, she was fleetingly conscious of Mogridge and of a tall, lean, affable stranger with oddly formidable-looking pale blue eyes; then the giddiness returned. Clutching at speech as the drowning clutch at straws, Helen spoke for the mere sake of it, careless of what she said or why. After that, oblivion.

The world she returned to was new, different, dream-like, all passion spent. She was aware that Casby was in the bar, and Colonel Babington; was aware of Mogridge proffering smelling-salts with an air of manly solicitude; was aware of being spoken to and of answering; was aware of the stranger's introducing himself, and of Casby's asking him some incomprehensible question about a Verger; was aware, finally, of being driven home by Casby and committed to the care of her servant Melanie. All these things she knew and afterwards remembered, but they were like scenes looked at through an inverted telescope: lucid, yet infinitely remote and infinitely unimportant. There was only one thing that was important. Helen Downing climbed the stairs, lay down on her bed, and in a moment was fast asleep.

CHAPTER 6

'AND now, Mogridge,' said Mr Datchery with firmness, 'you must answer me some questions, if you please.'

It was early afternoon of the following day. To say that Mr Datchery had not in the meantime been idle would be slightly disingenuous, for he was by nature a volatile man, readily distracted by trifles from any business which he happened to have in hand, and he had never found in total inactivity the tedium which proverbial wisdom ascribed to it. On his current mission, however, he had succeeded in keeping more or less to the point, and it was perhaps the consciousness of virtue, as much as Mogridge's natural talent for being victimized, which caused him to adopt his present rather hectoring tones.

Mr Datchery's virtue had taken the form of gossip, for as a stranger to Cotten Abbas he felt it essential to acquire at the outset some knowledge of the *dramatis personae* with whose lives he was proposing, if possible, to interfere. And the harvest so far had been good. About Beatrice Keats-Madderly's suicide, for example, he by now knew as much as anybody in the village, and he had in addition built up an adequate mental picture of Helen Downing and George Sims and the two Rolts. Casby alone remained, as a personality, elusive; no one, in the bar last evening or in the village this morning, had seemed to have any very decided views about him, and Mr Datchery's own acquaintance with him, in the few minutes after Helen Downing had recovered from her faint, had been too brief to reveal much more than the fact that he was shrewd and quick-witted. For on Mr Datchery's introducing himself: 'Oughtn't you,' Casby had pleasantly inquired, 'to be staying with the Verger?' And at Mr Datchery's calculated reply 'Ought I? Would it be better than here?' he had raised his eyebrows in polite surprise at this unlikely lack of awareness of a fictional namesake . . . Yes, Casby's was certainly a mind to be reckoned with. But apart from that – well, apart from that, the only thing Mr Datchery had noticed about him was that in an undemonstrative way he had seemed emotionally interested in Helen Downing; and for that interest there might, Mr Datchery thought, be more motives than one.

Mr Datchery had spent that morning, the morning of the Saturday, wandering about the village chatting to whomever he met; had lunched in Twelford; and had returned to 'The Marlborough Head' to find Mogridge in process of shutting up the bar. Mogridge was glum, a condition disagreeably familiar to him since his wife's discovery that he was 'friendly' (as in discussing the matter with intimates he decently termed it) with the buxom and rapacious Cora; that discovery had been communicated to him, by about the most public method conceivable, in this very room, and he was liable in moments of depression to feel that those who had witnessed it – which is to say, half Cotten Abbas – had only to set eyes on him for the event to monopolize their recollection to the exclusion of all else. He was troubled, moreover, by the irrational conviction that his undoing had been bruited about the nation like a rumour of war, and that in consequence the colleagues on his cherished Innkeepers' Regional Committee, coming to know of it, would expel him, ignominiously and for ever, from their elevating deliberations. These fears were as a matter of fact almost wholly unfounded, but they continued to bedevil him none the less for that. And although plump Cora had been spectacularly dismissed and an elderly woman prone to fits of causeless weeping substituted for her, although Eunice Mogridge had long since settled down to the pleasing routine of neither forgiving nor forgetting, although the Mogridge upheaval had some time ago been superseded in the general interest by other and more recent occurrences of a similar sort – despite all these things, the harrassed Mogridge continued, in his *mauvais quarts d'heure*, to plumb untold depths of embarrassment and social discomfort.

He greeted Mr Datchery wanly, therefore, and the prospect of catechism seemed not to cheer him very much. 'Newspapers, sir?' he echoed drearily in response to Mr Datchery's first question. 'There's no one sells them in the village, you'll find. Those the residents have on order come in every morning in a van from Smith's in Twelford. If you wanted to borrow one –'

51

'No, thank you, Mogridge. Is there a fishmonger in the village?'

'A fishmonger, sir? What sort of fish would you be requiring?'

Mr Datchery sighed; he had learned from hard experience that thanks to Mogridge's habit of reading between the conversational lines, instead of accepting what people said at its face value, communication with him almost always degenerated into a maze of cross-purposes. 'It isn't fish I want,' he said patiently. 'It's a fish*monger*. A purveyor, or tradesman.'

Mogridge made a half-hearted attempt to look knowledgeable. 'The finest turbot hereabouts,' he said, 'is to be had, if I'm not much mistaken, from Potter's in Twelford. As to Dover sole –'

'*But is there a fishmonger in this village?*'

The impact of this proved sufficient to jerk a negative out of Mogridge before his helpfulness had time to step in and prolong the misunderstanding. 'None at all?' Mr Datchery reiterated with emphasis. '*None?*'

'None,' said Mogridge peevishly. 'If people here should happen to require fish' – and his defensive tone implied that this whim seized them far more often than Mr Datchery imagined – 'they send for it from Twelford.'

'Well then, is there a *butcher* in the village?'

'If it was sausages you were thinking of –'

Mr Datchery groaned. 'Awful Mogridge,' he said. 'A butcher. Not sausages, a *butcher*.'

And Mogridge brightened slightly. 'There's Weaver,' he ventured.

'And he has a shop *here? In this village?*'

'Oh yes, sir. Quite an up-to-date little shop, too. It's in Cork Lane, round by the church. He's religious,' said Mogridge, 'is Weaver.'

'I'm very glad to hear it. And lastly, does anyone living in Cotten Abbas keep or own or work in a shop at Twelford, or anywhere outside the village?'

Mogridge thought not; he thought definitely not, and Mr Datchery, tiring of the inquisition, left him. Mr Datchery had learned that morning that the professional nurse who had looked after Beatrice Keats-Madderly during her illness, by name

Marjory Bonnet, lived on the outskirts of the village; and it was to her cottage that he now made his way. As he had expected, the inquiry with which he addressed her was not well received. But whatever her other qualities, Miss Bonnet was not subtle, and Mr Datchery's guileful approach induced her to give him his answer, by implication, as surely and as unambiguously as if she had put it into so many words. He came satisfied away from her door, meditating on violet ink; and although the association with that fluid, which certainly existed somewhere at the back of his mind, refused to reveal itself, he felt that in all other respects his affairs were decidedly prospering . . .

It was in this state of complacency that he encountered the tot.

The encounter did not, at the time, seem specially portentous, though events were to prove it so. Nor, all things considered, was the encounter surprising; where there are cottages, there will be tots also, squatting pensively in the dust or moving unsteadily about, absorbed in the tremendous adventure of proceeding un-aided from one point to the next. But Mr Datchery's tot was peculiar in this, that it seemed to be carrying something altogether incommensurate with its physical resources. It was female, Mr Datchery saw, and about three years of age; and it was staggering grimly towards him with a murderous-looking object clutched precariously in its arms.

'Hello,' said Mr Datchery. 'What's that you've got?'

The question was strictly speaking superfluous, since the nature of the object was plain enough; it was a large and formidable butcher's steel – that is, a heavy, rod-like bar of grooved metal with a sharp point at one end and a horn handle at the other. Its present possessor, on being accosted, halted, and surveyed Mr Datchery with gloom for a moment. She then immediately fell flat on her face.

But she was not, it seemed, the bellowing sort. Assisted by Mr Datchery, she got back on to her feet without breaking silence. And Mr Datchery, having noted with alarm that the point of the steel had only just failed to gouge out an eye, felt very strongly that it had better be removed before it had a second chance.

'Does that belong to your daddy?' he asked. The tot thought this over and presently shook its head. 'Where did you get it,

53

then?' Finding the question beyond its competence, the tot ignored it in favour of attempting, with a great display of knicker, to stand on its head. 'Will you,' said Mr Datchery, 'give it to me to look after?' The tot indicated that it would not. 'Well, then' – after some search Mr Datchery had produced and was proffering a personal point – 'will you change it for something to buy sweets with?' The tot accepted the coupon and put it in its mouth. 'No, no,' said Mr Datchery. 'You must take that to the shop, and then they'll give you the sweets – providing, of course, that you take money as well.' He gave the tot sixpence, and it put that in its mouth too. 'No, no,' said Mr Datchery again, retrieving the sixpence and the coupon with some difficulty from their moist concealment. 'What I mean is –'

But at this point the tot for the first time spoke. Scuffing the dust with one toe, and gazing abstractedly at a point in space somewhat to the right of Mr Datchery's left elbow, it embarked on a long diatribe having, as far as Mr Datchery could make out, nothing whatever to do with the matter at issue. 'Yes, that's all very well,' said Mr Datchery as soon as it seemed to have finished. 'But what I want to know is, are you or are you not going to swap your steel for my sixpence?' The tot contemplated him in simple wonder for an instant, and then, abruptly losing interest in the steel, the sixpence, the coupon, Mr Datchery and indeed the entire transaction, wobbled away dismissively into the gate of the cottage outside which they stood and was lost from view, leaving the steel where it had fallen.

Mr Datchery picked the steel up and looked at it dubiously. It might, of course, belong in the cottage – but for domestic purposes it was over-large, he thought, and in any case, the cottage appeared, apart from the tot, to be at the moment uninhabited. After a brief hesitation, therefore, he continued on his way, the steel swinging in his hand. And so it was that a few minutes later he rounded a bend in the lane and came in sight of a large and rather featureless house on the left-hand side. In front of the house was a gate; leaning over the gate, in a curiously furtive manner, was Colonel Andrew Babington, Chief Constable of the county; and parked just beyond the gate was a car which Mr Datchery recognized as Dr Helen Downing's. Mr Datchery received the impression that, as he came in view, Colonel Babington cast something hurriedly from him into the rhododendron bushes, and that a drift of pale blue vapour was hovering within measurable distance of his head. But by the time Mr Datchery reached the gate this had vanished. 'Still not smoking?' Mr Datchery inquired.

'The thing to do when you give up smoking,' Colonel Babington answered obliquely, 'is to tell everyone you're doing it. Then the only way your self-respect will allow you to smoke is in secret.' He produced a packet of jujubes and placed one with repugnance in his mouth. 'These things help.'

'Once *I'd* given up smoking,' said Mr Datchery smugly, '*my* self-respect wouldn't allow me to smoke even in secret.'

The Colonel regarded him with dislike. 'I dare say,' he said. 'It's easy to theorize. The trouble is, you get to feel so fit in such a short time that you can't imagine why you ever gave it up at all. And then before you know where you are –'

'Wouldn't it be better to just try and cut it down?'

'That's another thing you start thinking.'

'Well,' said Mr Datchery. 'So this is where you live.'

'Yes. Out for a walk, are you?'

'Here's a butcher's steel for you.'

'*A what?*'

'I took it from an infant.'

'Indeed. I've no doubt you think it very funny to –'

But by now Mr Datchery had thrust the steel into his hand, and this silenced him temporarily. 'Dangerous-looking thing,' he commented after examining it. 'Belongs to Weaver, I expect. Did you say an infant?'

'An infant.'

'Interesting,' said Colonel Babington. 'But I don't know what you want to give it to me for.'

'You represent the law, don't you?'

'I dare say I do, but I'm not a ruddy lost-property office.'

'Keep it,' said Mr Datchery generously. 'You keep it. Then you can return it to its owner when you go to fetch your meat.'

'I don't fetch my meat,' said the Colonel irascibly. 'It's delivered.'

'Well, then –' But here Mr Datchery broke off, for Helen Downing, emerging from the house, had come to join them. Her visit was apparently a professional one, for she carried a medical bag. 'Hello, how are you?' said Mr Datchery. 'No more faints, I hope?'

She smiled and shook her head – at which Mr Datchery, who liked to suppose himself too old now to look with wantonness at handsome young women, was much moved. 'But what's the trouble?' she asked. 'And what on earth's that?'

They showed her the steel and explained how they had come by it. 'Well, I'll take it if you like,' she said. 'I've got to pass Weaver's shop on my way home.'

The Colonel looked relieved. 'If you're quite sure it wouldn't be a nuisance...'

'Of course not ... Your wife's *very* much better, Colonel Babington, and I've told her she can get up to-morrow for an hour or two. But she's not to go out, or try to do anything.'

'I didn't realize Mrs Babington was ill,' said Mr Datchery. 'I'm so sorry.'

''Flu,' said the Colonel. ''Flu, if you please, in June.'

'Anyway, she's over it now.' Helen's smile did not quite disguise the effects of the strain she had undergone. 'Well, I must be getting back. I'll come again on Tuesday.'

They watched while she climbed into the car, pushed the steel into the leather pocket inside the door, and drove away. 'Nice girl,' said Colonel Babington appreciatively. 'They don't come any better.'

'And is she a good doctor?'

'I believe so. Haven't got much use for women doctors myself, but my wife swears by her. Well. You'd like some tea, I expect.'

'I'd rather have a drink.'

'So would I. Come on in, then.'

The garden was large – several acres, Mr Datchery thought; and the house had the mournful though heroic air, common in these days, of a dwelling which has to keep up appearances without the intervention of a sufficient staff. 'With my wife in bed,' said the Colonel, 'and only one girl to do the cleaning and the cooking, we're in a bit of a muddle at the moment. What we ought to do is abandon a lot of the rooms – shut 'em up – but I can't make up my mind to it. It's like an amputation, half the house dies on you. Of course, with me it's really money, not labour, that's the trouble; I sometimes think I must be in the same wood the country isn't out of yet ... Well, here we are. Look out for the mat inside, it slips.'

He opened the front door. A large and comely marmalade cat emerged in a hurry, careered to the step, and there stopped dead, peering apprehensively about it. 'It's funny he does that,' said Colonel Babington. 'Never been able to understand it. He has Enemies, I suppose.'

'A Kafka cat,' said Mr Datchery. 'Though it may be that what he sees is Martians.'

'Martians, poppycock. All this saucer business, I never heard such stuff.'

'What do you call him?'

'Lavender,' said the Colonel. 'His name's Lavender.'

Brooding over this instance of misplaced fancy, Mr Datchery was conducted into a large and airy study on the right-hand side of the hall, and while Colonel Babington fiddled with a tantalus, sat contemplating the cat Lavender, which had changed its mind and followed them in, and was now distractedly perambulating the furniture. Though beautiful, the cat Lavender did seem to be not very bright; it moved about with the hypnotic air of the feeble-witted, and unlike most of its species was scarcely able to take a step without knocking something over, so that at intervals, whenever its ramblings brought it into the vicinity of a clock or a vase, Colonel Babington closed his eyes and went rigid until the danger had passed. 'I can't think,' said Mr Datchery, 'why you *allow* it to walk along the mantelpiece like that. You could pick it up and put it down on the floor, couldn't you?'

'It looses its head if you try to do that, and makes a dash for it. You can imagine what happens then ... Soda?'

'Yes, please.'

Having dispensed the drinks, Colonel Babington put the cat Lavender unceremoniously outside the door, righted the things it had overturned, mopped his brow and sank into a chair. 'Damned hot,' he said 'Well, here's how.' They sipped gratefully. 'And now,' said the Colonel, 'let's hear how you've been getting on.'

Mr Datchery told him.

CHAPTER 7

SATURDAY, then, was on the surface uneventful. On the following morning, which was the morning of the third day of his visit to Cotten Abbas, Mr Datchery in his board-like bed awoke, not much to his gratification, at half past six, and when the communion bell began to sound, at a quarter after seven, rose hurriedly, dressed, and staggered across to the church. At half past eight, refreshed by an altercation with the Vicar about the unnatural rigour of the hour, he returned to the inn to eat breakfast, and subsequently, having bathed and shaved, made his way, by following Mogridge's laborious directions, to Beatrice Keats-Madderly's house, which he had not so far seen. His inspection of it confirmed a small but not wholly unimportant aspect of one of the theories he was incubating, and although the violet-ink problem continued to vex him intermittently, he still contrived to be fairly offensively pleased with himself by the time he set off homewards.

The route which he took in returning to 'The Marlborough Head' was more circuitous than the one by which he had come; and thus it fell out that he once again encountered Penelope Rolt, who was leaning over the parapet of a low bridge which spanned the main railway-line between London and Twelford. The bridge bore witness to a road long since abandoned and blocked up, for it led purposelessly from one expanse of grazing to another, and there was now nothing more than an ill-defined footpath where formerly carts and carriages had passed. The parapet was not high, and Penelope's thin figure was sprawled across it so as to enable her to gaze down at the metals below. The sunlight struck sparks of gold from her untidy hair, and her stained fingers caressed the warm, crumbling stone. She looked up as Mr Datchery approached.

'Hello,' she said. 'I wondered when I was going to see you again. You're Cotten's Public Mystery Number One.'

'Am I? Why?'

'You told Peter you were a Professor or something, and Mr

Mogridge says you told him you were a Mass Observer, and everyone else says you're from Scotland Yard.'

'And what,' said Mr Datchery, 'do you think?'

'I think you're what you told Peter.'

'Trustful creature.' Mr Datchery peered down at the railway line. 'Is this a favourite place of yours?'

'I come here *sometimes*,' she answered rather defensively. 'I say, does everyone feel they want to throw themselves over when they're on a bridge? I do.'

'I believe that to a small proportion of people the impulse comes naturally,' said Mr Datchery. 'Others acquire it as a result of reading about it in novels.'

'Do you feel it?'

'No.'

'It's stronger at night, of course.' Penelope rubbed her bare leg where a nettle had stung it. 'I love it here after dark, when there's an express coming through. You hear it first, a long way off, and then you see its boiler-fire yellow on the side of the cutting, and then the vibration starts and the train seems to go faster and faster as it gets closer, though of course it doesn't really, and then finally the whole bridge shakes as if someone had hit it and there's a gush of smoke and it's over and you feel quite flat again . . . You know, I can understand why people who want to kill themselves do it by chucking themselves under trains.'

'Can you?'

'Yes, I can. It's the what-do-you-call-it, the *crescendo*, and then like a terrific bang on a drum. If you poisoned yourself, or anything like that, you'd have to do it in cold blood, but a train coming up half does it for you.'

'Interesting,' said Mr Datchery with truth. 'I see what you mean.'

'And I've often wondered what it'd *feel* like if you *did* throw yourself over. I've stood here and tried to imagine it, you know the way one does, and whether it'd be better if the engine hit you while you were still falling or ran over you after you'd hit the rails.'

'I think,' said Mr Datchery without emphasis, 'that either way you'd probably feel a second or two of pain so much more

60

horrible than anything you'd expected that you'd die cursing yourself for the biggest fool who ever lived.'

'People who weren't killed have said afterwards that they didn't feel much.'

'Well, they *weren't killed*, were they? And apart from that, they were probably concussed and incapable of remembering. Human beings who propose doing something idiotic generally manage to persuade themselves that the laws of nature are going to be suspended for their benefit, and suicides aren't any exception: they imagine their act is such a stupendous and conclusive thing that in some occult fashion their capacity for feeling pain will vanish. But of course it does nothing of the kind.'

'The only thing is that if they're killed instantaneously –'

'That's a fine adverb, but it seldom means anything when applied to death. Death which is literally instantaneous is so rare as to be practically a miracle. Even a man who's shot in the heart has time to feel pain before he dies.'

'All right, Socrates,' said Penelope lightly. 'I give in. I s'pose you're going to tell me now that imagining suicide is morbid.'

Mr Datchery smiled. 'I expect it is, in excess. But most people above the level of morons do it at one time or another. In my case it brings my cowardice so nakedly to the surface that I daren't indulge in it nowadays, for fear of losing all my self-respect.'

A slow-moving goods train clattered into sight along the line, and puffed with deliberation towards them, its stoker placidly surveying the landscape through one of the cabin windows. And Penelope said abruptly:

'I had a row with my father last night.'

'Did you? I'm not surprised. You're probably very exasperating sometimes. Why do you have to tell me about it?'

'Oh, I don't know.' Penelope kicked peevishly at the long grass which grew beneath the bridge's parapet. 'I just wondered what you'd think, because when all's said and done you're quite sensible in some ways.'

'Thanks very much. But you haven't mentioned what the row was about.'

'Oh, it was *Peter*, of course,' she said petulantly. 'Pa said I

61

wasn't to see him any more, so later on, when I said that in spite of that I *had* seen him –'

'And had you?'

'No. He'd gone off hiking for the day, or anyway, that was what he was going to do. Me telling Pa I'd seen him was a Gesture.'

'Very proper,' said Mr Datchery without enthusiasm. 'Very proper and independent.'

'And the reason I'm here now is a Gesture, too. I've been here since six o'clock this morning.'

'You *must* be bored.'

'Yes, I am rather. But the point is, I hardly ever get up as early as that, so Pa'll be wondering if I've run away from home because of last night.'

'You're a nice amiable girl,' said Mr Datchery, 'aren't you? If I were your father, I should probably whack you for that.'

'Go ahead,' said Penelope airily. 'I don't mind.' She grinned, and Mr Datchery, without feeling any desire to take advantage of the offer, was pleased to see her so human and so normally naughty-minded. But then her face clouded, and for the second time she abruptly changed the subject. 'I say, what do they do to you for writing anonymous letters?'

'You get a prison sentence probably, but not, I think, a very long one. Why?'

'I just wondered, that's all. I suppose you've been hearing an awful lot about them.'

'The letters? Something.'

'Well, who do you suspect?'

'Anyone. Everyone.'

'Including Pa, of course.'

'Yes, including him. But I take it that *you* don't imagine –'

'No,' she said too quickly. 'I know him, you see, and it just isn't the sort of thing he'd ever think of. But people here don't like him, and he doesn't like them, so you could make out a case –'

'Of course you could. It wouldn't be impossible to make out a case against you.'

She stared incredulously. 'Me?'

'Or Dr Helen Downing. Or Mr Weaver, who is religious. Or

Inspector Casby. Or about a dozen other people I've met or heard of.'

Half to herself she said quietly: 'I think if they found it was my father I should die ...' And then with finality: 'Well, I'm sick of here. I'm going.'

'Home?'

'No, not yet. I'm not hungry enough yet. I'll go and potter about in the water-meadow, I think. There's a little glade in the copse there where Peter and I once – I mean, where I sometimes go to sit and think.' She turned away from the parapet. 'What are you going to do?'

'Meddle,' said Mr Datchery, 'in one way or another.' At which Penelope laughed delightedly, waved him good-bye, and ran off. A capricious child, Mr Datchery reflected as he left the bridge in the opposite direction; and at her age that was of course healthy and right. Mr Datchery had not much liked her talk of suicide, for he knew better than to subscribe to the popular fallacy that those who talk of suicide never commit it, but on the other hand he had not felt that that talk was morbid or dangerous, or would ever become so; unless – Mr Datchery scowled, thereby intimidating unawares a harmless old lady whom he happened to be passing at the moment: unless – so his thoughts ran on – Penelope's obvious fear that her father might be responsible for the anonymous letters should happen to receive confirmation, or what appeared to be that. In such an event she might need watching ... Thus ruminative, Mr Datchery ambled staidly back into Cotten Abbas.

Later, at half past eleven, Mr Datchery went to chapel.

During the short period of his stay in Cotten Abbas, his first impression of it had been confirmed: it was essentially a residential village for members of the cultured upper middle class – intelligent company directors, fashionable portrait painters and so forth – who needed to be within reach of London but who could dictate their own time of arriving there; and it was they who had been responsible, at some sacrifice to themselves, for preserving the village's amenities. They had restricted new building, and dictated its style when it proved inevitable; they had sat in judgement on inn-signs; they had pestered the Vicar to remove

63

the Victorian pews from the great church, and had paid for better ones to replace them; they had supervised restoration and rebuilding; by titanic wangling they had brought into being a by-pass to divert main-road traffic from the village's broad and airy street; they had ordained a minimum bus service from Twelford, and stringent anti-charabanc laws, in their determination to keep trippers at bay. But their best efforts had not succeeded either in preventing the erection of Rolt's saw-mill or in encompassing the destruction of a hideous yellow-brick conventicle, dedicated to the use of an obscure nonconformist faction called The Children of Abraham, which affronted the eye not twenty yards from the church. Against these two edifices the animus of the intelligent company directors, not less than of the fashionable portrait painters, simmered and bubbled perennially. And their schemes for the discomfiture of the persons most closely associated with the offending structures – Rolt himself on the one hand, and on the other the village butcher, Amos Weaver, who preached heterodoxy in the conventicle on Sunday mornings – imparted to the small community a liveliness which it might otherwise have lacked.

Now, it was one of Mr Datchery's peculiarities that he collected religious sects as other men collect stamps or butterflies; and The Children of Abraham being new to him, it was inevitable that he should make an effort to acquaint himself with them before leaving Cotten Abbas. The striking of the half-hour, then, found him seated on one of the hard benches with which the conventicle was furnished, among a motley group of worshippers most of whom had been conveyed to the village from outlying parts in a bus regularly chartered for the purpose. Though the place was small enough, in all conscience, they were still far from adequate to fill it, and the only company Mr Datchery had on his bench, which was situated at the back, was an ancient man who choked and spluttered uninterruptedly into an extremely dirty handkerchief. After five minutes of this Mr Datchery leaned across to him and said: 'You seem troubled with a cough, brother.'

'Ah,' the old man whispered painfully. ''Tis the Lord's will, sir.'

Mr Datchery thought this on the whole unlikely, but the

64

moment was not apt for theological dispute, and he contented himself with asking how soon the service was expected to begin; at which the ancient man, clearly taking this inquiry for an indirect form of supernatural prompting, got hurriedly to his feet, announced a hymn, and embarked solo on its first verse with such haste and immediacy that Mr Datchery suspected him of wanting to get through the maximum possible number of lines before the rest of the congregation could collect its wits sufficiently to join in. The key he had set resulted in the low notes being too low for the high voices, and the high notes too high for the low, so that a sinister drone alternated throughout with a surprised mewing; the text selected was of that lengthy narrative sort which almost always has to do with fish, apostles and storms on Galilean lakes; and the total effect gratified Mr Datchery extremely. In front of him, a spinster lady offered at irregular intervals a descant or faux-bourdon in thirds; to his right, a solitary pioneer was singing a bass part so wholly speculative as to really dissociate him from the proceedings altogether; and Mr Datchery himself, whose voice had range if no great beauty, boomed forth the tune with such power as presently to carry all before him.

At the end of the hymn a rather long pause supervened after they had all sat down, and soon Mr Datchery, tiring of it, once more lapsed into conversation. 'Which,' he demanded of the ancient man, 'is Mr Weaver?'

'Not here yet,' said the ancient man with unexpected pertinence and brevity. 'Preaching at Brankham, that's what he'll be doing now. But never you fear, sir. He'll be with us here at the last, to speak to us of sin and the Lord's work with the words of his tongue.' The ancient man paused, seeming to contemplate this last sentence and not, on the whole, to like it very much. 'Oh yes, he'll be preaching all right,' he amended more cheerfully. It was possible, Mr Datchery thought, that there were the rudiments of a literary critic here.

A prayer followed, of the catalogue type which by attempting to get everything in only succeeds in focusing attention on what has been omitted. 'For all miners, steel-workers, farmers' (the boot and shoe trade?), 'for all mothers in childbirth, sufferers from cancer' (herpes? Scarlet fever?), 'for all doctors, nurses,

65

surgeons, for all whose business lies upon the great waters' (does this include submarine crews? Does it include them when *submerged?* And if it doesn't, what have *they* done to deserve being left out? And if you can't mention *everyone* specifically, why mention *anyone* specifically?), 'for the King and Queen and all the royal family, for the sick and the homeless, for all those ...' It lasted for nearly a quarter of an hour, persons eventually unsupplicated for including, by Mr Datchery's estimate, musicians, tailors, greengrocers, and Mr Aneurin Bevan. Then there was another hymn, and then a selection of the moony fancies of the author of the book of Revelation, and then another hymn, and then the sermon.

Amos Weaver, who had somehow contrived to enter the chapel unnoticed by Mr Datchery, proved to be a tall, lean, powerful man with a long neck, unreadable but slightly mad-looking eyes behind thick horn-rimmed glasses, a sallow complexion, a blue chin, too-short sleeves revealing hairy muscular wrists, and too-short trousers revealing stick-like ankles; and the manner of his homiletic – a diarrhoea of 'thous' and 'thees', a twangling of seraphic harps, a laundryful of white robes, a Cumberland of lost sheep, an assault-course of pitfalls, a capricorn of goats, an ocean of tempestuous Galilean lakes, a Wall Street of money-changers, a pirate horde of unfruitful talents, an orchard of barren fig-trees, an Ecclesiastical Commission of Pharisees and Sadducees, a mass migration of flights into Egypt, a warren of snares, a Ritz bar of gins and lime and adulteresses – the manner of his homiletic was nothing novel. But for all that, he had a certain authentic rhetorical power, and Mr Datchery heard him out with attention. Mr Weaver hated sin, it seemed. His text was the twenty-third chapter of Ezekiel, and he made no secret of hating sin with as much vehemence (and with nearly as much gross allusion) as the prophet hated those symbolical daughters of joy Aholah and Aholibah. And the choice of text was significant, Mr Datchery thought: the distinction between sin and sinner, so easy to recommend but in practice so difficult to achieve, could be side-tracked very conveniently by the use of allegorical prostitutes; a pretended impersonal abhorrence of evil could be stated in decidedly personal terms; and if the congregation elected to identify those wanton damsels of Ezekiel with actual young ladies living in the neighbourhood – well, so much the worse; no one, at least, could accuse the preacher of lacking a proper Christian charity ... So Weaver denounced, and Mr Datchery listened. 'Oily sort of fellow, Weaver,' Colonel Babington had said when on Mr Datchery's leaving his house the previous afternoon they had spoken again of the steel. 'Can't stand that sort of religion myself, all this showy piety and riding about on the tops of buses reading tracts. Nasty obsequious way of doing business Weaver's got, too – though I suppose in a tiny place like this he can't afford to risk offending people or they'd put him out of business ...' Obsequious perhaps, Mr Datchery reflected, to his customers in the week and to God on Sundays. But Mr Weaver was certainly not obsequious to sin ...

But now he was perorating; several previous 'lastlys' had been duds, but Mr Datchery had hopes of this one, and they were not disappointed ... The only thing was that *now* he seemed to be going to pray. 'For all that have erred from Thy ways; for all that have offended against Thy laws; for all that are sick and in sorrow; for her who took her own life, that it may please Thee to forgive her great trespass; for the young soul torn from us this day in our village by hideous murder; for the aged and infirm; for ...'

Mr Datchery was not the only person there to jerk upright and stare incredulously; but he was the only one immediately and unceremoniously to leave.

CHAPTER 8

By seven that Sunday morning Helen Downing was out of doors.

On the Friday night, that following the suicide of Beatrice Keats-Madderly, she had slept long and deep. But the Saturday night had seen a recurrence of her old habits of wakefulness, and such little sleep as she had been able to snatch had been troubled by nightmares – nightmares the more distressing in that she seldom dreamed at all, and since early childhood had not dreamed of terror. At six o'clock, then, she got up, dressed, and went out, turning right outside her garden gate – away, that is, from the direction of the main street – and following the road out of the village to where, beside the raw, aggressive pile of Rolt's saw-mill, it crossed the stream on the back of an ancient stone bridge. Here she turned left through a gap in the hedge, slithered cautiously down a nettle-covered bank, and with the mill behind her crossed the first of the water-meadows towards the coppice at its far side, intending to walk on beside the stream as far as the point at which the boundary wall of Sir Charles Wain's estate (through which the stream flowed) made further progress impossible. From there she could cut across country through Satchel Farm, and by rejoining the Cotten Abbas-Brankham road near the ruins of Brankham Priory be back at her house in good time for an early breakfast.

The sun promised another day of intense heat. Scarlet of poppies flared in the ripening corn, and the osiers with their sky-pointing branches were like shocks of uncombed silver hair. Water-insects, blind to lurking trout, volplaned ecstatically on the surface of the water; fledglings babbled incoherently in their nests; at the edge of the coppice bloomed showy foxgloves in bowers of fern. And presently, as Helen approached the uneven drift of small trees through which she must pass, she became aware that she was not the only inhabitant of the village thus early abroad, for a hatless figure pushed its way out from under the birches and stood there for a moment, in apparent indecision, before noticing her. Then it looked up, saw her, and spoke.

It said: 'Hey! Hey, you!'

Now to be addressed as 'Hey, you!' is an experience apt to exasperate even the mildest-tempered of adult human beings; and Helen's temper, after a worried and sleepless night, was far from being mild. She veered deliberately from the path in order to move away from the direction of the man who had called to her, and walked on without pause or reply, biting her lower lip in a spasm of annoyance. There was a moment's silence; then, more civilly this time, he called to her again.

'Hey, lass! Dr Downing!'

With considerable reluctance Helen halted. But she made no attempt to join him, which was what he seemed to expect; if he wanted to talk to her, it was up to him to do the walking.

'What is it?' she answered curtly.

He came up to her mopping his brow with a damp and grubby handkerchief – for although the day was still cool, he was sweating profusely, and his breath was as laboured as if he had been running.

'Have you seen my girl?' he demanded.

'Penelope? No, I haven't. What's happened to her?'

'That's what I'd like to know.' Harry Rolt's North-country accent was usually not more than just perceptible, but the effect of excitement on speech is regressive, and this morning the accent was much broader than commonly. 'Ay, that's what I'd like to know myself.'

He was a large man, gross as to body and ill-favoured, with small close-set eyes and a limp, wet mouth distorted by badly fitting dentures. There was coarse grey-black stubble on his cheeks and neck and chin, and the sweat had matted his thick eyebrows. His hands were large, the nails bitten and grimy, and his clothes had apparently been thrown on anyhow. Like most people in Cotten Abbas, Helen had little use for Harry Rolt; but in his manner this morning, though superficially it was as offensive as usual, there was an undertow of anxiety which held her repulsion temporarily in check.

'But I don't understand,' she said. 'What makes you think there's anything wrong?'

He laughed, shortly and unpleasantly. 'Ah, you'd like to know,

I dare say. Then you could go and blab it all to your fine aristo-cratic friends. But Harry Rolt's not quite such a fool as all that. Let me tell you, lass –'

At any other time Helen would simply have abandoned the conversation at this point, and walked off; but on this occasion she was too tired to make the gesture, and what she said was:

'For God's sake, don't be such a damned fool. I don't care a brass farthing about your domestic troubles, and nor does anyone else. If you want to tell me about Penelope, get on with it. But I've got quite enough worries of my own without bothering my head about yours, and if it wasn't that I like Penelope I shouldn't have listened to you as long as this.'

He was taken aback. 'Easy, now,' he expostulated. 'No need to jump down a man's throat like that. I was a bit hasty, I dare say, but that's Harry Rolt's way and always has been.'

'You,' said Helen vulgarly, 'are telling me.'

At that he unexpectedly grinned. 'I like a lass as speaks up for herself. You're all right.'

'Dear, dear, what flattery.'

The grin broadened – but there was not the least trace of salaciousness in it, and it occurred to Helen for the first time that whatever his other faults, Rolt was no philanderer. 'You're all right,' he repeated – and there was an odd note of satisfaction in his voice. 'Your high-and-mighty pals, now, they don't answer back. Oh no. That'd be beneath their dignity. But you –'

'Mr Rolt, if you imagine I like being commended at the expense of my friends, then you'd better think again.' Helen was angry now. 'If you've anything to tell me about Penelope I'll listen to it, but I'm not in the mood for general conversation.'

'Freezing, aren't we?' said Rolt. 'Quite the little duchess. All right, then, here's how it is. And by God, if you blab it about –' He paused, awaiting a disclaimer, and was disconcerted to receive none; in a milder voice he went on: 'What do you say we sit down on the bank a minute, eh? I'm not as young as I was, and all this chasing up and down has taken it out of me.'

'The bank will be damp.'

But he was already leading the way there, and Helen, cursing herself for letting herself become involved in this distasteful *tête-à-tête*, slowly followed. Arriving at the water's edge, he stripped off his coat and spread it on the ground. Then he slumped down heavily beside it. He made no comment or invitation, Helen noticed, and when she settled on the coat appeared to expect no thanks.

'That's more like it,' he said, and again wiped sweat from his face. 'And it's a pretty view from here.'

'It was till you stuck your mill in the middle of it ... But as far as I remember, it wasn't scenery we were going to talk about.'

'Beg pardon, your highness, I'm sure,' he said with heavy and infuriating facetiousness. 'You'll have to forgive a poor uneducated man like me for not being up in all your lordly etiquette.'

Helen shook her head wearily. 'I can't be bothered with fourth-form repartee.'

He glanced at her inquisitively for a moment. 'Ah,' he said. 'Not sleeping too well, are you?'

'Do I look as bad as all that?'

'Yes, you look pretty bad,' he said, with a candour which was even more depressing than offensiveness would have been. 'And mind you, I know the signs.'

'Why do you know them?'

He sniffed loudly. 'Ellen – that's my wife – she couldn't sleep much either. Sometimes it nearly broke my heart to see how thin and sick she looked ... But that's women for you. There's always summat amiss with them. Penny, now –'

'Yes, it's about time we got to her.'

'Keep you hair on, Duchess; I'm coming to it.' But for all that he seemed at a loss how to begin. 'Well,' he said at length, and more awkwardly than he had spoken yet, 'the first thing is, Pen's been running after a gormless little twerp of a foreign schoolmaster.'

'You mean – what's his name? – Rubi?' Helen's question was disingenuous, since like everyone else in the village she knew perfectly well that Penelope was infatuated with this reputedly rather tedious young man.

'Ay,' said Rolt grimly. 'That's him. Well, I'll tell you straight, I don't approve of it. Pen's still too young for boy-friends, and

71

even if she wasn't, I'd want her to be walking out with a decent lad, not a pansy little foreign gramophone record.'

'So?'

'So I told her yesterday morning she wasn't to see him again.'

'That,' said Helen drily, 'was very subtle of you. And I suppose the result was that she went off and saw him straight away.'

He nodded. 'Ay. That she did, the unnatural little –' But in the mid-flight of imprecation he checked himself. 'No. That's wrong. She's got a will of her own, my Pen, and good luck to her. But I'm asking you, lass, what was I to *do*? There's this dirty-minded letter I had –'

Helen gestured impatiently. 'If we all took the things in these anonymous letters seriously, we'd be crazy, certifiable.'

'Granted. But you can't deny there's been some truth in them. Pen's a decent lass, and she'd not have done what that letter said she had . . .'

'Then why worry?'

'There's always a danger, isn't there?' he said obstinately. 'Pen wouldn't do it, but then again she might . . . Ay, it's all very well to smile: I know what I'm saying isn't logic. But if you had a girl Pen's age, you'd worry just as hard as I do.'

'Anyway, what happened?'

'Happened? I'll tell you. Damned if she didn't come to me last night and say straight out to my face, "Dad", she said, "you told me not to see this chap again. Well, I've just come from him. So what are you going to do about it?"'

'And what *did* you do about it?'

Rolt shrugged. 'What'd any man do? I took a slipper to her.'

'You mean' – Helen stared at him incredulously – 'you mean you *beat* her?'

He stared back in equal surprise. 'Ay. What else'd I mean?'

Helen controlled her feelings with an effort. 'And do you make a habit of that?'

'Habit? Of course I don't,' he said with obvious truth. 'Do you take me for one of these sadists?'

'I take you for a very great fool,' said Helen angrily. 'An occasional walloping doesn't do a *child* any harm, but you seem to have forgotten that Penelope isn't a child. She's at an age when girls are terribly shy and self-conscious about their bodies, and anything more indecent than beating the poor kid it's impossible to imagine.'

Rolt flushed, and his bewilderment was certainly genuine. 'Indecent?' he muttered; and then vehemently: 'As God's my witness, Dr Downing, there was nothing of that about it.'

'Well, anyway, it's done,' said Helen resignedly. 'And I dare say Penelope's sensible enough not to take it too much to heart. Unless . . . What's happened to her *now?* This morning, I mean?'

'God knows. She's gone off somewhere.'

'Run away?'

'I hadn't thought o' that,' he said slowly. 'And after what you've just told me . . .'

'Well, but where did you imagine she's gone?'

'What I was afraid was, she'd arranged to meet her boyfriend again, and he'd be tumbling her somewhere in the bracken.'

Coarse but not prurient, Helen reflected; and aloud she said: 'Oh, rubbish. I expect that in actual fact she's simply got up early and gone for a stroll.'

'Ay. I dare say it's that.' But his voice was expressionless and Helen knew that he did not really believe what he said. Well, serve him right, she thought unsympathetically; fathers who are imbecile enough to spank their sixteen-year-old daughters deserve everything they get . . . 'I was worried, y'see,' he went on after a moment's silence. 'I don't ever have much heart for punishing Pen, so last night I didn't sleep any too well myself. That meant I was up at five, and something made me take a look in her room, to make sure she was all right. That's when I found she'd gone. So I've been out ever since, trying to find her.'

'If you'd had any sense,' said Helen, 'you'd have employed a woman to take care of her after your wife died. I don't suppose it's ever occurred to you, but Penelope's wretchedly lonely.'

All at once he was hostile. 'Mind th'own business, lass,' he said insolently, 'and I'll mind mine. Pen and me can manage all right without criticism from outsiders, thanks very much. What I do after my wife dies is my own affair and no one else's. And as to Pen, if you put her on the rack you wouldn't get her to say a word against her father.'

Helen stood up. 'You certainly wouldn't,' she replied with heat, 'but I can assure you it's no thanks to you. If you had even an ounce of tact in you, you'd realize – Oh, what's the use?' She turned to go, but he too had risen and was holding her by the sleeve. 'And for God's sake,' she said in sudden uncontrollable rage, 'take your hands off me, you – you money-grubbing guttersnipe!'

His arm fell to his side as though paralysed. 'Thanks,' he said quietly, 'thanks very much. So I'm a guttersnipe. All right – granted. But at least I don't pretend to be anything else, like some of your friends I could name.'

'If you're going to start that again –'

'"Again"? I wasn't aware as I'd mentioned it up to now. But since you're so free with your tongue, you might as well know one or two things I know. For instance –'

'Good morning, Mr Rolt.'

'Oh no, you don't, lass.' He caught at her sleeve again. 'Fair's fair, and tit for tat. If you're going to talk like that about me –'

'Let me go, please.' Helen was trembling, but it was with anger and not with fear. 'Whatever it is you're trying to say, I don't want to hear it.'

'I believe you.' Though his voice remained quiet, monotonous even, he was manifestly as enraged as she, and as indifferent to the consequences of what he said or did. 'And you'll like it even less when you know what it is, I can promise you that. Your Miss Beatrice Keats-Madderly –'

'Even you couldn't have the revolting bad taste to –'

'To speak ill of the dead? But I'm only a guttersnipe, remember, and there's no telling what *they'll* say, particularly about someone as never hesitated to speak ill o' them. Your Miss Keats-Madderly was rare proud of her family, wasn't she? You'd have thought they were kings, the way she talked about them. But the fact is, she didn't legally belong to that family at all. She was illegitimate. She was a bastard.'

For perhaps half a minute there was complete silence. Two feet below where they stood, the stream flowed on towards Twelford. The morning mist had almost completely gone, and the dew was drying on the rough grass. The clock of Cotten Abbas church, its tower high above the trees and houses, struck the quarter after seven, and a moment later the bell began ringing for early Communion. Flashing green and blue, a kingfisher swooped in a whir of wings. And Helen said:

'I don't believe a word of it.'

'Don't you?' Rolt smiled unpleasantly. 'But you'd better, you know, because it happens to be true. When I was a lad I worked in the same part of Yorkshire the Keats-Madderlys lived in. Fine haughty folk, they were. Lots of pride and lots of brass. But no children. So one summer Sir George Keats-Madderly started paying visits to a lass who worked in one of his own mills, and the year after that she pupped. Round there we all knew whose baby it was, and I'll say this for Sir George, he never tried to disown it. Beatrice he called it, and it was sent to Leeds to be brought up in style, no expense spared. Lady Mary Keats-Madderly, she knew all about it. She was a cold, snubbing woman, but when I was a bit older my dad told me she didn't mind what her husband had done – the only thing was, she wouldn't have the brat in their house. Well, in 1929 Sir George and Lady Mary were both killed in a motor smash. By that time, I'd left Yorkshire and set up in business on my own, so I'd no reason to think much about the family till ten years ago, when I came here. But when I found there was a Beatrice Keats-Madderly living here, I started to think a bit, and the next time I was in London I took myself to Somerset House and looked up Sir George's will, and there it was: all his brass left to Miss Beatrice Dodgson, such-and-such an address in Leeds, on condition she took the name of Keats-Madderly. So if you still don't believe me, you can look it up for yourself – and there's still plenty of folk in Yorkshire'll tell you the same as I have.'

The recital had quieted him; he no longer spoke as vehemently as at first. And as to Helen, the effect of his story on her was unexpected. The revelation of Beatrice Keats-Madderly's illegitimacy did not, of course, in any way diminish her affection for that brusque, imperious woman; what was surprising was that although Harry Rolt had plainly intended to wound, his narrative had left her with a far greater respect for him than at its outset she would have believed possible. For intolerable though he doubtedly was, Beatrice *had* treated him particularly badly; their mutual hatred had been as intense as any hatred that human beings are capable of – and yet in spite of that he had never, as many a better man might have done, used his knowledge of her birth as a weapon against her ... Helen said abruptly:

'You're not so bad, you know, as you paint yourself.'

'Guttersnipe,' he reminded her – sulkily, but at the same time with an air of vague discomfiture, like a man caught out in some venial and preposterous sin. 'That's what you said, and that's what you meant, so don't try to go back on it.' He became suddenly aware that he was still holding her by the sleeve, and took his hand away as if it had been stung. 'Ay. Maybe I shouldn't have said what I have said, but you riled me ... Well, she's dead now, and you can't expect me to howl my head off about it.'

Helen said: 'I'm quite glad you told me.'

'Are you?' He laughed uneasily. 'That's one shot missed the target, then. Well, I'd better be getting back. If you should see Pen, or hear of her –' He hesitated.

'Yes, I'll let you know. And at the risk,' Helen added, 'of being ticked off again as a critical outsider, I'd still advise you to think a bit about the sort of life she's leading. She's got nothing to occupy her, she won't make friends with people like me because she knows we don't get on with you, and if she runs after foreign schoolmasters it really isn't to be wondered at. In my opinion you ought to send her away from here till she's got over her growing pains and can see things in their right perspective.'

'See me, you mean?'

'You among other things,' said Helen coolly.

He was pensive for a moment, staring across at the osiers on the far side of the stream; then:

'It mightn't be such a bad idea, at that – though Lord knows I'd miss her. The trouble'd be, getting her to agree to it. How about you having a talk with her?'

'Me? I see no reason to imagine she'd take any notice of anything I said.'

'Wouldn't she, though. Pen admires you, Dr Downing, I can tell you that much. Mind you, it may be what they call a pash, but it's real enough for all that. And if you and I both said the same thing –'

'Oh ... all right.' And if Helen hesitated before consenting, that was rather because she mistrusted her own capacity than because she was not anxious to help Penelope. 'But it's all a bit vague, you know. What *exactly* is it that you want me to do?'

'That's up to you, lass. All I'm after is what's best for Pen, and you'll be able to find that out better than I would.'

On the whole, Helen doubted this. It was pleasant, of course, to be credited with so much wisdom and discernment – not so pleasant, on the other hand, to be obliged to put those qualities to the test. Moreover, she thought it unlikely, in spite of what she herself had said, that Penelope Rolt was quite so green, and in quite such a complex of spiritual difficulties, as this suggestion of a heart-to-heart talk implied. At the age of sixteen it is of course shaming to be walloped, disturbing to dote on Swiss pedagogues, trying to be lonely, upsetting to be innocently involved in a feud between one's father and one's neighbours. But Helen was aware that the mentality of most human beings possesses a great deal more of stamina and resilience than the solicitude of others will usually allow, and she was conscious of a lurking suspicion that Penelope would see through this whole manoeuvre at a glance, and be considerably amused by it ... 'I don't,' said Helen, 'quite see how it's going to be arranged.'

Rolt waved this aside. 'See her professionally, that's the first thing. I've an idea she may have been having a bit of' – quite delicately – 'trouble just recently. You know. Some sort of thing she wouldn't want to tell me about ...'

'Yes. Well, if that's so, it certainly ought to be seen to. I think the best thing will be for you to ring me up as soon as you've talked to Penelope, and then we can make some arrangement ... All this is assuming, of course, that she hasn't run away from her home.'

'Be damned to that for a lot of poppycock,' said Rolt rudely, his earlier uncertainty on this score having apparently vanished in the course of the last few minutes. 'She'd not run away, not if I know anything about her.'

'I thought you'd just admitted that you didn't.'

'All I admitted was that she could do with a woman to advise her. That's fair enough, isn't it? No, if you ask me, she's out with that pansy schoolmaster. And if they're up to mischief, and I get my hands on him –'

'Yes, all right,' said Helen impatiently. 'I don't care what you do about him, but as far as Penelope's concerned, keep your hands to yourself. Now I must go. You'll ring me up?'

'Ay.'

'Good morning, then.'

'Good morning, Duchess. Behave tha'self.'

... Damned impertinence, thought Helen as she strode towards the coppice; but perhaps because she was so tired, the whole interview had had a curious dreamlike quality which inhibited serious resentment and left her vaguely inquisitive rather than decisively annoyed. Picking her way along the narrow path between the birches, however, she found herself reluctant to think seriously about what had been said, and it was only later, when exercise had freshened her mind as well as her body, that her thoughts reverted to the story of Beatrice Keats-Madderly's birth. It was overwhelmingly probable, of course, that that was what the burned anonymous letter had been about: odd, Helen reflected, that anyone should feel so strongly about illegitimacy as to prefer death to exposure – and a death, at that, which must have been agonizing, for Beatrice's heavy body had certainly dangled from the banisters for a full minute or two before consciousness was lost ... You never quite get used to the sight of any dead person, thought Helen, remembering the revulsion and pity with which she had looked at that cyanosed face; but when it's someone you know and like, that's a thousand times worse – as bad, in fact, as if you'd had no training and no experience of death at all ... But the whole trouble, Helen now saw, had been Beatrice's incessant boasting about her family. *That* was why the prospect of the truth's becoming known had so appalled her; if she could only have refrained from *that*, no one in these tolerant days would have cared twopence whether she was legitimate or not. But she had been unusually sensitive, as many tactless souls are, and unusually proud, so that a motive which most people would have thought trivial had been quite sufficient to drive her to the fatal, conclusive act. The pity of it, though, the *pity* of it. And all because of an anonymous letter announcing, presumably, that –

Helen stopped short.

An anonymous letter announcing that the writer knew Beatrice to be illegitimate.

And apparently the only person in Cotten Abbas who knew that was Harry Rolt.

CHAPTER 9

THE majority of us are permitted to cope with the important events of our lives in a decently leisurely manner – with ample breathing-space, that is to say, in which to assimilate one shock and recuperate before the next. But it does sometimes happen that a series of such events is compressed into a few electrifying weeks, days, or even hours, each one treading so closely on the heels of its predecessor as to create a sort of momentous blur, like telegraph poles seen from an express train, rather than (after the fashion of mountains viewed from the same standpoint) a slow-moving recession of isolated and significant peaks. So it was with Helen Downing this Sunday. Looking back on it afterwards, what surprised her most was her own unnatural equanimity. It is doubtful if this was quite so unbroken as she subsequently imagined, but there was a certain justification for her surprise in the fact that the day's happenings succeeded one another so rapidly as to give her mind no chance of reacting fully to any of them. The result of this was a slightly misleading air of level-headedness, and the man who three weeks later became her husband has been heard to assert, in amiable mockery, that he was decidedly uncertain that day as to whether the recipient of his proposal was flesh or marble. (But he has not, he adds – to Helen's mild confusion – been in the least uncertain about it since.)

At breakfast-time, however, destiny's preparations were still not quite complete, and Helen was able to eat the meal undisturbed – undisturbed, that is, except by the suspicion that Harry Rolt might be responsible for the epidemic of anonymous letters. Of course, there was no guarantee that he and he alone knew of Beatrice's origin – no guarantee, even, that a reference to that origin had been what the burned anonymous letter had contained. But the latter qualification was thin to the point of invisibility, and although to some extent the former held, Helen found it difficult to believe that anyone who had not lived in the relevant area of Yorkshire at the relevant time – and Rolt was

80

almost certainly the only person in Cotten Abbas who had – could possibly be aware of so remote and long-buried a scandal. There was the chance that Rolt had told someone else in the village about it; but his manner in bludgeoning Helen with the tale had been the manner of a man driven by extreme provocation to violate a hitherto inviolable confidence, and Helen felt convinced that until this morning he had kept it strictly to himself . . . Well, yes; on the other hand, if he had written the anonymous letter to Beatrice, and if that letter *had* referred to Beatrice's illegitimacy, then it had been most unwise of him to tell Helen what he knew – so unwise as to seem, in a criminal whose care had up to now kept him invulnerable, almost incredible. To that objection in Rolt's favour there was, however, an answer of sorts: whoever had written the anonymous letter to Beatrice might well have relied on her destroying it so that its contents would never be known – must, indeed, have heard that a burnt letter had been found, and possibly had forgotten that burnt paper, unless reduced to fragments, can be reconstituted and read. In which case . . .

Oh damn, thought Helen: this drifting round in circles isn't any good. The point is, what motive would Rolt have in writing anonymous letters to start with?

And there was no difficulty about finding a reply to that. If the anonymous writer was not certifiably insane, and operating without any rational motive at all, then his intention, in which to a disastrous extent he had already succeeded, must almost certainly be to disrupt the contentment of Cotten Abbas as a whole. In the case of the merely obscene letters, accusing people of practices at which, as Colonel Babington had once remarked, Gomorrah would have looked slightly askance, the writer's object was probably nothing more subtle than his own sexual gratification. But that explanation left out of account the other type of letter, the tell-tale sort whose matter and manner were by no means invariably erotic. For those, as far as Helen could see, the only conceivable interpretation was that they were inspired by a generalized malevolence against the entire community – and if you were looking for someone with a grudge against that community, then of course the first person you thought of was Harry Rolt.

Helen frowned. If anyone had asked her to choose the individual in Cotten Abbas whom she would most like to be found guilty of writing the anonymous letters, and so indirectly of Beatrice Keats-Madderly's death, she would almost certainly have chosen Harry Rolt. But honesty compelled her to admit to herself, after this morning's conversation with him, that in two important respects he didn't at all fit the part. In the first place, she was certain that sex, far from obsessing him in the way that it obviously obsessed the letter-writer, interested him scarcely at all; up to a point, such a preoccupation can of course be concealed – but overtones of it are apt to leak out when the person concerned is talking directly about the matter, and Helen had been particularly struck by the complete absence of these overtones in Rolt's references to Penelope and her schoolmaster. And in the second place, Rolt's whole mentality had seemed to her leagues removed from the sneaking, stab-in-the-back mentality of the letter-writer. He was repulsive, yes; he was malignant, yes; he was dirty and rude and stupid. But despite all that it had been evident to Helen that he did order his life in accordance with some kind of moral code, and what she had sensed of this code convinced her – illogically yet still powerfully – that any such hole-and-corner business as anonymous letters would be completely alien to it. *Fair's fair*, he had said; and again, *That's fair enough, isn't it?* As proof of good character, neither of those *clichés* would carry much weight in a court of law, but they had impressed Helen as being, on Rolt's lips, something more than mere catch-phrases.

She ate the last of her toast and marmalade, poured more coffee, and lit a cigarette. The sun, strong now and likely to be oppressive at its zenith, freaked the room's sombre furniture with gold, and garden scents drifted in through the open windows, riding a light breeze which stirred the stiff chintz curtains and fluttered the roses in their vase. A bluebottle fulminated round the alabaster bowl which shaded the centre light. From the kitchen, the voice of Melanie Hogben, the seventeen-year-old girl who mismanaged Helen's house for her, could be heard raised in heartfelt, unfocused song. And Helen, watching the grey smoke of her cigarette turn vivid blue where it crossed a bar of sunlight, asked herself for the hundredth time what exactly she ought to do. What she now knew, Inspector Casby ought to know likewise – but tale-bearing, even where no promise of secrecy had been exacted, was as repugnant to her as to most people, and like the majority of Britons, she regarded it as one of the functions of an organized police to exempt her from such squalid necessities. On the other hand, her anger at Beatrice Keats-Madderly's death went very deep, and if there was anything she could do about it, then in honour that thing must be done . . .

Stubbing out her cigarette when it was only a quarter smoked, she got impatiently to her feet, and, still fretting, went to the window and looked out. Casby, in his back garden next door, was peering suspiciously at a rose-bush. The sun gleamed on his dark hair, and the expression on his face was of the blankest incomprehension. 'Green-fly!' called Helen, and 'What the devil does one do about it?' he called back.

'One sprays it. But it looks to me, from here, as if that wretched thing's too far gone.'

'Is it? Had I better root it up?'

'I'll come and look if you like.'

'I wish you would. I know nothing about flowers, nothing whatever.'

So Helen climbed out of the window – not ungracefully either, she thought with a touch of complacency – and having passed through a gate which for some reason linked the two gardens, joined him in sober contemplation of the offending plant. 'It's dead,' she told him.

'Yes, I suppose it is. What's that mould all over it?'

'That's not a mould, it's *green-fly*.'

'Oh, I see.'

'And if you don't kill them off they'll soon be all over everything – my roses included.'

'Oh, Lord . . . You know, it's beginning to occur to me that I'm not a very desirable neighbour to have.'

'It can't be said that you're excessively sociable.'

He gazed at her in dismay. 'No, I suppose I'm not. It's working in Twelford that's the trouble.'

'Do you actually *work*, all the time you're not here?'

'I think so. Apart from meals, that is, and the odd pint. But it isn't a penance. I enjoy it.' He gave her a rather worried smile. 'I do hope you haven't been thinking me horribly uncivil. I can never really *believe* that people are anxious for my company – and that isn't modesty, by the way; it's a peculiarly vicious form of inverted conceit.'

'Well, since you like working so much, I've got some information for you.' As was usual with her, Helen had reached her decision on impulse, independently of reasoning or argument. 'It's probably quite unimportant, but –'

'About the letters?' he asked quickly.

'Yes. But don't get excited. I'm afraid it'll turn out to be a mare's nest.'

'This does seem to be the season for them. The number of fledgling foals ...'

'*Listen.*' And Helen recounted what was relevant of her conversation with Harry Rolt. He heard her out attentively, and when she had finished said:

'Yes. I rather suspected that, but I couldn't be sure.'

'Suspected ...?'

'Inferred, anyway.'

'But how?'

'Well ... It's quite a long story.' There was something of speculation in his glance, and it struck Helen that he was wondering how far to confide in her. Slightly irritated, she said: 'If you don't want –' but he interrupted her with: 'Please don't be offended. With policemen, being secretive gets to be a habit.'

'Of course. There's no need –'

'There's no need for me *not* to tell you. The fact is that after the letters started, I investigated – for obvious reasons – the background and history of everyone living here who didn't one way or another fit in with the life of the place.' He hesitated a moment, and then added, with a lightness which his steady look belied: 'You, for instance.'

It was at least five seconds before Helen grasped what he had said – and five seconds can seem a very long time.

'Me?' she said. 'You thought that I –'

'I was looking for misfits, and it would have been stupid to leave anyone out. One doesn't hunt one's thimble only in the obvious places.'

'I see.' Helen battled with her anger and held it precariously at bay. 'But for a misfit I have quite a reasonable number of friends here, don't you think?'

'In your case,' he said levelly, 'it was a question of money. I understand that you don't get as many patients as you deserve.'

'Do you really?' Helen was trembling now. 'And I suppose you thought that because I was over thirty, and still not married, I had just the right sort of unsatisfied urges for an anonymous letter-writer . . . I think you said you enjoyed your work?'

There was a pause before he replied. Then he said quietly: 'I find it worth while to help clean up the mess made by malevolence and folly. But I do try not to like the mess for its own sake. Liking the mess for its own sake is a – an occupational risk, and better policemen than I am have succumbed to it from time to time. That's one of the reasons why the Force isn't keen on imaginative types: they get too interested in the sewers they have to dabble in . . .' But he was talking, Helen thought, less for the sake of justifying himself than with a view to keeping bitterness in check. And it flashed across her mind, fractionally dissipating the haze of resentment with which it was clouded, that it was strange a man should be so zealous to palliate a hurt he need never have administered in the first place. She said:

'Why have you told me this? There wasn't the slightest nece.-sity, that I can see.'

And for the first time in their brief acquaintance she saw him confused, embarrassed, uncertain. He evaded the question, saying: 'I'm sorry. Routine sounds rather a threadbare excuse, but it's a real one just the same. I hope you'll forgive me.'

'It's your job,' said Helen slowly.

He smiled. 'Rather a qualified sort of pardon – but of course I'm lucky to get that . . . Let's see, where was I? Oh yes – Rolt. Rolt's childhood, I found, was spent in a certain part of Yorkshire – which discovery didn't interest me very much at the time I made it. But then, after that wretched business on Friday, I read in the burnt anonymous letter we found in the grate that Miss Keats-Madderly had been illegitimate; so naturally I investigated *her* childhood, and discovered that it had been spent in the same area as Rolt's – the obvious inference being that Rolt knew the circumstances of Miss Keats-Madderly's birth.'

Cooler now, and beginning to feel a little ashamed of her pique, Helen laughed. 'After all the soul-searching I've been through . . .'

'Soul-searching?'

'About whether to be a good citizen and turn copper's nark, or just keep my mouth shut. And it seems you knew, all along.'

'Not *knew*. I haven't talked to Rolt yet. If you hadn't told me this, he'd be in a position to lie, and get away with it.'

'Actually,' said Helen, 'I very much doubt if he would lie.'

'He impressed you like that, did he? Me too, what little I've seen of him.'

'And I don't consider he has anything to do with any of the letters. By the way, what *exactly* was in that letter of Beatrice's? Or mustn't I ask?'

'It was a simple statement, backed by some convincing detail, that Revelations Would Be Made.'

'Made unless?'

'No. No blackmail. Just devilry penny plain. And I don't think it came from the same source as the other letters.'

Helen was surprised. 'Why shouldn't it have?' she demanded; but he only shook his head. 'I may be quite wrong about that,' he said. 'The only thing is, there are one or two small indications such as –'

'Oh, and another thing I wanted to ask you.' Helen had interrupted him before she clearly realized that he was on the point of telling her something interesting; and felt obliged, once having embarked on the interruption, to push it through. 'What did you mean when you told that man in the bar he ought to be staying with the Verger? I never knew we *had* a Verger.'

'And you never read *Edwin Drood* either, I take it.'

'*Edwin DROOD*? Dickens?'

'Dickens. It wasn't finished, you remember, so one can only guess at who and what the Mr Datchery in it was going to turn out to be. But he crops up at Cloisterham, lodging with the Verger, soon after the mystery gets under way, and it occurred to me when this man introduced himself as Datchery that a literary-minded bloke might adopt that name if he wanted to hang about here incognito investigating *our* mystery.'

'Only he didn't react.'

'You think not?'

'Well, he was puzzled, as far as I could see.'

'Yes. His error. If you're a cultivated man, as he obviously is, and you happen to have the same name as a character in a celebrated novel, then it's very unlikely you won't be aware of that character. And from what I've seen of this chap, I'm inclined to pay him the compliment of believing that he responded wrongly out of deliberate carelessness – which argues a rather frightening degree of self-confidence.'

'But who do you think he really is?'

'Haven't the vaguest.' Casby chuckled suddenly. 'But in case he's up to mischief, I shall keep an eye on him.'

Helen regarded him thoughtfully. 'I'm damned if I can make you out,' she said. 'One moment you're competent and adult and a bit stand-offish, and the next you're friendly and naïve and – and –'

'*Puerile* would seem to be the antonym you're looking for.'

'What's more, I don't believe any policeman uses words like "antonym". I don't believe you're a policeman at all.'

'I am, though. The new sort: minor public school and Hendon Police College. As to the rest of your analysis, the friendliness and so forth are the natural man, and everything else is that ignoble kind of timidity which people politely call shyness.'

Helen smiled. 'A shy policeman?'

'It is absurd, isn't it? But of course, you get just as many different types of men in the Force as you do in any other profession.'

'But why should you be shy?'

'Well ... A psychologist, I suppose, would put it down to an unhappy childhood.' He raised a hand to stroke his scar. 'And this ugly thing hasn't helped.'

Their eyes met.

A tremor passed through Helen's body; she desired to look away and could not.

'You fool,' said Helen calmly. 'Oh, you fool.'

Later – after what might have been a second or an eternity – she released herself from his arms to become conscious that Melanie Hogben, paralysed with amazement, was staring out at them from the kitchen window of the adjacent house with the saucer eyes and gaping mouth of an unarmed hunter confronted with a rogue elephant. In half an hour, thought Helen dazedly, this is going to be all over the village; well, and does it matter? In a shaky voice she said:

'For a shy man you don't do so badly.'

He was regarding her with an incongruous mixture of earnestness and pleasure: an artist, Helen reflected, in process of dealing with a novel and fascinating technical problem. Clearing his throat impressively, he said:

'Would you say we were going to get married?'

'I most certainly would.'

'In that case . . .'

'*No*.'

'But, darling girl, I've always understood that all sorts of liberties –'

'Not in the open air. Not in public.'

'We'll go into my house?'

'Perhaps . . . You know, I see now why you told me that.'

'Told you what? I think . . .'

'*Not here*. What I meant was, you told me about me being a suspect because you wanted to be honest. I'm not sure that a husband as upright as you won't be rather intolerable.'

'I shall study to degenerate. The depths I haven't yet sunk to aren't extensive. And now –'

But at this point they were interrupted by the sound of laughter. The laughter proceeded not from Melanie Hogben, who by now had recovered the use of her limbs and departed from Helen's kitchen window, but unmistakably from Mrs Flack, that monument of domestic incompetence who looked after Casby, and who at the moment should have been engaged in her diurnal labour of sweeping dust under carpets. It was one of Mrs Flack's most notable characteristics that her laughter had in some fashion got itself detached from her sense of humour, so that it bombinated irrevantly in an emotional vacuum. Perhaps as a consequence of this, it had developed a regular, mechanical tone, as though Mrs Flack were *reading* laughter – ha! ha! ha! – aloud from a book: an implausible sound which thanks to existing independently of Mrs Flack's emotional condition had frequently disconcerted funeral-goers and such of Mrs Flack's acquaintances as had tales of woe to purvey.

The noise which Helen and Casby now heard, then, indicated no more than that Mrs Flack had company – and a moment later she was ushering it out of the back door. It proved to be Burns, the village Constable, a bright, up-and-coming young man deficient in the conventions of slow rusticity which fiction commonly attaches to his office; but on this occasion he was pale and distraught, and when he hurried up to Casby and Helen they saw that he was breathless as well.

'Beg pardon, sir,' he said. 'But it's urgent. That schoolmaster – Rubi, or whatever his name is – we've found him down in the coppice near Rolt's mill. I didn't find him, that is. It was Miss Penelope Rolt who gave the alarm. I'm afraid it's serious, sir.'

'Well?'

'That's to say, he's dead. And from what I've seen of him, sir, I'm pretty certain the reason he's dead is because he's been murdered.'

CHAPTER 10

LAUGHING rowdily at nothing, Mrs Flack had retired into the house: curiosity was not one of her vices, and there was yet much dust requiring transference from the centre of rooms to the corners. Burns, still panting after what had evidently been a hectic ride, twitched off his helmet and ran stubby fingers through his damp hair, and Casby, glancing at his watch, made a rapid note of the time in a pocket diary.

'I must phone Sims and Colonel Babington,' he said. 'After that we'll go along there. Shan't be a moment.' He turned towards the house, hesitated, glanced back at Helen, and smiled. 'So sorry,' he said. 'And I don't imagine this will be the last occasion, either. You see what you've let yourself in for.'

'I'll try to bear it.'

He said 'Thank you' seriously, and went into the house. Burns, at no loss to interpret the exchange, gazed interestedly at the heavens and ventured the fatuous comment that it was a fine day. 'Beg pardon, Doctor,' he added, 'but did you happen to be acquainted with the deceased?'

Helen, conscious of a rummaged appearance, was making ineffectual efforts to remedy it. 'I only knew him by sight,' she said. 'He lived in that cottage out beyond Beedon's, didn't he?'

'That's right, ma'am. Fiveways, in Ascot Lane. He was a bit of an oddity, by all accounts.' Burns coughed uneasily. 'And I don't know if you've heard about it, but Miss Rolt –'

'Oh, my God.' Now belatedly digesting Burns's first words, Helen stopped preening herself abruptly. 'Didn't you say it was Penelope who found him?'

Burns nodded. 'Couldn't hardly be worse, ma'am, could it?'

'What sort of state is she in?'

'No tears or hysterics, Doctor, if that's what you're meaning. Nothing so healthy as that, I'm sorry to say. She come up to my cottage calm and collected as you please, but her eyes all glazed and dead-looking, and her voice high and quick like a record that's playing too fast. Gabbled it out, she did, and then the wife took her in for a cup of tea or that, and that's the last I've seen of her.'

'I'd better look in,' said Helen, 'and find out if there's anything I can do.'

'Might be as well, ma'am.'

'Of course, there's no suggestion that *she* could have –'

'No, ma'am. I can't think she did it. He was only a little chap, I grant you, but spite of that, I still doubt she'd have the strength.'

'How was he killed, then?'

'Some sort of knife, ma'am, I think, though I didn't see no sign of it. Anyway, there's a fair-size wound in his chest, over the heart. What it seemed to me might have done it was some sort of thing like a –'

But here Casby rejoined them, and Burns fell silent. 'I can't get hold of Sims,' Casby said. 'He isn't at home. I've left a message asking him to come along if he gets back within the next hour or two, but it's a damned nuisance just the same.'

'If it's a doctor you want,' said Helen, 'there's me.'

'You would be very useful, if you felt up to it. Time of death, and so forth.' And 'Thank heavens,' thought Helen, 'he doesn't insult me by trying to coddle me.' Aloud she said:

'My forensic medicine's a bit rusty, I'm afraid, but I think I can remember enough about it to give you some sort of idea.'

'Good ... Burns, I don't want to be tiresome, but I rather doubt if you ought to have left him unguarded.'

Burns went red. 'I know, sir. Trouble was, I didn't see a soul about I could have sent a message by. And by the time I'd got to a telephone, I was so near to here I thought I might as well come on. Ought I to have waited, sir, till someone happened along?'

'No, I think in those circumstances you did quite right. Delay's always a hindrance.'

'I took a good look at him, sir, and I think I'd know it if anyone's meddled with him in the meantime.'

'Sensible. We'll go, then. Unluckily, Colonel Babington wasn't at home either when I rang him, but I got on to the Station at Twelford, and their people will be on the spot almost as soon as we are.'

'I'll fetch my bag,' said Helen.

She rejoined them a minute later in front of Casby's house, and they drove in his Morris down to the bridge by Rolt's mill, and alighting there, followed the path across the water-meadow which Helen had taken early that morning immediately prior to her meeting with Rolt. It being Sunday, the mill was of course silent, and apart from a solitary angler just visible a considerable distance up-stream, they had the place to themselves. By now – the hour was nearly ten-thirty – the sun shone really hot, and Helen, who had intended after breakfast to substitute a cotton frock for her light-weight coat and skirt, began to wish that she had delayed long enough, when fetching her medical bag, to make the change. But about the unpleasantness awaiting her among the trees they were approaching she thought little, for Rubi had been no more to her than a name and a spare, small, neat figure rarely glimpsed on his way to and from the school at Twelford where he taught. What sort of life had he led? she wondered. And to Casby, as the three of them moved in single file along the narrow track with the rank grass proliferating on either side, she said:

'He *was* a bachelor, wasn't he?'

'Oh, yes. Unless, that is, he's got a wife tucked away in Zürich. His parents live there, by the way, and I must remember to cable them as soon as possible, poor souls.'

'You seem to know quite a lot about him.'

'Well, it wasn't so very long after he came here that the anonymous letters started, so I had to find out what I could.'

'Negative reaction?'

'Oh, yes, I think so. Unless he was a first-rate actor, his English wasn't idiomatic enough for him to have written the letters. He was a good deal interested in them, though.'

'Yes, Beatrice told me that, though I can't say I paid much attention at the time. He went to Colonel Babington, didn't he, and suggested the police should co-opt him as a psychiatry expert?'

'He did. I'm sorry to say that Colonel Babington was half in favour of the idea, though I talked him out of it in the end. The trouble was, I was making so little progress myself that I couldn't afford to be too snooty when help was offered. But I said that if we *had* to get in outsiders, I'd much rather they were Scotland Yard people than amateurs.'

'We've all been wondering,' said Helen, 'if Scotland Yard was going to be called in.'

'Scotland Yard isn't called in nearly as often as detective novelists seem to think,' Casby replied with a trace of heat. 'They're not all that good, you know – if you look at the improvements in criminal science during the last twenty years, you'll find that nearly all of them originated not in the Metropolitan C.I.D. but in the provincial ones, places like Coventry. That goes for elaborate laboratory work, too. The only real advantage the Metropolitan C.I.D. has is that it's big ... Am I right, Burns?'

Burns, in the lead, turned his head with a grin of professional understanding, not unmixed with pleasure at having his opinion canvassed. 'I'll say you are, sir. I was talking to Dr Larkin in Twelford last week, and he tells me our County C.I.D.'s miles ahead of anyone else with the new blood-group tests. What he said was, they're finding so many new groups and sub-groups that in ten or twenty years you'll be able to identify a chap straight away just by his blood, like as if it was his fingerprints. But then as soon as we've done all the donkey-work, the Yard'll pinch our results and go bossing about the country as if us police as don't live in London was just a lot of thick-headed hayseeds. Ma'am,' said Burns earnestly, 'you just wait and see if they don't.'

This warm apologia for criminal investigation in the provinces, which pleased Helen not a little, took them past the spot on the bank where she had sat with Harry Rolt, and in among the trees. The coppice was not a large one, and about ten yards along the path which traversed it Burns turned off to the left, and they pushed their way through bracken and bramble, by a route no more defined than children will mark out in going to and from their private dens and bowers, until the trees thinned momentarily to reveal a tiny glade, grass-floored and open to the sky. The moss-grown stumps of two or three birches, with charring still visible on the free surfaces of the wood, showed that the clearing was the result of a small fire which either had been speedily checked or else had burned itself out without spreading further.

93

Wild flowers, accessible here to the sun's rays, grew more luxuriantly than in the shadier parts of the little wood. Hazel-leaved brambles bloomed about the circumference.

And at one side, half hidden from them by couch-grass, lay the body of Peter Rubi.

Both Casby and Burns halted at the edge of the glade to survey it carefully and so avoid eliminating, in their approach to the body, any suggestive traces which might remain. But to Helen's inexpert eye, at least, no clue offered itself. The ground was bone-dry, the undergrowth tangled, the grass sprawling and prolific: a herd of elephants passing through would probably have left the place looking very much as it had before, and foot-prints were out of the question.

'I didn't cross over from here when I went to look at him, sir,' said Burns. 'Though of course there's no knowing what Miss Rolt did. My idea was, I pushed my way round outside the clearing to where he is, and had a dekko at him from there, where there isn't any sort of path.'

'Good. We'd better do the same, I think.' Casby moved away to the right, adding to Helen: 'Sorry about your clothes, but we mustn't trample all over the clearing till we've made sure there's nothing to be got from it.'

So they forced their way round to where the body lay, and presently were standing over it. After scrutinizing it attentively for a few moments, Burns said:

'I don't think he's been moved, sir, since I saw him. That little flower that's bent down under his head – some sort of campion, isn't it? – that's lying exactly the way it was, and it'd have changed its position if he'd been moved.'

'Good man,' said Casby with approval. 'I'm inclined to think you're wasted here – you'd be very useful in the County C.I.D. Appeal to you?'

Burns flushed with pleasure. 'I'll say it does, sir.'

'I'll put in a good word for you, but don't rely on anything. As you know, there are plenty of hindrances.'

'Not fair,' said Helen. 'Having got a first-rate policeman in the village, we want to keep him.'

Burns was overwhelmed. 'Well, anyway,' said Casby, 'this is

hardly the moment for meditating careers. Burns, will you go back to the bridge, please, and bring my Twelford people along here when they arrive? They won't know where we are. But don't bother about Sims. He can find us on his own.'

Burns saluted and took himself off. 'Nice lad,' Casby murmured. 'He ought to do well.' Helen felt the gentle pressure of his hand on her waist, and he said: 'There are lots of things I'd rather be doing than this. But all the textbooks tell one that the Investigating Officer must guard against becoming – what's the phrase they use? – oh, yes, "emotionally involved" in whatever case he's handling. They add rather gloomily that such an event will "cloud his judgement and result in the formation of prejudices".'

Helen smiled. 'What you mean is that this must remain a business trip.'

'Emphatically. Don't you agree?'

'Darling, of course I do.' Helen looked down dubiously at Rubi's body. 'And in the circumstances it's rather unnatural of us to be even as cheerful as we are. But the thing is, he looks so peaceful, more as if he were sleeping . . .'

It was true. Rubi lay stretched out on his back, the legs straight and natural-seeming, the left arm at his side, the right hand resting lightly on his body just below the ribs; and although his mouth was a little open, showing white teeth, his eyes were closed. With his glasses askew on his nose, he looked astoundingly like a man in slumber, a man whom the beauty of the weather has tempted to lie down in a pleasant spot and who, immune from interruption and so careless of appearances, has allowed himself to doze off. But no trickle of breath came from those parted lips, no slightest movement of the rib-cage gave hope of air in the lungs; and in the open-necked shirt, just over the heart, there was a rounded hole nearly half an inch in diameter, smeared round with blood – a clean hole, a hole matter-of-fact rather than repellent, but wide enough and deep enough to let death in.

'It looks like a bullet-hole at first sight,' said Helen. 'But Burns was quite right: it isn't.' She bent down, only to feel Casby's restraining hand on her arm.

'Don't touch him yet,' he said pleasantly. 'Photographs first.'

Helen straightened up quickly; it was nothing more creditable than pride, of course, but she was desperately anxious not to make any sort of mistake. 'I'm very stupid,' she said humbly.

'You're a highly intelligent young woman, not to say ...' He checked himself in his swift defence of her, and added more lightly: 'But no, I mustn't get amorous: unpolicemanly lusts would undoubtedly cloud my judgement and result in the formation of prejudices, if I did. Business, then: why shouldn't it be a bullet-hole?'

Helen was remembering the forensic medicine lectures she had been to at St Thomas's, the notes gleaned at midnight from Taylor and Sydney Smith – remembering them not badly, either, considering how little use she had had for them since. But then, like most of her contemporaries, she had found it a particularly fascinating branch of her training.

'It isn't a bullet-hole,' she said carefully, 'for the simple reason that it's much too big. It might be that size if it were an exit wound: but it isn't that, because then the edges would be pushed outwards, and they're not.'

'Yes, I see. There seems to have been surprisingly little bleeding.'

'There's certainly less than I'd have expected.' Helen stared at the body in some perplexity; something about it was subtly *wrong* – and the next moment she realized what that something was, saying excitedly: 'You know, I don't think he was killed here at all. That streak of blood down the left side of his shirt – well, surely there ought to be signs of it on the grass, and as far as I can see there aren't. Of course, you'd have to move his arm to be sure, but just the same ...'

'Yes,' he said mildly. 'I quite agree.'

Helen sighed. 'In fact,' she stated in a rather flat tone of voice, 'you've realized it all along.'

'Practice, that's all ... Yes, as soon as we've finished here we shall have to start trying to find out where he was actually killed. And I wish those Twelford people would hurry up. I want to know about the time of death.'

They did not, however, have much longer to wait. Two minutes later Burns was conducting a miscellaneous troupe of men, hampered by a variety of equipment, to where they stood, and the ensuing quarter of an hour was devoted to stationing a harassed photographer in positions from which he could take photographs without trampling his boots on supposititious clues – a series of manoeuvres which he took in very bad part, saying 'That one isn't going to come out' and 'The light's terrible from here' and 'Why I don't leave the Force and do studio portraits ...' until, having finished his job, he resumed his former affability, packed up his camera, and climbed a small tree at the edge of the glade, from whose lower branches he emitted a sardonic commentary, *sotto voce*, on the subsequent activities of his colleagues. These consisted primarily of quartering and searching the glade, while Casby, having given some considerable time to examining the ground round the body, slowly and pensively circumambulated the body itself. And presently he said to Helen, who still remained just outside the clearing where he had left her:

'Would you like to look at him before I shift him, or doesn't that matter?'

Two or three of the men glanced at Helen as he asked the question, and for a moment she was smitten with a blind panic of self-consciousness. For heaven's *sake*, she thought desperately, what do I answer to that? And – damn him! – why does he have to ask it, in front of all these people ...?

But he had seen that she hesitated, and before she could reply he went on without haste: 'Most doctors don't mind about it one way or the other, but a few of them make a fuss.' The men looked away again – wholly uninterested, as Helen, recovering her wits, now saw – and she said briefly:

'As far as I'm concerned, go ahead. The only thing is, don't shake him about more than you can help.'

He made her a little mock-bow, but she sensed pleasure and respect underlying the mockery, and was happy, her earlier nervousness gone. She watched him as he went slowly and carefully about the job, and when he had finished, and had restored the body more or less to the position in which they had found it, she said:

'We were right, then.'

'About there not being any blood on the ground? Yes, we were. No weapon, either.'

'My turn now?'

'Fingerprints first. Though I'm afraid the only possible surfaces are his shoes and his glasses and his buttons and the little buckles at the back of his trousers. If chaps who proposed to get themselves murdered would only have the sense to put on a suit of nice shiny armour ... Briggs!'

The fingerprints man joined them, did his job, and provisionally expressed himself displeased with the results. 'Hardly any prints at all,' he said, 'and what there are look like turning out to be his own. I always have great hopes of bodies, miss,' he added to Helen, 'because it's surprising the number of murderers who'll wipe their prints off everything round the body for miles and miles, and completely forget about the body itself. But this ...!' He went off in disgust and settled down on a tree-stump with a magnifying glass and a note-book to make a start with the job of classifying Rubi's prints. 'They're re-showing an old Betty Grable film at the Rialto to-night,' he said in explanation of this assiduity, 'and I don't want to have to miss that.'

And now it really was Helen's turn. Casby made no attempt to watch or supervise her, but went off (the combing of the glade having proved it barren of evidence) to organize a more extensive but less detailed examination of the locality. When he returned, a quarter of an hour later, Helen had done, without pleasure but also without repugnance, all that could be done.

'The weapon's some sort of rod-like thing,' she told him, 'about the width of the wound. I wasn't able to measure it, I'm afraid, because I haven't got –'

'Oh, that's easily managed.' And presently, getting to his feet again: 'Seven sixteenths of an inch. What else?'

'It must have had a good sharp point, because there's hardly any tearing.'

He was making notes in the Memoranda section of his pocket diary. 'Yes. And then?'

'Well, I can't be sure about this, but I've a strong suspicion that the weapon was grooved, all round.'

'Longways, you mean?'

'Yes. There are little ridges which suggest that. The autopsy will give you a better idea, though.'

'Any notion how long this weapon would be?'

Helen shook her head. 'You can't possibly tell that till you find out how deep the wound goes. And of course, even then you only get a minimum length.'

'I suppose,' he said vaguely, 'that if one inserted a stick or something, and measured it afterwards ...'

'I certainly don't advise it. You'd probably alter the shape of the wound and destroy most of the information you'd normally get from it at the autopsy.'

'My mistake.' He smiled at her. 'You know, you're getting far too good at this ... But I suppose the weapon did pierce his heart.'

'There's no particular reason why he should have died if it didn't ... Oh, well, internal haemorrhage, of course. But I'm pretty sure it's not that.'

'Would he die as soon as the blow was struck?'

'Oh yes. There are cases of people lasting quite a long time after heart wounds, but not, I think, after a wound as big and violent as this.'

'For an engagement morning, this must be one of the most incongruous dialogues ever spoken ... Well, and now we come to the most important thing: how long ago did he die?'

'About five hours ago.'

He looked at his watch. 'Seven to seven-thirty this morning, in fact. Is that based on rigor?'

'M'm. It's only half complete, and the fact that he's been lying in the sun would speed it up – any heat does.'

'Did you make any other tests?'

'Well, the hypostasis confirms it. Temperature's no guide, because he's hot from the sun. I could see how his eyes react to physostigmine, if you like, but if they *do* react, that'll only mean he's been dead less than ten hours or so, and we know that anyway, from the rigor.'

'Right.' Casby snapped the diary shut and returned it to his pocket. 'Then that's all about that. If Sims turns up I shall get a second opinion from him – but that won't be because I distrust your verdict: it'll be because Sims is, after all, police-surgeon for this district ... Oh, here he is now.'

Dr George Sims pushed his way into the clearing. For a man engaged on his present errand he was somewhat oddly costumed, for he wore tennis shorts and shirt. 'Sorry about these,' he said to Casby. 'But when I got your message I thought I'd better not stop to change.' He smiled politely but not familiarly at Helen. 'I'm glad you were able to hire a guest expert. Knows a hell of a sight more about it than I do, I imagine. Well, well. Shall I have a look at him now I'm here, or do you know all you want to know?'

'For the record,' said Casby, 'I think you'd better make an examination.'

Sims stared at the body, and his humorously ugly face twisted in a grimace. 'Do I know him? Is he local?'

'He lives – lived, rather – at a cottage called Fiveways, in Ascot Lane. Swiss. A schoolmaster. Name's Rubi.'

'Oh yes, I remember,' said Sims cheerfully. 'Poor devil. Well, here goes.' He dropped to his knees.

And when, after a few minutes, he gave his conclusions, they matched with Helen's, even to the point about the grooves on the weapon. In conclusion he said: 'You're going to want a P.M., I suppose?'

'I'm afraid so,' said Casby. 'How soon will you be able to do it?'

'I can make a start on it after lunch. Good thing it's Sunday. In the meantime, if there's nothing else you want, I'll go back and try to squeeze in another set before I eat.'

With that he departed, wiry, vigorous, and undeniably attractive. The routine of search, tedious now, went on interminably; the sun shone ever hotter. 'I suppose I can't do any good by staying,' thought Helen; but she stayed none the less, warm and sticky and uncomfortable on the tree-stump which the fingerprints man had vacated, until at last, as the church clock struck one, Casby called off the search and sent for stretcher-bearers from the waiting ambulance to carry the body away. He was obviously exhausted, and he spoke little as with Helen he made his way out of the coppice into the water-meadow, bringing up

100

the rear of the file of his men. His car, and the ambulance, and the big police car from Twelford, were parked in a line near the gap in the hedge, and a little group of staring villagers were loitering round them. 'This,' he said abruptly when they were half-way across the meadow, 'will give them something to talk about.'

Helen put her hand timidly on his arm, and then, thinking better of the gesture, withdrew it again. 'Any clues?' she ventured.

'Precious little.' He was curt, withdrawn, and had not acknowledged her touch by so much as a glance. 'The next thing I must do is see Penelope Rolt.'

'I think,' said Helen quietly, 'that I'd better see her first. From what Burns said, she's in a pretty bad way.'

He agreed to this, though not very graciously. Well, damn it, he's tired, thought Helen; and said: 'I wonder *why* he was killed?' Rolt was at the back of her mind, as he had been ever since Burns had brought the news of Rubi's murder; Rolt saying: '*And if they're up to mischief, and I get my hands on him ...*' But she pushed the memory aside. 'Could it,' she added, 'have anything to do with the letters? If Rubi was playing at detectives, he might have stumbled on the truth about them, and – and been put out of the way.'

'That's possible, yes.' Casby turned his head to give her a wan smile. 'I'm sorry to be brusque,' he said, 'but I'm a bit on edge.'

'You mean you're worried about whether you can clear this up.' And after a pause he murmured:

'I haven't been doing so very well just recently.'

He doesn't want to talk, Helen told herself: well, then, shut up, like a sensible girl, and leave him alone. But even as she issued this judicious fiat, some demon prompted her to say: 'I interrupted you back at the house when you were going to tell me something about Beatrice's letter. Something which made you think it wasn't in the same class as the rest of the letters.'

'Yes,' he said; and there was a long silence before he went on: 'All the other letters have been made up of words cut from a considerable number of different newspapers. The words in Miss Keats-Madderly's letter had been cut from only two ... By the way, you told me when we first met that you took only one newspaper. Which is it?'

'*The Times*. But I sometimes buy the *Express* as well - just casually, you know: I don't order it.' Helen laughed, not very spontaneously. 'I hope those weren't the two newspapers used in Beatrice's letter.'

'As a matter of fact, they were.'

'Oh, but –'

'But what?'

Helen laughed again, even less confidently than before. 'I expect lots of people buy that particular combination of papers.'

'Yes, of course.'

'And besides, I wouldn't have any motive for sending Beatrice a letter like that, would I? We were very fond of each other.'

They were only a few yards, now, from the waiting cars, and already the stretcher-bearers were manoeuvring Rubi's body up the slippery bank to the gap in the hedge, while the older men in the little crowd doffed their caps and the women muttered together in agitated speculation. Casby halted.

'Motive?' he echoed. 'You haven't seen Bland, I take it?'

'I don't even know who he is.'

'He's a solicitor in Twelford. I got in touch with him yesterday because he was Miss Keats-Madderly's solicitor. Among other jobs, he drew up her will.'

With a tightening of the throat, Helen said: 'What has that got to do with me?'

'You're her legatee, that's all. She's left you her money. Forty, I think, or fifty thousand pounds.'

CHAPTER 11

CONSTABLE BURNS took crime seriously. He had been accepted into the Police Force soon after his demobilization in 1946, and most of his spare time since then had been spent poring over works of criminology with a view to fitting himself for the day when his longed-for transfer to the Criminal Investigation Department should be achieved. Hans Gross he had read, and Taylor on medical jurisprudence (though his ignorance of anatomy and of general medicine had made that particular book heavy and in the upshot not wholly satisfactory going), and Wilton on fingerprints, and Burrard on firearms and Rhodes on forensic chemistry. Mindful of the convenient omniscience of such heroes of detective romance as Dr Thorndyke and Mr Reginald Fortune, he had made random forays into the territory covered by Egyptology, speleology, religious heresy, and the habits of mollusca. He had attempted at considerable expense to train himself in identifying perfumes; he had peered at fabrics through lenses; he had taken casts of footprints, and on one momentous day, which nearly wrecked an otherwise ideal marriage, had dusted all his furniture with lampblack, copper powder, and metallic antimony in order to bring out latent prints, the afternoon he unluckily elected for his experiment being subsequent to a morning which Janet Burns had devoted to polishing ... Constable Burns took (I repeat) crime seriously; and it was therefore a little unkind of the gods to decree that his contribution to the solution of the Rubi affair should result from anything so banal as plain observation and ordinary, unscientific common sense.

From the water-meadow he cycled back to his cottage for Sunday dinner, which in his excitement he ate without, as Janet rather irritably noted, being in the least aware of its many rare perfections. She was mollified, however, by the sensational nature of his news.

'Dr Downing came in five minutes before you got back,' she said when he had finished his account of the morning's work. 'The Inspector brought her here in his car. She was looking for

Pen Rolt, but of course, I didn't know where she'd gone. Home, probably, was what I said.'

'Ah.' The recollection of Penelope sobered Burns's professional elation somewhat. 'She was in a pretty bad way, wasn't she?'

'Wouldn't stay here, though. Nor she wouldn't let me go with her when she left. "I'll be all right," she says over and over, "I'll be all right" ... Will, you don't think she'd ... well, do herself a mischief, do you?'

'Lord, no.' But he was uneasy for all that. 'It's shock, that's all.'

'She was keen on him, though, and that'd make it worse. And Mrs Cuddy says that place where she found him was where they used to meet.'

'Ah,' said Burns again. 'But you know what sort of a dirty-minded old bag Mrs Cuddy is. Some of the things she's told you –'

'Still, but what I mean is, he might have been put there deliberate-like, so as the girl should find him.'

Burns was interested. 'That's an idea. If that's what happened, then it looks as if whoever did the murder wanted to show he disapproved of their goings-on ... not,' he added hastily, 'that I believe there *were* any goings-on, not at her age, and not with him the faddy, chatterbox sort he was ... Yes, and *that* looks like our friend who's been writing the anonymous letters, doesn't it? I wonder.'

He wondered to such effect that they finished the meal in silence – a silence broken only by the sound of Burns eating feathery pastry as if it were carpet. Finally he pushed his plate aside, swallowed his tea, consulted his watch, and stood up.

'Well, I'm off,' he said. 'The Inspector's meeting me' – he considered this, and then amended it to 'I'm meeting the Inspector' – 'at Fiveways, where this chap lived in Ascot Lane. Says he'll need me for the local detail and so forth. So keep your fingers crossed. This business might do me a bit of good if I handle it right.'

'Just the same, don't you go acting the great detective, Will, or you'll only annoy people.'

Burns chuckled. 'Don't you worry, love. I may be green, but I'm not that green. Expect me when you see me.'

'Enjoy the pork, Will?'

'Never better.'

'What you ate,' said Janet demurely, 'was lamb.'

Burns looked blank; then, awareness dawning, he grinned. 'I'll deal with you,' he said with cheerful menace, 'when I get back. And don't let me find any lovers in the cupboards, either.' After more than three years of marriage, this joke still kept its virgin charm.

'Oh, but I'm always finished with *them* by tea-time,' said Janet, winking. Then she backed away in mock-terror. 'No, go on, Will, you've got *work* to do ...'

So ten minutes later, Burns, cycling in the statuesque, un-ruffled manner of his kind, turned out of the village street by the west end of the church and proceeded at a dignified pace towards Ascot Lane. Just beyond Weaver's shop he met Helen Downing, who was on foot, and stopped to ask if she had been able to find Penelope Rolt.

'No, I haven't, I'm afraid,' said Helen. 'I went to her house, but she wasn't there. It's really rather worrying. If you get any news of her, let me know, will you? She oughtn't to be wandering about on her own, after what's happened.'

'I'll let you know, miss.' But then, with his foot on the pedal in readiness to remount, Burns checked himself and stared. 'Hullo,' he said jocularly. 'Going to do an operation, are you?'

'Operation ...? Oh, *this*.' And Helen displayed what she was carrying. 'No, it's not as bad as that. Colonel Babington gave it me yesterday to take back to Weaver, and I completely forgot. So I'm returning it now.'

And that was when Burns had his great inspiration. A butcher's steel; grooved, with a sharp point; just about the right width to have made a certain wound ... He was so startled that he did not, for the moment, pause to consider the implications of his guess, if it should turn out to be correct: his lie which immediately followed stemmed from the habit of discretion rather than from mistrust.

'I'll take it, miss, if you like,' he said casually. 'Passing the shop just now made me remember there was something I wanted to see him about anyway. So if it'll save you trouble ...'

'All right,' she said readily enough. 'Visiting Weaver isn't a thing I do for choice. By the way, there's nothing fresh, I suppose?'

'About the murder, miss? Not that I know of.'

'I see. Well, don't forget about Penelope, will you?'

'I won't, miss.'

But in point of fact Burns had forgotten about Penelope within fifteen seconds; because this steel business, he reflected as he wheeled his bicycle back along the road, looked as if it might turn out to be something big. Colonel Babington had given Dr Downing the steel yesterday, so she'd said; and presumably she'd had it ever since. Well, then: by her own evidence, as well as Sims's, Rubi had been killed about seven that morning; and that meant – here Burns slackened his measured stride, frowning – well, of course, what it *must* mean was that someone had pinched the steel from Dr Downing, and then returned it afterwards. The only trouble was, why should they have returned it? So as to try and incriminate Dr Downing? Could be ...

The simpler possibility was one which Burns was not, at the moment, prepared to face.

Thus rather inchoately brooding, he came to his destination – a little Georgian house standing on its own, whose ground floor had been converted with tasteful unobtrusiveness into a small shop, the single word 'Weaver' in faded gold-scrolled lettering above the window. It being Sunday, the shop was of course shut, and empty of wares; but the blinds had not been drawn, and Burns, glancing in as he propped his machine against the wall, could see the bare marble shelves, the scrubbed wooden tables, the knives, the massive door of the electrically operated cold-storage room, and the sawdust-strewn floor. Skirting the house, on a cinder-covered path between its west wall and the garage where the delivery van was kept, Burns arrived at, and portentously knocked on, the back door.

It was opened to him, by Weaver in person, with disconcerting promptness. Seen at close quarters, Weaver was not a handsome man: his narrow, slightly equine face was perched on his long neck like a too-heavy flower on a too-slender stem, and the eyes behind his horn-rimmed glasses were as small and black as currants in a cake. His smile showed large, discoloured teeth; his body moved with the suppleness of an india-rubber doll; his decent black serge was ostentatiously sabbatical. But in spite of his failure to prepossess, he was at once all deference, all gratification, when he recognized his visitor.

'Mr Burns!' he cried. 'Come in, sir, come in! No, no, I insist ... insist. Come along! There's a step down, so be careful not to trip and fall. I've only just this moment finished my bachelor repast, so you must excuse the muddle. This way, this way. The ladies in my little flock sometimes tell me my house badly needs a woman's touch, and I'm sure they're right, certain of it. But who, I ask them, would ever marry an ugly fellow like me? Here we are, then. Goodness, it does look rather a mess. If you'll just allow me a moment to clear away ...'

The room into which Burns had been unwillingly conducted was the kitchen, and it contrived in some mysterious way to be at once perfectly clean and entirely squalid. The window was closed, and the air frowsty with the smell of many meals; a tap dripped persistently; a mangy black cat sharpened its claws on the dresser. An old-fashioned black iron range occupied almost the whole of one wall, and the pictures were of Biblical personages who pointed dramatically with one hand at distant sheep, Galilean lakes, and so forth, while with the other they clutched providently at unmanageable-looking robes. On the centre table were the remains of a small cold lunch, and Weaver bustled about removing these to the neighbourhood of the sink while Burns looked on helplessly.

'There!' said Weaver, in transit with the last plate. '*That's* better! And now we must find you a chair. Dear, dear, what a wretched host I am, to be sure! Keeping you standing all this time! And you could do with a cup of tea, I expect.' He darted to an electric kettle. 'I wonder if you would oblige me by fetching out the plum cake from the cupboard in the corner?'

Burns, who up to now had been almost literally hypnotized by this hospitable agitation, managed at long last to voice a disclaimer. 'Very good of you, Mr Weaver,' he said with a considerable effort, 'but I can't stay, I'm afraid. Official business is what I'm here on.'

'Official business?' Replacing the kettle, Weaver shook his head in humorous perplexity. 'Well, what have I been up to now, I wonder? Or is it' – all at once he was serious – 'is it perhaps to do with the horrible crime which I understand to have been discovered this morning?'

'You've heard about the murder then, sir?'

'Indeed yes. Mrs Cuddy spoke to me of it when I was on my way to preach in our little temple here.' And at this, Weaver closed his eyes and levelled the point of his nose at the ceiling; he was praying, Burns assumed. 'Dreadful, dreadful,' he murmured after a moment. 'The wickedness of the human heart is indeed infinite, without God. In the midst of life –'

Burns found him not unimpressive; but at the same time he was anxious to get to the point. Producing the steel, he said abruptly: 'But as to why I'm here, sir . . .'

Weaver opened his eyes; he nodded deferential encouragement, his head bouncing back and forth on his long neck like a knob on a spring. 'As to why you're here . . .'

'Well, sir, what I want to know is, is this yours?'

'The steel? Certainly it's mine.' Weaver was emphatic. 'I have owned it ever since my apprenticeship. But where did you . . .'

'It was found, sir,' said Burns impressively. 'Found. Down by the river,' he improvised, feeling that something more explicit was called for. 'Have you any idea how it can have got there?'

Weaver wiped sweat from his forehead; inside, as out, the afternoon was certainly insufferably hot. 'Little rascals!' he said somewhat obscurely; and grinned, though without convincing Burns that he was much amused. 'It would be some of the village children who took it, I don't doubt.'

'Just exactly how do you mean, sir – "took it"?'

'Why, from the shop, Mr Burns, when my back was turned.'

'I'd hardly have thought,' said Burns mistrustfully, 'that that was possible.'

'Indeed yes. As you know, I have no assistant in the shop, and so naturally I am sometimes obliged to leave it unattended for a

108

few moments while I am in the cold-storage room or elsewhere in the house. At such times ...'

'I see, sir. Yes. But what makes you think it was children specially? Could have been anyone, couldn't it?'

Weaver shrugged. 'There are two reasons, Mr Burns, why I suggest that it was probably children who took the steel. The first is that I cannot see why anyone *else* should take such a thing. And the second is that – as I think you may remember – the village children have tried to play such jokes on me before.'

Burns did remember; Weaver had complained of that particular nuisance two or three months ago. There had been little Burns could do about it, and that little he had done grudgingly, for he disliked Weaver and felt that in any case the man ought to be capable, where children were concerned, of looking after himself. Still, the complaint had had substance, Burns was bound to admit.

'High spirits,' Weaver was saying now with a consciously wry smile. 'High spirits ... The little ones think me a very comical fellow, and an excellent butt for their tricks. Of course, they mean no harm by it, but none the less ...'

'Just which children,' Burns interposed, 'do you have in mind, sir?'

But he got no clear answer to this. Children, it appeared, were a class of being not much more individualized in Weaver's recollection than so many ants, and his conjectures, on this occasion as on the previous one, were vague and lacking in confidence. Moreover, he had not, he said, particularly noticed *any* children lingering near the shop yesterday morning, when the steel had disappeared. 'All I can tell you, Mr Burns,' he concluded, 'is that I went for a moment into the cold-storage room, there being at the time no customers in the shop, and that when I came back the steel was gone. I was annoyed, of course, and was intending to notify you of the theft, but since the steel is now found ...' He tentatively stretched out his hand for it.

'Sorry, sir,' said Burns, 'but I can't let you have it back just yet awhile.' Weaver's hand dropped to his side. Burns swallowed, plunged. 'It'll have to be tested first, sir,' he said, 'to find out if it's got anything to do with the murder.'

Weaver closed his eyes again.

'Do I understand, then,' he said quietly, 'that you believe it to have been used to kill this unhappy young man? Horrible, horrible. And but for my carelessness ...'

'Come, come, sir.' Burns was discomfited by these scruples and moreover was already beginning to regret the precipitate statement which had given rise to them. 'There's no need to take on so, no need at all. Matter of fact, the odds are ninety-nine to one against this having anything to do with the murder. All I meant ...'

But Weaver was not listening. Without opening his eyes, he said: 'I have put temptation in the way of some wretched sinner. You will say that his crime would have been committed in any case. But can you be sure? Perhaps it was only the fact of the instrument's being at hand that drove him to his appalling deed. If that is so, I have much to answer for.'

He dropped suddenly to his knees. In hideous embarrassment Burns fled. And his faith in his inspiration, as he pedalled under the blazing sun towards Ascot Lane, waned disastrously. The steel which he now had buttoned up inside his tunic might well be the *sort* of weapon that had killed Rubi; but that it was the *actual* weapon seemed increasingly doubtful – unless, of course, you were going to accuse Dr Downing of using it, which Burns, as one of her admirers, most certainly was not. It could have been stolen from her, of course – that had been his first idea – but stabbing weapons weren't like firearms, difficult to lay hands on, and a murderer who went so far out of his way as to procure one by those means wasn't very credible, to say the least. And besides, if stealing it had been unnecessary, *returning* it was ten times more so. No, the fact was that he'd been barking up the wrong tree, and this particular steel had nothing to do with the case: a queer coincidence, if you liked, but that was all. And I hope to God, thought Burns, that Weaver doesn't pass on what I said to him about it; that was damn-foolishness all right, and if the Super gets to hear of it, I'm cooked. What was it Janet had said? '*Don't go acting the great detective.*' And that was just exactly what he had been doing ... Constable Burns came to the small house named Fiveways with the spark of life in him burning rather low.

Fiveways was the only house in Cotten Abbas that had been built since the war. A writer had had it put up in the first place, had lived in it for a few months, tired of it, gone to live abroad, let it furnished; Rubi had been in it not much more than four months. It stood solitary in a small, neglected garden, its militant newness as yet unmitigated by wind and weather, with a dispiriting view from its front windows of cows in a field; and its name – since there was no cross-roads of any sort within half a mile – was distinctly fanciful. 'B-but my dear fellow,' its owner had once said to Burns when remonstrated with about this anomaly, 'the absence of c-cross-roads is p-precisely the *p-point*. D-don't *you see*?' Burns had not seen, and did not see even now; but then, he was scarcely, as he parked his bicycle against the hedge and trudged up the diminutive path to the front door, in the mood for sophisticated little jokes.

It was Sergeant Pound who let him in – a gawky officer who like half the police force considered himself long overdue for promotion, but who was unusual in having allowed this persuasion to sour him. 'Ah, here you are,' he said unwelcomingly. 'High time, too. The Inspector's been here an hour already.'

'He can't have had any lunch, then.'

'He hasn't. Too busy for it – not like some I could name.' The sergeant paused to allow this thrust full penetration; then, since Burns only glowered: 'Well, get a move on, can't you? I'm not going to stand holding the door for you all day.'

With this he led the way to the sitting-room, where Burns, glancing at the book-shelves, saw works by Freud, Jung, Adler, Ernest Jones, and other authors with the import of whose names his more modish criminological text-books had familiarized him. These clearly were Rubi's; but the impression left by the rest of the room, at a first glance, was no better than a blurred, unilluminating composite of his personality and the owner's, like two photographs taken on the same plate. Casby was seated at a desk by the window, looking through the pages of a note-book or diary which he seemed to have found there.

111

'Sorry if I'm late, sir,' said Burns, saluting. 'But you didn't say any definite time, so I assumed . . .'

'Yes, that's all right,' Casby answered abstractedly; and then with more vigour, after finishing his perusal in silence: 'Oh, damn this thing, it's *all* in German. Pound, you don't speak German, do you?'

'No, sir.'

'Burns?'

'Well, yes, sir, I do a bit. Learned it at school for three years, and then I had a chance of keeping it up when I was stuck in Hamburg at the end of the war. I'm a bit rusty now, mind you. Still . . .'

Pound made a whiffling noise, patently intended to express disgust. But Casby was pleased.

'Good,' he said. 'I'll be getting a translation later, of course, but in the meantime it may be useful for me to have a rough idea of what it's all about.' He handed the diary – for it was that – to Burns. 'Sit down and have a look through it, will you? I'm going to prowl about upstairs. Pound, have you been out to the shed yet?'

'Well, no, sir, not *yet*. The fact is . . .'

'Then for heaven's sake do it now.' Hugely aggrieved, Pound saluted and went. 'Take off your coat if you like,' said Casby to Burns as he followed Pound out through the door. 'It's too hot to stand on ceremony.' He vanished, and Burns heard him clattering up the stairs.

For all its alienist's jargon, Rubi's diary proved to be fairly easy going, and by the time Casby returned, after bumping about for ten minutes or so overhead, Burns had read all of it once and parts of it a second time.

'But I'm afraid it's a bit of a disappointment, sir,' he said. 'More like a notebook, it is. There's a lot to do with his teaching, theory mostly, and a lot to do with the anonymous letters, but all of that's theory too, psychological stuff: he seems to have thought it was an unmarried woman writing them, but only – if you see what I mean – because of what his books told him; he obviously didn't *know*. Then there's some bits about Miss Rolt.' Burns flushed slightly. 'There's got to be science, I suppose, but it seems nasty cold-blooded stuff to me. No hint, though, that he thought of her as anything but a – an object of study; there's one place where he actually admits that he's pretending to be fond of her so as to be able to watch her.'

'Rather unappetizing, yes.' Casby nodded. 'Anything about anyone else in the village?'

'Well, yes, sir, there is, about quite a lot of people. But nothing *personal*, as you might say: just analysing them.'

'I see. No note of engagements?'

'No, sir. It's not that sort of diary. Abstract ideas, that's all there is in it. Except perhaps just this last entry.'

'Well?'

'He's been theorizing about the letters, you see, all just usual But then it breaks off and you suddenly get this bit.' Burns read the German aloud. '*Die Zeitüngen: drei (vier?) Art von Geschäft. Ausfragebesuch (Gemütsbeschaffenheit ändert sich natürlich nach der Entdeckung).*'

'And that means?'

'"*The newspapers*,"' Burns translated: '"*three (four?) kinds of business. Visit for questioning (the mental condition isn't of course the same after detection).*"'

'Well, well.' Casby was pensive. 'So perhaps after all he did have a definite suspicion as to what person was writing those letters. And perhaps that person didn't like the sort of questions he asked ...' Then more briskly: 'Well, that's something, anyway – namely a motive. Thanks very much, Burns; you've helped enormously. There are just one or two questions before you go – not about this, about other things. In the first place, do you happen to know who looked after this man?'

'Yes, sir. It was Miss Tuffill.'

'What was the arrangement, then? I mean, when did she come and how much did she do?'

'Three times a week, sir, she's been coming: Mondays, Wednesdays, and Fridays. And all she's been doing is the cleaning – he did his own cooking, it seems, and the bed-making and the washing-up.'

'I see. And I imagine that if he did the cooking, he did the shopping as well.'

'So I believe, sir. But as to that, Miss Tuffill, she told my wife he got most of his food in parcels from Switzerland. Tins galore, she said, and he as good as lived out of them.'

'Yes, the kitchen confirms that. Even his milk seems to have come out of tins. Did *any* tradespeople deliver here? What I'm trying to get at is when he was last seen alive.'

'Quite so, sir. But as far as I know he bought his bread and so forth from the shops, and carried it back here himself.' Burns paused dubiously. 'There's the postwoman,' he suggested.

'I met her when I was on my way here, and spoke to her then, by way of routine. But apparently he got very little mail; she hasn't been here since Wednesday. This house is out of *sight*, too, and I imagine that as often as not he approached and left it on the side away from the village – which means he wouldn't be seen about much . . .' Casby pondered, sucking at an unlit pipe. 'Well, I think that's all for the moment,' he said presently, gesturing dismissal, 'unless, of course, anything else has occurred to you that might help.'

Burns hesitated, and the words *great detective* chimed cautionarily inside his head. But their chime, though still distinct enough, was fainter than before. For in the meantime Burns had made himself useful; he had translated German; like the psalmist, he had seen the ungodly – meaning Sergeant Pound – smitten upon the cheek-bone. In short, he was by now feeling a renewed, if limited, piety with regard to his Inspiration, and if he was going to mention the steel at all, this undoubtedly was the psychological moment . . . 'There's just one thing, sir,' he blurted. 'It's about the weapon.'

'Yes? What about it?'

'I may be quite wrong, sir' – Burns was fumbling at the buttons of his tunic – 'but it did occur to me that it might be something like this.' He produced the steel. 'It's the right size, sir, or near enough, and it's sharp, and there's the grooves on it . . .'

Casby had taken the steel and was examining it intently. Presently he took out a lens and made use of that. 'Blood, I think,' he announced, 'in the crevice between the steel itself and the handle.'

'Well, sir, it is of course a *butcher's* steel.'

Casby smiled. 'Oh, quite.' He found pocket callipers and

adjusted them to the steel at its widest diameter. 'Seven sixteenths of an inch,' he said. 'Well, well. Pound can take it to the laboratory while I go and see Rolt ... You're right, Burns. This does look very much like it.'

Burns was not a little taken aback. 'The – the actual one that did the job, sir?'

'Why not?' Casby looked up, struck by the incredulity in Burns's voice. 'Whose is it? Where did you get it?'

Constable Burns told him.

CHAPTER 12

THE Chief Constable's study was slightly shabby – as a room initially well-furnished can be allowed without offensiveness to become: the chintz a little faded; the ceiling smoky; the rugs, though still serviceable, frayed. Long lattice windows looked towards the front gate, and opposite to them were double doors which led into the drawing-room. The chairs and sofa were Edwardian, with a frail look; Edwardian, too, the massive roll-top desk. The only decisively modern things there were the green metal filing-cabinet and the telephone, and these, you felt, were interlopers, suffered there for their utility alone. The mantelpiece had photographs on it, many photographs; the decanters on the side-table wore necklace labels, shallow-incised lettering on rectangles of thin silver; the books were behind glass. At wood and fabric, brass and paint, the years had picked with delicate, untiring fingers, and the felts tacked on to eliminate draughts were like patches on an old ship.

It was half past five. Inspector Edward Casby, his face so white with fatigue that the scar hardly showed, sat in an armchair by the fireplace, and Colonel Babington, fidgeting with his clipped moustache, was pacing the carpet. The heat was less now: westering, the sun had gained definition and no longer hurt your eyes.

The Colonel glanced surreptitiously at Casby, halted.

'My dear chap, you're overdoing it,' he said abruptly. 'Get some food and some sleep, that's my advice. There's nothing that won't keep till to-morrow.'

'I'm afraid I can't be sure of that, sir.' Casby remained quietly dogged. 'And that's why I feel I must make some sort of interim report. There'll be' – he hesitated – 'there may be action you'll want to take.'

'Action?' The Colonel stared. 'What sort of action, for God's sake?'

'About me, sir.'

'About you?'

'You'll understand what I mean, sir, when I've told you the results I've got so far.'

'Oh, very well, then.' The Colonel shrugged. 'If you must, you must. But you'd better have a drink first.' He went to the decanters, poured whisky for both of them, carried it back to the fireplace. 'Now,' he said, 'what *is* all this?'

'As you know, sir, there are three separate problems.' Casby spoke with deliberation – with too much deliberation, Colonel Babington felt; what he was going to say plainly had an interest for him above and beyond his professional concern with it, and he was using logic to shut that interest out. 'Three problems: the letters in general, the letter sent to Miss Keats-Madderly in particular, and the murder of Rubi.

'It may be that those three problems are quite separate and distinct; or it may be that two of them are connected, and the third is separate; or it may be that there's a nexus involving them all.'

The Colonel looked at the ceiling. 'Yes,' he murmured. 'Yes, I see.'

'I beg your pardon, sir.' Casby smiled faintly. 'Perhaps I am overdoing it rather. I didn't intend to imply ...'

'No, no, go on – my dear man. It's your report, after all.' Colonel Babington returned the smile. 'And I dare say that sometimes I am a shade slow-witted about these things. So don't mind me. Go ahead.'

Casby sipped whisky and returned the glass carefully to its place on the bricks of the hearth. 'First, then, the letters in general,' he said. 'As you know, one doesn't, in the normal way, expect to be held up long over a problem like that; not these days. But the fact remains that we've drawn a blank every time. The paper and envelopes – to start with them – have all been the same sort, cheap stuff that you can get at any Woolworth's; the paste used to stick on the bits of newspaper has always been Gloy, which half the population buys; the scraps of brush-hair we've found mixed in with it from time to time have all come from the sort of brush that's supplied with the stuff; and the newspapers – well, they've just been newspapers: various newspapers of various dates, and not all the snippings in any given letter have been of the same date, necessarily. Place of posting, in three cases here, in

117

seven Twelford, in two Brankham; but quite often people have destroyed the envelopes – and of course there must obviously be letters which have never been handed to us at all. Time of posting, variable. And none of that helps, because people from here are constantly going into Twelford and Brankham to do their shopping. The pen used in addressing the envelopes has always been a blue-black Baby Biro, which is tricky, because with a Biro there's practically no difference between the width of the up, down, and cross strokes, and that takes away half the writing's individuality before you begin; anyway, the graphologists say they can't possibly indentify the writing on the envelopes with any of the various handwritings we've submitted to them, so we're foxed there. What's more, none of the obvious suspects uses a Baby Biro in the normal way, and although we've tried to trace recent purchases of Baby Biros in the local shops, it's been a hopeless business – the girls in Woolworth's, for instance, wouldn't be likely to remember any particular purchase.

'So far, so bad. But there did seem to be just three possible lines of investigation we could try.

'The first was analysis of dust and hair in the envelopes. Well, the dust so far has proved absolutely nothing, and the one and only hair we found turned out to belong to the woman to whom the letter had been sent. As far as hair's concerned, this letter-writer has either been extraordinarily careful or extraordinarily lucky ... Oh, and I was forgetting fingerprints. None – and that, of course, means care: the writing and sealing and posting must all have been done in gloves.

'Secondly, there was the marked-stamp idea – individualized twopenny-halfpennies to be sold to each of half a dozen suspects when they asked for stamps in the local post office. And you know what happened to *that* scheme.'

Colonel Babington nodded. 'Someone came across it in a detective story,' he supplied, 'and in a day or two half the village had heard of it. Ample warning. So it's hardly surprising that it got no results. Of course, our choice of suspects was pretty arbitrary; we just picked people we knew to have, or thought might have, a grudge against the community, and hoped for the best. And that's really been the trouble all along. All our prying's been concentrated on those six, more or less, and quite likely the culprit isn't one of them at all.'

'Just so, sir. But it's difficult to see what else we could have done. And naturally it was on those six that we experimented when we tried out the last of our possibilities – I mean the blood-group business. That looked promising, because very few people realize that you can tell a man's blood-group from his saliva, provided he doesn't belong to the fifteen per cent they call "non-secretors", and there was plenty of the letter-writer's saliva on the gummed-down flaps of the envelopes and the backs of the stamps. Well, it was tested: group A, it turned out to be. And that was when the idea began to look rather *less* promising, because forty-four per cent of the population are A. However, we went ahead and managed one way and another to get a blood or saliva sample from our six – and damn me if five of them, *five*, weren't just that, group A.'

'The odd man out,' said Colonel Babington, 'being –'

'Being Rubi. He was B, we found, a rare group that only about eight per cent of Europeans belong to. So *he* hadn't been writing the anonymous letters, or anyway he hadn't been sticking the stamps on them, and finding that out wasn't much help to us, because for other reasons he was practically eliminated already. All of which leaves us – well, leaves us where it leaves us, to wit, nowhere.'

Colonel Babington grunted. 'You certainly seem to have had the devil of a job. Fingerprints, blood-groups, hair, dust, pen, marked stamps – as far as I can see, the chances are a million to one against that combination failing to get results. Still, it's the odd chance that comes off, and there's no use moaning about it. If it's any consolation to you, I don't see what more you could have done. But now, what about this letter that was sent to Beatrice?'

'As regards that, sir, we've very little to work on. It was burned, as you know, and the envelope's missing. But I'm still inclined to think that it wasn't sent by the person who sent all the other letters. For one thing, the envelope – if Miss Pilkington's to be relied on – was different: violet ink, and script, not capitals. For another, only two newspapers (both of them dated the first of this month) were used to make up the message.'

'Yes,' said the Colonel thoughtfully. 'Interesting, that. And particularly about the envelope. The form of the letter itself suggests that whoever sent it was making some effort to make it seem to have come from the same person who wrote the other letters. But then, why didn't he bother to make the *envelope* seem the same, too? Everyone round here *knew* about the envelopes, about the block capitals and so forth.'

Casby nodded. 'That had occurred to me, too, and I confess I don't know what the answer is. Just carelessness, perhaps. But now, about the message. You know what that was –'

'My God, I do,' said the Colonel with feeling. 'Amazing thing. I suppose it *is true?* Some of these letters have accused people of the most unlikely –'

'Well, sir, but if it isn't true, the suicide becomes quite pointless.'

'Yes,' the Colonel assented gloomily. 'Yes, I see what you mean ... The trouble was, poor Beatrice would *swank* about her family so. If she hadn't done that, no one would have cared a brass farthing what side of the sheet she was born on, except perhaps that dolt Mogridge.'

'But in any case, sir, there's proof. Rolt, you see, knows the history of it – of Miss Keats-Madderly's birth, I mean.'

'Rolt?'

'Yes, sir.' And Casby repeated what Helen had told him of her meeting with Rolt in the water-meadow. 'I've been to see him this afternoon,' he added, 'and he certainly didn't try to *deny* knowing. What's more, he insisted that he'd never told anyone else about it – not even his daughter.'

Colonel Babington frowned. 'Well, that doesn't look much like guilt, does it? If he sent that letter, then he certainly wouldn't want you to think he was the only person who knew about Beatrice's birth.'

'Quite so. And of course, someone else may have found out about it quite independently of Rolt. But that's stretching the long arm of coincidence rather far.'

'It's pulling the damned thing right out of its socket,' said the Colonel emphatically. 'And yet ... Oh Lord, what a muddle. There's one other possibility, though: Beatrice *might* have confided in a particular friend. And I suppose you'd have to say that her best friend here was –'

'Was Helen Downing.'

If there was any alteration in Casby's tone as he said these three words, Colonel Babington failed to notice it. 'Helen Downing,' the Colonel reiterated moodily; and then: 'No, damn it, I don't believe for a single second that she'd do a thing like that. After all, anyone who knew Beatrice would realize there was quite a danger of her acting rashly if she got a letter like that, so unless you had a motive for wanting her dead –' He checked himself, suddenly remembering; and in a flat voice Casby said:

'Fifty thousand pounds.'

There was a silence. Colonel Babington, fretting, went to a silver cigarette-box on the desk, opened it, peered into it, and then closed it again with a bang. And the cat Lavender, which had hitherto been slumbering in a chair, took advantage of his pre-occupation to leap up on to the side-table and pursue Martians among the cut-glass decanters there. With an exclamation of annoyance, the Colonel seized the cat Lavender and thrust it out of the room. 'No, I don't believe it,' he said, returning to the fire-place. 'Do you?'

Casby made no direct reply. He said: 'She was in Miss Keats-Madderly's house at the time when the envelope disappeared.'

'So were you. So were a lot of people.'

'It's not conclusive, of course.' Casby still spoke tonelessly. 'All I was trying to convey was this, that Helen Downing is apparently the only person with motive, just as Rolt is apparently the only person with the necessary knowledge. I'm assuming, mind you, that the letter sent to Miss Keats-Madderly was *intended* to incite to suicide, and that assumption may be quite wrong. If it is wrong, then obviously Rolt is the chief suspect.'

'And he was one of our original half-dozen, wasn't he? But if this letter to Beatrice was in fact different from the others, then presumably it wasn't he who wrote the others.' Colonel Babington made a gesture of despair. 'It couldn't,' he suggested, 'be much *more* confusing, could it?'

'Finally, there's the murder of Rubi.' Casby was talking more

121

rapidly now, and the Colonel sensed that they were approaching a crux. 'My information about that still has a lot of gaps in it, but I'd like you to know what I've got so far ... The worst gap, I think, concerns when he was last seen alive. Friday afternoon, when he left his school after taking a gang of boys out to test a grandstand or something, is the best I've been able to rake up so far.'

'*Friday?* But good heavens, that's two days ago. Wasn't he teaching yesterday?'

'No. Apparently his time-table happens not to involve any work on Saturdays. I gather that what he told one of his colleagues was that he was proposing to spend yesterday doing a long hike, but there's no evidence as to whether he carried out that intention or not, and I understand from Rolt that there's a possibility he didn't.'

'Oh? How's that?'

'Rolt told me, when I saw him this afternoon, that his daughter told him yesterday evening that she'd seen Rubi during the day; I gathered there had been a row about that. But I can't check it, because at the moment neither her father nor anyone else seems to know where the girl is.'

'Yes, I see ... But does all this matter very much?'

'I beg your pardon, sir?'

'I mean, we *know* more or less when Rubi was killed, don't we? Early this morning.'

'Quite so, sir. But there's one factor which makes it essential that we should find out where he's been recently, and whom he's seen.' And Casby explained about the final entry in Rubi's diary. 'Of course, there may be nothing in it, but plainly it's got to be looked into.'

'Plainly,' the Colonel agreed drily. 'You may remember that at the time he came to us, and offered to help us over the letters, he was very positive he could find out who was writing them. And it rather looks now as if he did.'

'We can't be certain of that, sir,' said Casby defensively. 'He may have been murdered for some quite different reason.'

'As, for instance, what?'

'Well, for one thing, there's no possible doubt that Rolt

disapproved of his going about with Penelope. Disapproved strongly.'

'Tcha! You don't kill a man for that. You send the girl away for a month to forget about him; or else you give him a large piece of your mind; or both. And from what I know of Rubi, he wasn't the sort of suitor to go on hanging around after the girl's father had warned him off.'

'But if the girl still insisted on seeing him –'

'Oh well, it's *conceivable*, I suppose. I'm not suggesting you should put it out of your mind altogether. But it sounds very thin to me ... Who else in the village was this wretched young man friendly with?'

'To the best of my knowledge, nobody. He kept himself to himself, as they say. You'll remember, sir, that we made inquiries about him not long ago, in connexion with the letters, so we do know something about him in advance; and I quite agree that apart from Rolt he doesn't seem to have had any enemies. But there's still a lot of ground to be covered – his relations with his colleagues at school, for example. The diary's suggestive, yes, but at present not *more* than that.'

'He said he thought the anonymous letter-writer was an un-married woman, didn't he? That seems to have been the line he was working on. And out of our six suspects only Helen Downing is that.'

'As you said yourself, sir, our list of suspects was quite arbi-trary. And there's no evidence that Rubi didn't change his mind – about the unmarried-woman theory, I mean.'

'There's no evidence that he did, either ... Oh, damn it.' Colonel Babington bunched his brows in annoyance and per-plexity. 'Well, anyway, go on with what you were saying. I don't for a moment believe Helen's a murderer, but these snags have got to be explained away somehow.'

'There are others, too, sir.'

'Are there, by God!' The Colonel, who had wandered to the window and been gazing out, swung round abruptly. 'About Helen Downing, you mean?'

'I'm afraid so.' The flatness was back in Casby's voice. 'For one thing, she was certainly very close to the spot where we found

123

the body, at about the time the murder must have been committed. That – between seven and seven-thirty this morning – was when she met Rolt.'

Colonel Babington sat down heavily in a chair at the other side of the hearth; for a moment he seemed not to know what to say. 'But that,' he ventured at last, 'tells against Rolt as much as against Helen, doesn't it? And besides, I thought it was certain that Rubi wasn't killed in the place where he was found.'

'The chances are, sir, that he wasn't killed very far off.'

'Why? I don't see that. If you haven't *found* the place where he was killed, then –'

'We haven't. But the point is this: even allowing a wide margin of error for what Helen Downing and George Sims say was the time of death, Rubi was pretty certainly killed in daylight (all else apart, he's not very likely, in summer, to have got up and dressed while it was still dark). All right. But there's nowhere you can take a vehicle within three hundred yards of the coppice, on any side. So if Rubi wasn't killed in the coppice, or in the water-meadow close to it, then the murderer must have had to *carry* his body there, a considerable distance, in broad daylight, and all the time within view of the windows of several houses – not to mention the saw-mill. Well, I can't for a moment believe that any murderer would be so idiotic as to do that, and that's why I say that Rubi was killed somewhere within hailing distance of where he was found.'

'But why – in that case – should the body ever have been moved at all? It seems senseless to me.'

'Well, sir, it's possible that the actual murder was done in a relatively exposed place – say at the edge of the coppice – and that the murderer shifted the body because he didn't want it found too soon. We shall go on searching, of course, and I've no doubt we shall find the spot eventually.'

'Yes ... You're pretty sure, I take it, that the scene of the murder wasn't anywhere very close to the glade where the body was found?'

'Yes, sir, fairly sure. We've searched a thirty or forty-yard radius already.'

'That's a point in Helen's favour, then. Corpses don't weigh light, and I can't see her carrying this one, single-handed, over any very great distance – or dragging it, even.' The Colonel paused to reflect. 'Of course, she could hardly avoid telling you the true time of death, even if she'd wanted to, because she knew Sims was going to make an examination too ... Look here, Casby, didn't she *realize?*'

'That she must have been about when the murder was committed? No, sir, she apparently didn't. And I can understand that, in a way.'

'Yes, yes, so can I. It's devilish awkward, though.' The Colonel sought reassurance in the hearth-rug, and seemed to find none. 'Well, what next? What about the weapon?'

'I think we may have found that, sir.'

'My dear chap, admirable!' The Colonel was temporarily cheered by this intelligence. 'And what exactly is it? The wound was unusual, I gather, and –'

But here he was interrupted by the ringing of the telephone. 'Babington speaking,' he said into it. 'Who ...? Yes, he's here.' And to Casby: 'For you.' He handed the instrument across.

'Yes,' said Casby. 'Yes ... Just a minute, please.' He fished out a pencil and settled his notebook open on his knee. 'All right, go ahead.' He listened, taking down what was said: and Colonel Babington, who had thought his face white enough to start with, saw that it was whiter now. 'Thank you,' Casby said presently. 'Blood from the crevice in the weapon group B and rhesus-positive. Blood from the body identical. Can you give me a rough idea of what the chances are that the two lots of blood are the same ...? Yes, I see ... Yes, please, test for the M N S and P groups, and for the rhesus sub-groups; we may as well be quite certain about it ... Certain now, you think? So do I ... All right. Thank you.'

He got up to replace the telephone in its cradle. 'That was our laboratory, sir,' he said. 'I took the liberty of asking them to try and find me here if I wasn't at my house.'

'My dear chap, of course ... And I think I got the gist of it. Your weapon that you've got is in fact the murder weapon, eh?'

'They say the chances of that are about two hundred to one on. Or to be more exact about it, they say it's two hundred to one against the blood on the weapon not being Rubi's. Fairly long odds. And as the weapon happens to fit an uncommon sort of wound uncommonly exactly –'. Casby shrugged. 'Well, that would seem to be that.'

'But you still,' said Colonel Babington peevishly, 'haven't told me what it is. Or where it came from.'

'It's a butcher's steel, sir.'

'A butcher's steel? Well, but damn it, it was only yesterday that –'

'Yes, sir. That's the one. It's got the finger-prints of half Cotten Abbas on it, so there's no lead there.' Casby picked up his glass, drained it. 'But at the time of the murder for which it was undoubtedly used, it was in the possession of Dr Helen Downing.'

For long seconds the room was as though in trance. Outside the windows, the leaves of rhododendrons stirred in a faint breeze. The sun was lower now, an orange ball streaked by the branches of the oak at the gate, and there was a blurring on the horizon which might mean cloud. Colonel Babington lifted one hand in instinctive protest and then dropped it again. 'Tell me,' he said.

So Casby related the history of the steel from the moment of its presumed theft from Weaver's shop, yesterday morning, to its appropriation, earlier this afternoon, by Constable Burns. 'On my way from Fiveways to Rolt's mill,' he said, 'I dropped in at – at Dr Downing's house and spoke to her about it. She told me it had been in a pocket of her car from teatime yesterday up to lunch-time, or later, to-day; and that during the whole of that period her car was locked up in the garage.'

'And you mean to say' – the Colonel, stammering, was almost beyond speech – 'that she still didn't *realize* . . .'

'She realized *then*,' Casby answered. 'But she hadn't realized before – not, I mean, when she was looking at the body. And I can understand that, too; the steel, to her, was so close and – and trivial a thing that it must have been quite invisible in the context of the murder . . . That is assuming,' he added with difficulty, 'that she is in fact innocent.'

'But she *must* be innocent!' the Colonel exclaimed. 'Damn it, man, if she were guilty she'd never dream of telling you the steel had been locked up in her possession at the time of the murder. Saying that is as good as putting a rope round her own neck. No, she's made a mistake, that's what it is. The steel must have been get-at-able all along. The murderer took it, and returned it afterwards, and ...' He faltered, aware, even as he spoke, of the extreme unlikeliness of this. 'Well, but did you look at the garage, to see if anyone had forced an entry?'

'No, sir, I didn't.'

'Then for God's sake,' said Colonel Babington, 'go and do it now.'

Casby went ...

Half an hour later he was back again.

'Nothing,' he reported. 'It's a modern garage, solidly built. No windows, and a Yale lock which I'm pretty sure hasn't been tampered with. And consider, sir: even if the murderer *knew* the steel was in the car inside, why the devil should he go to the trouble of pinching it and the even more fantastic trouble of returning it? It's beyond belief. It just can't have happened. But if it didn't happen, then –?'

'If it didn't happen,' said the Colonel staunchly, 'then there's some other factor in the equation that we've got wrong: the time of death, for instance.'

'But three doctors agree about that – Sims, Helen Downing, and Larkin, who's been helping Sims this afternoon with the autopsy. It's not likely that they're *all* wrong. And even supposing they're as much as twelve hours out in their reckoning, we're still left exactly where we were before.' Casby was slurring his words: he had touched the limit of his endurance. He said: 'I think you'd better know, sir, that just before I got news of the murder this morning I asked Helen to marry me; and that she accepted.'

The Colonel went rigid; all colour vanished from his cheeks. 'My dear chap,' he said helplessly. 'Oh, my dear chap.'

'So you see why I felt I had to tell you all this. I can't go on with it, of course. Even if it means resigning, which I imagine it may, I'm still bound to abandon the case.' Casby stared with vacant eyes at the carpet. 'But at the same time, I can see just how it's going to look to someone whose sympathies aren't involved. You and I – well, we've talked about it with kid gloves on, seeing all the objections to Helen's guilt and skating over the things that tell against her. But to an outsider it's all going to look very much simpler. There's a foolproof court-case now – you could get a warrant and a committal and a verdict without any trouble at all. And the *little* things – my God, how they pile up!'

'Yes, but they can be explained away. Even taking them all together, they're nothing like conclusive.'

'I'll tell you what is conclusive, though, and that's that blasted steel. I know Helen didn't kill the man. That isn't guessing – I *know*. But I can't see – *can't* see – how anyone else can have done it ...'

And that was when a new voice spoke, from the double doors which led from the study into the drawing-room.

'*Can't you?*' said Mr Datchery. '*But I rather think I can.*'

CHAPTER 13

At eight o'clock that Sunday evening Helen Downing was alone in her house by the churchyard, fighting down panic.

Outside the windows of the room in which she sat, clouds were hastening across a yellowish sky. During the past hour they had multiplied much as a rabble, scenting riot or loot, will multiply in city streets, and now, in drunken-seeming confusion, they were being driven reeling towards the east by the wind's pursuit, their shadows flickering on the mounds and stones of the waiting dead like unquiet ghosts. Below, it was still calm; only rarely did a fringe of that furious movement of the upper air catch and shake a tree-top, or pause to whisper in the grass. But the sun had disappeared, and in its place a moon just past the full hung flat and unreal behind the hurrying vapours, passing them, it seemed, in listless or hostile review. Dusk was setting in; few, this evening, had lingered long in the church-porch to gossip after Evensong; and as for the birds, they in their wisdom had apparently gone early to bed ...

A storm, Helen told herself: there's going to be a storm. And with her coffee-cup cradled warm between her hands, she moved closer to the window, staring out. But her thoughts were not such as may be fettered by the spectacle of a sultry, threatening twilight; they too had their storms in prospect, and of a vehemence to surpass anything an English wind could do. Helen Downing looked out at the clouds and the saffron sky – and looked away again. Among the dark, heavy mahogany furniture, she moved back to her chair.

'*Forty, I think, or fifty thousand pounds.*'

Melanie Hogben, the servant, had Sunday afternoons off; the house with its solitary occupant was as still, now, as if it had stood untenanted for years. There was movement enough, outside in the waning light, but since that movement was soundless, the impression it conveyed was much less of animation than – disagreeably – of stealth. Helen finished her coffee, lit a cigarette, and began prowling about the room, struggling to turn her mind outwards, to prevent it, by fixing it on material surroundings, from reverting again to the narrow circular path of fear and mistrust which it had traversed that evening a hundred times already. Here the desk at which her father had worked in his draughty Essex rectory; here his heavy silver-plated inkstand, a parting gift from the parishioners of his first living; here –

'*Forty, I think, or fifty thousand pounds.*'

That was when it had started: a stretcher being carried awkwardly up the nettle-grown bank; men from the village with their caps off, and a waiting ambulance. She had exclaimed involuntarily, then fallen silent as memories returned; and the silence had lasted until, after their fruitless call at Burns's cottage, Casby had put her down at her door. He too had been preoccupied; his kiss had been formal, almost cold. But there was little mistrust in Helen's nature, and she had attributed their slight temporary estrangement to the fact that as yet they knew too little of each other to have learned for any but intimate occasions the *modus vivendi* of lovers. She had humility enough, too, to be prepared to efface herself whenever (as now) his work must obviously be paramount, and for the time being she had forgotten his disturbing questions about newspapers in the larger shock of learning of her inheritance. So she had not been unhappy when she went in to lunch – perplexed, perhaps, and for no very compelling reason a little uneasy, but not unhappy.

So far, so good. And over lunch her buoyancy had increased, for now she could look without the old misgiving at the unpaid bills stuffed into the pigeon-holes of the secretaire, could make splendid plans and dream gallant dreams. Callous to be so elated? No, surely not. Helen knew that if renouncing the money could have brought Beatrice back to life, she would have renounced it without a second thought – with eagerness, indeed, and with gratitude. But that was impossible. And that *being* impossible, to grieve at the gift – as opposed to grieving at its occasion – would surely be a kind of insult to the giver...

Helen was conscientious – a dull virtue, but an immensely practical one – and to fail in a promise, however trivial, had always distressed her much more than, in this expediency-worshipping age, such sins of omission distress the great majority of people. Lunch over, she had therefore gone at once to unlock the garage and fetch the steel from her car, where it had stayed forgotten since yesterday. In the upshot Burns had relieved her of it, and at the time she had certainly not for a moment suspected him of any ulterior motive in doing so; not until several hours later had she looked back on the incident and seen it in a new and less reassuring light. No, the fact was that the meeting with Burns had set her mind moving in an altogether different direction: had reminded her again of Penelope Rolt. And it was with Penelope occupying her thoughts that she had strolled back to her house under the baking afternoon sun. Penelope had got to be found, and found quickly. To an already complex disturbance of mind had been superadded the appalling experience of finding her young man's murdered body, and that at a spot where, according to Janet Burns, rumour had it that they – Helen checked the thought, frowning; it was impossible to think of the relationship as having been in any sense an adult one, and yet – well, after all, Penelope was sixteen or seventeen, an age at which marriage, and other things than marriage, are by no means inconceivable. Marriage ... Penelope would have money, Helen supposed, when her father died; Rolt was the sort of man who did make money, and (what was more important these days) who had started making money before penal taxation made the accumulating of it impracticable. Had money been what Rubi had been after? A surprising number of girls stay faithful to their first loves, and to get in early might be a calculated act based on the knowledge of that. In any case, Penelope, as an heiress, would have to be exceedingly careful about the *bona fides* of anyone who proposed to her; any girl with money, or the prospect of it –

And that was when Helen suddenly woke up.

It has been said that mistrust was foreign to her nature, and that is the truth. But there are limits. Standing stock-still, with her hand on the latch of the gate, she for the first time realized, sick at heart, that Edward Casby had known of her inheritance when he proposed to her that morning.

131

Realized that he had never made the least attempt to become friendly with her before.

Realized that she had agreed to marry him on the basis of precisely four short meetings.

Her loyalty fought back. Well what of it? If he had not made friends before, that was because he was diffident. And there had been nothing of the casting of accounts in the morning's embrace. But oh God, thought Helen, women have been sure of that sort of thing before, and specially if they've been like me and missed love in their first youth, because then they've wanted it so much that they've seen it in a man's eyes when it was never there at all. Auto-hypnosis, that's called; what you look for and long for you're sure, sooner or later, to think you've found ... Her thoughts grew inchoate, unmanageable. She went slowly indoors, and there attempted to distract herself with business matters. But the savour of her inheritance had turned to repulsion; it had come to her by evil means, and its first effect had been evil, and for all her difficulties Helen now passionately desired herself quit of it. Debts, good Lord! If having debts will restore love and confidence, let's have debts and be grateful, because love and confidence are cheap at that or any price. Money, someone had said, may not make you happy; but it does at least enable you to be miserable in comfort. Cheapjack stuff, thought Helen with anger. And then the rows of figures at which she was staring blurred as anger turned to tears.

She had got a grip on herself presently, for she knew in her heart that she was making a great deal of fuss about a suspicion which as well as being quite unsupported by evidence was essentially treacherous. By the time – half past three or thereabouts – that Casby dropped in to speak to her, her emotional condition had reverted to nearer normal, and she had forced herself to suspend judgement. But there had still been that in her superficially equable greeting which caused him to look askance at her for a moment before stating his errand; and such composure as she had succeeded in achieving had been swept away like straw when she heard the few questions he had come to ask.

At the outset, those questions had only bewildered her.

'The steel? Yes, Colonel Babington asked me yesterday to take it back to Weaver. Only I forgot, I'm afraid. But why –'

'Can you tell me where it's been in the meanwhile?'

'Yes, of course. In my car.'

'Lying on one of the seats, I suppose?'

'Well, no. Actually it was tucked away in a pocket – you know, the sort on the inside of the door, with an elastic top to it, that you get in most old cars . . . But look, darling, what *is* all this?'

He had attempted a smile. 'Probably nothing important. I'm just checking up, that's all. When did you last have the car out?'

'Yesterday afternoon. I didn't have any patients to see this morning, so –'

'You mean yesterday afternoon at the time Colonel Babington gave you the steel?'

'Yes.'

'Did you drive straight back here from his house?'

'Yes. Mrs Babington was my last call. I put the car away about tea-time and haven't had it out since.'

'Do you keep your garage locked?'

After a long pause Helen had said quietly: 'I see. Stupid of me not to have seen before. You think the steel was what killed Rubi.'

'*No*,' he had answered with some vehemence. 'I realize now that it can't have done. But it's been hanging about, and it's the sort of thing that could have made the wound, so I had to ask about it. You see, it occurred to me that someone might have had the chance of pinching it from you.'

'That's impossible. I didn't stop anywhere on the way back from Colonel Babington's house, and I locked the car up immediately, and it's been locked up ever since. How does this particular steel compare with the wound for size?'

'It's the right size exactly.'

'Quite a coincidence,' Helen had said stiffly. 'Are there any traces of blood on it?'

'A few. They're being tested now . . . Helen, you're *certain* no one could have stolen it?'

Beneath her surface equanimity Helen was desperately afraid: it needed an almost physical effort not to lie in self-protection.

'And returned it as well?' she had responded coolly. 'That's asking a bit much, isn't it?'

'I'm wrong, then,' he had said half to himself. 'And yet –'

'And yet it looked *so* promising.' Helen's fear broke suddenly through the mask. 'Why don't you say straight out that you –'

'It may have been planted on you.'

'My dear man, how? How?'

'All right, then. I *am* wrong about it – must be. But you can surely see that I had to follow it up.'

'A little trustfulness would have saved you the trouble.'

'A little trustfulness would put the police out of action for good.'

'Damn the police!'

He had not answered that. 'I'd better go,' he had said. 'We're in the hell of a mess, and we shall go on being in it till this whole filthy business is cleaned up.' Then his voice had grown gentler. 'I'm sorry, Helen. If it's any consolation to you, I can tell you that I shall probably chuck the case up in the next few hours.'

'Thanks. I can understand that. Because you wouldn't want me hanged, would you?'

'Of course I wouldn't want –' And then, looking into her eyes, he had suddenly realized what she meant. 'I see. Yes, I see how our marriage might look to a certain type of mind. Good-bye for now.'

With that he had gone. For a time you could shut out the shame of your own wretched, indefensible innuendo by indulging your resentment at that '*certain type of mind*'. But the more dreadful thing which underlay shame and resentment alike was such as no amount of emotional juggling could suppress. For Helen knew that whatever he might have said, Casby had gone away still believing, in spite of everything, that that damnable steel was what had killed the Swiss schoolmaster; and where the steel was concerned, not love and confidence were at stake but life itself . . .

It was only later that she learned of his return to examine the garage; and that was well, for if she had seen what he did she would have known how to interpret it, and she was already quite close enough to panic without the addition of that. Moving restlessly about her sitting-room, while the daylight failed and the dull moon took lustre from its failing, Helen experienced positive loneliness for the first time in her life: it seemed to her that with Beatrice gone there was no one, no one, to whom in this extremity she could turn. A lawyer, she thought vaguely: I ought to get a lawyer. But long hours of wretchedness had so sapped her energies and her resolution that she was by this time incapable of action, incapable even of making plans.

The room was wholly in shadow; light lingered only on the massive silver-plated inkstand and on the glass front of the corner-cupboard. In the whirligig of memory and emotion Helen had been oblivious of the besieging darkness. But now, as reflection petered out in misery and she raised her eyes from the desk at which she had been vacantly staring, she became all at once aware and afraid of the thickening gloom, so that her movement, when she swung round abruptly to turn on the lamps, had the quality of an animal's when it scents a trap.

Quietly, almost timidly, someone knocked on the front door.

CHAPTER 14

LIGHT filled the room as the switch clicked; the sullen, ponderous furniture, whose replacement – much as she hated it – Helen had never been able to afford, absorbed the light without refracting it, deadening it as sound is deadened in a building which lacks resonance. During the heat of the day Helen had left her front door standing open. In a village where two decades had not produced a single theft, that was often done, though it had not been done so much since the anonymous letter-writer had started work: the communal mistrust wrought by the letters had proliferated irrelevantly into every department of normal life. But the habit still prevailed so long as conscious defensiveness did not interfere, and Helen could hear soft footsteps, now, as her unknown visitor accepted the open door's invitation to stroll into the house. In the hall outside the sitting-room, a voice called inquiringly.

'Hello!' it said. 'Anyone at home?'

Inwardly cursing her nervousness, Helen strode to the sitting-room door and flung it wide.

'Oh, *there* you are,' said Dr George Sims. 'I thought everyone must be out. Whatever were you doing – meditating in the dark?'

When Helen had last seen him he had been in tennis kit. Now he wore an ancient, baggy hacking-coat with ancient, baggy grey trousers and a pink tie which clashed deplorably with his untidy ginger hair. His pale, straggling eyebrows were lifted in humorous inquiry; the summer sun had reddened his face (he had the sort of skin which can never acquire a tan) and had brought out orange freckles round the root of his irregular nose; a curved briar pipe, unlit, projected solemnly, with an air of self-parody, from a corner of his ugly, attractive mouth. As Helen stood aside, he ambled into the room with the nonchalance of perfect physical health; and for all that she hardly knew him, his coming seemed to her then like the magic of a fine hot fire in a chilly room, so that she laughed in sheer relief.

'Meditating?' she said. 'Well, as a matter of fact, I was. Do sit down, and I'll get you a drink ... Oh Lord, though, I don't believe there's anything but beer. I'm so sorry. The fact is –'

'I like beer,' he said argumentatively, as though someone had accused him of the contrary. 'I drink a lot of it, especially in the evenings. The only trouble is that it makes one so hellish fat ...' He looked round him with the naïve curiosity of a child. 'So this is where you live. It's nice,' he said politely.

Helen, busy at the sideboard, laughed again.

'You know perfectly well it's quite awful. If I had any money, I'd burn every stick of furniture in the place, and buy a new lot.'

'Not these days you wouldn't,' he responded a little absently. 'Not with quality and prices what they are ...' Then with more interest: 'I say, though, it might be quite a good notion to put in a window-seat. There's room enough, and –'

'I don't like them.' Helen was pouring beer into pint pewter tankards. 'If you want to look out of the window they give you a crick in the neck – and what's the good of that?'

'Oh, nonsense,' said Sims vigorously. 'The whole point of them is –' And for two or three happy minutes they argued zestfully about window-seats, so that Helen temporarily forgot her wretchedness, and wondered – at last recollecting it again – that so small a thing could succeed where all her solitary efforts had so pathetically failed. The effect lasted, too. There was a refocusing: her difficulties, when she thought of them again, seemed not quite so large or so immitigable as they had done in solitude. And the reason for that was that with George Sims you could never be other than uninhibited, since his own extravagance, his total absence of self-consciousness, made your social defences seem so petty and unnecessary that it was child's play to abandon them.

'Well, all right, have it your own way,' he said impenitently at last. 'But I still don't believe a single word of it.' And then all at once he was serious, with a seriousness as large and unqualified as his controversial mood had been. 'Still, I mustn't go on all night about that. You'll be wanting to know to what you owe the pleasure, et cetera, and I'm afraid the reason I came here isn't particularly cheerful – rather the reverse, in fact ...

'Helen, I'm worried.'

It was the first time he had ever addressed her by her Christian name, and he used it diffidently – the tone in which it was spoken an implicit apology for not asking permission, so that the touchiest person could hardly have taken offence. Moreover, Helen sensed then – and knew for certain later – that the words which followed it were true: George Sims was really perplexed and uneasy on her account – so much so that for a moment he was unable to find more words with which to continue.

'Look here,' he said presently, plunging where calculation had failed, 'I've been getting about a bit this afternoon, and talking to people. And to be frank with you, I haven't much liked what I've heard. Mind you, I'm not saying there's anything to be seriously alarmed about, but I do think that in common fairness you ought to know where you stand ... For instance, I met Burns an hour or two ago, and he handed me out some rigmarole about a butcher's steel.'

Helen's dread returned. She nodded.

'I know.' And she explained how she knew. 'I don't pretend to understand,' she said in conclusion, 'and I can only assume that the particular steel I had wasn't in fact the one which –'

'Only apparently it was.' Sims got up from the chair into which he had lapsed on entering, and slouched moodily to the window, his hands thrust deep into his jacket pockets. 'Larkin and I have been doing the autopsy on Rubi this afternoon – as you know. While we were at it, Walton traipsed in to get a blood sample from the corpse, and of course I asked him what it was for, and equally of course, I saw him before I left Twelford to find out what results he'd got. They're pretty conclusive, I'm afraid.'

'But that's *impossible!*'

He turned back towards her, smiling. 'Now, for the Lord's sake don't get panicky. No one's going to believe *you* killed him.'

'But I've thought and thought, and there isn't a loop-hole anywhere!'

'No?'

'Well, can you see one?'

'Certainly I can. Several. For instance, we've no means of knowing that the steel Burns gave to Casby – the one with Rubi's blood on it – is the same steel you gave to Burns.'

138

Helen stared. 'Burns? But surely you can't believe that Burns would –'

'No, I don't, as a matter of fact. But you said there weren't any loopholes – so I was just giving you a sample. Another would be that the steel Casby gave the laboratory wasn't the same as the steel Burns gave Casby.'

Helen's heart was beating very fast. 'Absurd,' she said levelly.

'Perhaps. But I'm still inclined to think there's more than steel involved in this business. They're more or less standard in size, you know, and some sort of deliberate duplication isn't at all inconceivable.'

Helen considered this. She could not bring herself to suspect Burns of trickery, and as for Casby – well, better not think about that for the moment. But the point was that George Sims had shown her escape-routes where none, earlier, had seemed to exist; and if there were these, there were probably others too. Her spirits rose; she even managed to smile.

'Thanks,' she said. 'I've been needing a little common sense.'

'Welcome, I'm sure,' he answered in Cockney. 'And as I see it, the next thing is: where were you at the time the murder was done?'

'That's easy. I was –'

And then, for the first time, Helen realized. 'Oh, my God,' she said quietly.

Sims had lifted his tankard and was about to put it to his lips; now he replaced it without drinking.

'Well?' he said.

'I was – I must have been there. In the water-meadow. I – I went for a walk, you see. Rolt was there too, we talked and ...'

The blood had ebbed a little from George Sims' sun-reddened cheeks, leaving them a dirty pink.

'Not so good,' he said. 'Definitely not so good ... There's one thing, though, Rolt's in exactly the same boat. And as between the two of you –'

'Rolt,' Helen interrupted, 'hasn't had anything to do with any butcher's steel.'

'That we know of ... Look, Helen, I don't want to interfere in what isn't my affair, but I think that just for safety's sake you ought to get in touch with a solicitor straight away.'

Helen regarded him steadily. 'Do they in fact suspect me?' And he shrugged uneasily as he replied.

'God knows. No one's said anything definite to me.'

'But if they do suspect me' – and for Helen, a world of pain lay hidden in that seemingly impersonal 'they' – 'if they do suspect me, whatever do they imagine my *motive* can have been? After all, I've never even spoken to the wretched little man.'

'He left a sort of diary, you see.' Sims was at the window again, gazing at his own reflection in the darkened panes. 'That's another thing Burns told me about – thanks to me being police-surgeon, he feels it's ethical to confide in me. And that diary –' He gave her an account of what was in it.

'But then, if they think I killed Rubi, they must think I wrote the anonymous letters as well.'

'Yes. That would seem to follow. But of course, it's all of it utter nonsense, and you're not to let it worry you. All I'm trying to do now is explain how the official mind works – or to be accurate, may be working.'

The official mind ...

Helen said: 'Yes, I do understand that. And I'm grateful to you for coming. I was – I was feeling a bit lonely.'

He swung round to face her, twitching the pipe out of his mouth. 'We've never seen very much of one another, have we?'

'No. It's – it's been my fault.'

'And for that reason I certainly oughtn't to say what I'm going to say. In the circumstances, it's conceited and tactless and discourteous and altogether mad, but I've still got to say it. Helen, will you marry me?'

Outside, the wind was rising. It rattled a pane and woke sighs among the bold new leaves of the trees at the bottom of the garden. A tracery of hurrying clouds flecked the moon, and the stars were coming out, like sparks kindling, dying, kindling anew. In the sombre sitting-room it was very still.

'It's hopeless, I know,' George Sims went on after a fractional pause. 'I'm an ugly devil and a rotten catch. But ever since you

140

came here I've wanted to – to be friends with you. You've always avoided me, and that's made it worse, of course. I shouldn't have blurted it out now if I hadn't been afraid that as soon as all this mystery was cleared up we should go back to the old footing ... Please forgive me. It's an impossible sort of question to ask, when you hardly know me at all, but if you could – well, keep me in mind, perhaps ... What I mean is,' blurted Dr Sims, fierily red, 'that I don't want an answer. I mean, I don't want an answer straight away. Well, of course, I do *want* an answer straight away, but I quite see that you – I mean, I want it if it's the answer I *want*, if you see what I mean ...'

'Thank you,' said Helen simply. 'I'm very grateful, and if it didn't sound old-fashioned and – and insincere, I'd say I was honoured, because I am. But you see, Edward Casby asked me this morning to marry him, and I said I would.'

It was as if she had struck him. Not a muscle of his face moved, but the sun's reddening stood out on it like rouge, and his hands grew taut with the effort of self-control. After a brief but unendurable silence he said shakily: 'I'm sorry,' and she saw with horror – almost, for a moment, with repulsion – that tears had started into his eyes.

'I'm sorry,' he repeated meaninglessly. 'I didn't know. I – I think I'd better go.'

Helen scrambled to her feet. 'No! Please don't go! I never realized –'

'I must.' He had turned his head away. 'I'm sorry, but I must. I – I can't –' Two seconds later the door had slammed behind him, and Helen was alone again.

His behaviour was not destined to be the last shock of that eventful Sunday: but certainly it was the most unexpected, and in that sense the most terrifying. Helen was dumbfounded. Standing helplessly, motionless, in the centre of the carpet, while his rapid steps receded down the path to the gate, she found herself scarcely able to believe that the whole swift episode had not been a kind of hallucination; the refusal of an offer of marriage could only seldom in the world's history have provoked so violent and sudden a reaction as that. And Helen was not flattered. That short, astounding scene had had a quality which even the most

141

conceited woman would have found it difficult to interpret to her advantage – a quality almost animal in its ferocity. Shaken, Helen crept back to her chair, groped for a cigarette. Consolation, and its instantaneous sweeping away; hope, and its immediate annihilation. She was as near now to breaking-point as she would ever be. Loneliness had returned the stronger for its temporary exile, and her only thought was to find, at all costs, someone to come to her whom she could trust.

Presently she went to the telephone.

The telephone was in the hall, recessed beneath the stairs. With unsteady hands Helen sought a number and took the instrument from its cradle.

'Exchange? I want an Oxford number, please. 317723.'

She waited, her heart thudding uncomfortably in her breast. If Alice Riddick didn't happen to be in ...

But Alice Riddick was in.

'Helen? How nice to hear your voice, child. How are you?'

'Alice, I'm in horrible trouble. I suppose you couldn't possibly come?'

'Come when, child? And what is the trouble?'

'Now. To-night.'

'My dear, I certainly would if I could, but it's out of the question, I'm afraid. I'm stuck in bed, as it happens, with a broken toe. What's the matter, though? What's happened?'

'Alice, I think the police suspect me of killing a man.'

There was a pause; then: 'Do they? More fools them. But I can quite see that you need company, and since you're phoning me, I take it there are reasons why you can't find it in your own village ... Look, why don't you come here?'

'I daren't. God knows what they'd think if I was to clear out. And besides – well, I've got to be here, don't you see, so as to know what's happening. And – oh Lord, it's all so complicated ... Alice, I'm frightened.'

'So I gather,' said Alice Riddick grimly. 'Listen, my dear – will you be all right for to-night? Because I'll get to you by lunch-time to-morrow, even if I have to steal one of the Radcliffe ambulances and a driver with it ... Will that do?'

Helen's heart sank. It wouldn't do, of course; it wasn't nearly soon enough. But she still had reserves of pride to draw on, and she drew on them now.

'Yes, thank you, Alice, that's marvellous. Bless you.'

'And in the meantime, get yourself a lawyer, and don't go making statements to the police, even if they happen to be true.'

Helen laughed tremulously. 'It's Sherlock Holmes I really need, not a lawyer so much. Alice, it's all so –'

'Sherlock Holmes? Now I wonder if – Oh no. He's away.'

'What were you going to say?'

'I was going to say I might have brought Gervase along with me. It sounds as if it might be in his line. But I was trying to get in touch with him yesterday, and apparently he's been out of Oxford since Friday, and no one seems to know, quite, where he is.'

'Gervase?'

'Gervase Fen. Didn't you ever come across him when you were up?'

'No, I don't think I did. He's Professor of English, isn't he? I've heard of him, of course.'

'Yes . . . Well, I shall just have to see what I can do on my own. Helen, it is – it is manslaughter, isn't it? I mean, they just imagine you've been careless about a prescription, or some nonsense like that?'

'No, Alice. It's murder.'

There was a second pause – a longer one.

'Oh . . . Well, you're still not to worry, child. No certainly innocent person has been executed for murder in England or America for the past fifty or a hundred years, and I see no reason at all why they should abandon the precedent in your case.'

'Then you don't believe I'd –'

'Tush, child! Of course I don't. *Nemo repente fuit turpissimus*, and your extreme lack of turpitude when you were reading medicine here was one of the most depressing human phenomena I've ever come across. If you've murdered anyone, I'm a Dutchman. So what I should do now, if I were you, is lock all your doors and windows, drink a bottle of gin and go to bed soused. In the morning you'll feel horrid, but benzedrine'll cure that.'

This time Helen's laughter was sincere.

'Thank you, darling. I dare say I'm just being a nervy fool, and

143

I'm sorry to be such a nuisance, but – well, if you only knew the things that have been *happening* to me . . .'

'Tell me in the morning. I'll be there. And if you want to ring me in the night, go ahead. I can't sleep a wink with this bloody toe, anyway.'

'Oh, Alice, I'm so sorry about that. However did it happen?'

'An old fool of a don called Wilkes ran over it on his bicycle.'

'Oh, Alice!'

'Yes, child, I know it's funny. That's been borne in on me with increasing force every time I've mentioned it to anyone. But you just try it, that's all I say.'

'I'm sorry, dear. I didn't mean to giggle. I know it must be damnably painful.'

'It belongs,' said Miss Riddick philosophically, 'to the same class of affliction as warts on the behind. One doesn't expect sympathy; all one hopes is that people won't actually make themselves sick with laughing . . . But that's enough about me. Keep cheerful, child, and I'll see you in the morning.'

'Well, Alice, if you're *sure* . . .'

'I'm sure. God bless.'

Helen rang off. And that was when a man's voice, immediately behind her, said:

'I'm so sorry, but –'

She swung round, her brief spell of reassurance dissolved on the instant in panic terror. 'Who –'

'Please.' He put strong hands on her shoulders to steady her. 'Your front door was open, and I heard your voice, so I came in. I'm sorry if I frightened you.'

Helen went limp. 'Mr Datchery,' she said, and began to laugh. She laughed quietly, without hysteria, until the laughter turned to tears. With her head on Mr Datchery's shoulder she cried some of the wretchedness out of her; and when her sobs began to diminish he said briskly:

'Without at all wishing to alarm you further, I think I ought to mention that the hall is flooded and we're both of us about to go under for the third time.'

She broke away from him, flushed beneath her tears. 'I – I don't know what you'll be thinking of me,' she said with a doleful sniff. 'I – I d-don't always weep on the s-shoulders of strange men. And every time we've met so far –'

'Every time we've met so far,' he said gravely, 'I've felt, I admit it, a little like a feast at a skeleton. But that's hardly been your fault.' He offered her a silk handkerchief. 'You look awful,' he added more cheerfully. 'There, there, don't drop it about. Wipe your face with it, and if you smear your lipstick like that it'll look as if you've been drinking blood. Your collar's undone. Your hair's coming down. As soon as you're ready you can offer me some beer, if there is any in the house.'

'Oh, don't bully me,' said Helen. 'I've been so miserable, and –'

'No doubt you have. But just as it happens, there's very little left for you to worry about now. What I've come to ask –'

'*Wait*,' Helen told him, and fled upstairs.

Five minutes later she returned, looking, except for the pallor, her normal self again, to find Mr Datchery in the sitting-room, loudly singing a hymn to the accompaniment of her father's harmonium. 'Greenland's icy mountains,' he murmured, desisting from this performance as she came in. 'And they're not quite so irrelevant as you might at first think. That looks better, I must say. Will you take my word for it, please, that no one suspects you any longer of murdering dominies or writing anonymous letters? I've just come from talking to Colonel Babington and Inspector Casby about it, so I ought to know.'

Helen said: 'Who are you?'

He chuckled. 'I'm a friend of a friend of yours. But never you mind who I am. The point is, do you believe what I've just said?'

'Yes!' cried Helen. 'Yes! But in that case, the steel I had –'

'Ah. The steel. You've been fretting about that, have you? Quite right, too. Of course, it was in fact your steel which killed Rubi,' he added dispassionately, as an afterthought.

'But –'

'But there's still a loose end to be tied in, you were going to say. I quite agree. And that's why I'm here. There's only one question I need to ask, so you must answer it very carefully.'

Helen braced herself. 'Yes?'

'What sort of books' – Mr Datchery's pale-blue eyes were

145

directed ruminatively towards the ceiling – 'what sort of books did Beatrice Keats-Madderly read?'

'I – I beg your pardon?'

'Who,' Mr Datchery elaborated with a gracious air, 'were her favourite authors?'

Helen stared helplessly at him. 'But you can't be *serious!*'

'Of course I can be serious. I often am. I am now.' Mr Datchery had by this time left the harmonium in order to lower his long, lean body into an armchair, where he sprawled gracelessly. 'Do *answer*,' he said waspishly after a moment.

'Well, I – I suppose,' said Helen in a daze, 'that Emma Paton was her favourite *novelist*. She used to enthuse about her an awful lot, and –'

'*So!*' exclaimed Mr Datchery in a guttural, Teutonic manner. '*Also gut!* That, you know,' he said more mildly, 'is just the answer I wanted.'

'But what has it got to do with –'

'With the Cotten Horror? A good deal. You'd be surprised. May I use your telephone?'

'Yes, of course. It's – oh well, you know where it is, don't you?'

She sat bewildered for a while after he had gone out of the room, trying vainly to assemble her thoughts into a coherent pattern. But there was renewed hope for her now, and she was content to struggle no longer, to let events carry her wherever they would ... Mr Datchery had left the sitting-room door open, and she realized presently that she could hear him talking on the telephone.

'Look here, Emma, when I take the trouble to ring you up I don't expect to be treated to a great diatribe about not writing for six years.'

'Yes, yes, that's all very well, but we were both much younger in those days.'

'I don't regard it as an unchivalrous thing to say, at all.'

'No, I haven't read any of your books for decades. I've read some reviews of them.'

'Do let me get to the point, or you'll be running me into another one-and-ninepence. What I want to know is whether you've had a fan-letter recently from a woman named Beatrice Keats-Madderly, living in a place called Cotten Abbas.'

'Nonsense, you don't get as many fan-letters as all that.'

'Well, go and look, then.'

A pause.

'You have? Did you answer it?'

'No, I know *I* don't answer letters, but that's not the point.'

'Well, when?'

'You think Thursday definitely. And it'd be posted that day?'

'It would. Excellent. In your own hideous scrawl, I take it.'

'Well, there's no need to jump down my throat like that. Violet ink as usual?'

'Yes, good. And of course, it wouldn't be the sort of letter that'd invite or imply any further correspondence between you.'

'My language is *not* pedantic.'

'Yes.'

'No.'

'There are the pips.'

'Well, if you want to go on talking we must reverse the charges.'

'Quick, or it'll be another three minutes.'

'Of course not. Good-bye.'

'I said, good-bye.'

An extremely long pause.

'Oh, do listen, there are the pips *again.*'

Half a minute later Mr Datchery returned to the sitting-room, counting out three-and-sixpence from his trousers pocket into the palm of his hand. This sum he deposited conscientiously on the mantelpiece. 'Did you hear?' he asked. 'You were meant to.'

Helen nodded. 'All except the very beginning. But' – she gestured helplessly – 'but what does it all *mean?*'

He might have explained it then, had there been opportunity; but as it turned out, there was not. Even as Helen spoke, a car, driven fast, pulled up outside the house with a squeal of brakes, and they heard its occupants hurrying up the path to knock violently at the front door. With Mr Datchery at her heels, Helen ran to meet them. The thick, unshaven face of Harry Rolt loomed up in the dim light of the hall, and Constable Burns was behind him.

'My girl,' said Rolt succinctly. 'Not here, is she?'

Helen shook her head. 'But what –'

'Not been home all day, not since she found that chap's body. But Burns here, he says he saw her eavesdropping at the window when the Inspector and me were having our talk.'

Burns started to explain: 'She ran off, though, when I called to her, and by the time I got round the side of the house –' But Mr Datchery interrupted him.

'Your talk,' he said sharply, 'about what?'

Rolt eyed him with momentary hostility. 'I don't know who the hell you are to ask questions,' he said unpleasantly, 'but if you must know, we happened to be talking about me being the only one in the village as knew about Beatrice Keats-Madderly's birth. And what I'm afraid of –'

He stopped, for once irresolute and unsure of himself.

Very distantly, on the main-line railway which skirted the village, they heard the whistle of a train.

CHAPTER 15

'A BRIDGE,' said Mr Datchery. 'A railway-bridge stuck in the middle of a field, somewhere out in the Brankham direction. I'm not sure that I could find my way back to it, but you'll know where it is. And I suggest we get there quickly.'

There are some voices you do not think to question. Looking back on it afterwards, recreating in her mind's eye the shadowy hall with the wind still rising in the darkness outside the open door, Helen realized that neither to herself nor to the other two, in that moment of crisis, did it occur to require of Mr Datchery the why and wherefore of his unexplained assurance. The door had slammed behind them, and they were out in the night, before another word was spoken – and that word was addressed by Rolt not to Mr Datchery but to Burns, by way of confirming the whereabouts of the place that had been described. Then, silent again, they were hurrying down the path to the gate, and with Rolt at the wheel – Burns beside him, Helen and Mr Datchery in the back – the big, battered car leaped forward, twenty horses strong, to skid with a screech of stretched tyres round the angle of the church and accelerate fiercely along the main street.

Helen never kept any clear impression of that short and hectic ride. She could remember the smell of petrol and of stale cigar smoke; could remember that by a common trick of the retina it was the clouds which seemed to her to be fixed and the moon which seemed to be anchorless; could remember her finger's finding and enlarging a hole in the leather upholstery of the seat on which she sat, her nail scratching at the soft, damp kapok inside. But these were isolated images; the sum of them she could never recall. And the silence which lay heavy on them was broken only once, when Mr Datchery said abruptly:

'Is there an express due?'

The dashboard light was in a hollow hood projecting above the instrument-panel. Burns leaned forward, twisted the hood to turn it on, glanced at his wrist-watch. The small glow-worm of light vanished again.

'In five minutes,' he said.

Then they were out of the village, among trees, meadows, hedges. All of them had known where they were going; all of them now knew why. The headlamps converged to a white splash on the empty road, and fitfully, whenever the clouds uncovered her, the moon blanched them with her own light, as a fire in a room will grow cold under the sun's rays. The wind was blowing not uniformly but in violent, unpredictable gusts, like buffets from the ragged hem of an immense rough garment, and the trees seethed with it. Dust, piled up during the long, windless drought, whirled round them in clouds, eddying violently wherever the thrust of their progress conflicted with the direction of the wind. And all along the banks, the June wildflowers bent their thready stems as the car passed. 'Easy, sir,' said Burns, as the Humber approached a sharp bend without slackening speed. 'Easy does it ...' And then Mr Datchery grunted as Helen was flung against him, and the hedges wheeled in dizzying ellipse, and they were in the straight again ... Helen lost all sense of time; at one moment it seemed to her that they had already covered many long miles, at another that the slam of the front door, as they left the house, was still vibrating in her ears. She found out afterwards that in sober fact the whole journey had taken them three minutes exactly.

Helen, Burns, and Mr Datchery were out of the car before it stopped, and scrambling over the stile which gave access to the right-of-way across the field they sought. Gasping painfully from the unaccustomed effort, Rolt followed, and then they were all of them running, stumbling in the darkness on tussocks of un-cropped grass at the path's verge, in the direction in which they knew the old bridge to lie. Knew, and presently saw. For now the moon was unveiled again, and they could make out the flattened arcs of the stone parapet, and the geometrical belt of shadow, at the field's crest, which marked the shallow cutting. For an instant they paused, straining their eyes for what more the moon might show. But they were still too far off for certainty, and so in another moment they were running again, running to-wards a shadow whose edge – as more cloud spread like a stain over the bright disc overhead – raced to meet them

150

across the uneven slope. In six strides the darkness reclaimed them.

It was uphill the last part of the way. They struggled on, spaced out now according to their physical capacity: Burns ahead, then Mr Datchery, then Helen, with Rolt a good way to the rear. The wind blew hard against their faces, thrusting their expired breath back into their mouths and overfilling their lungs when they sucked air in; where there were drops of sweat on their foreheads it struck chill. Helen tripped, and only recovered her balance by a convulsive movement which strained a muscle in her thigh. Then the ground became level again, and the wire fence which guarded the cutting's lip loomed up in front of her. In the black depths below, the metal of the rails gleamed very faintly, and far along to the right was the single eye of a green signal-light. She heard again the whistle of the approaching engine, and from behind her, as if released by the sound, Rolt's voice spoke.

'Pen!' it called in agony. 'Pen, girl! Pen!'

The clouds were like smoke, without depth or cohesion, spindrift-thin. Through a rent in one of them the moon looked out again. And Helen saw.

In the last stages of the ascent she had evidently strayed unawares from the path, so that the bridge was now a hundred yards to her left, with the blurred figures of Burns and Mr Datchery between her and it. You could distinguish details – weeds sprouting from crevices in the crumbling stone, a flustered night-bird clapping his wings on the bare bough of a dying oak, the wind-whipped swaying of the tall brome-grass. But Helen had no attention to spare for any of these things; they somehow found lodgement in her mind, so that later she was able to recollect them, but the whole of her consciousness was fixed, in that moment of revelation, on the slender figure, ghostly in the moonlight, which stood at the centre of the bridge, gazing across the nearer of the two parapets in the direction from which the train would come. Its hair was tangled. Its eyes glittered like a cat's as the head turned. And in the instant that Helen became aware of it, it moved, climbing swiftly on to the parapet to stand there balanced precariously against the wind. Burns started to run

151

again, with Mr Datchery after him. But they had not taken half a dozen steps before words from the poised figure, shaky yet shrill and clear, halted them.

'Don't come near!' called Penelope Rolt. 'Don't come near or I'll jump!'

'Pen!' Rolt shouted. His voice choked as he sought breath. 'Don't do it, Pen! Don't do it! Oh, my Christ!' He staggered to Helen's side, his hand pressed hard against his ribs and his cheeks blotchy with tears. 'Do something,' he whispered. 'For God's sake do something.'

In their several ways, they added their voices to his. But it was hopeless; in that rough, fickle wind they could not even be sure they were heard – for there were times when Penelope seemed to be calling back to them, and yet they could distinguish no articulate sound. 'Your father is cleared!' Mr Datchery was shouting. 'He had nothing to do with the letters!' And that at least Penelope heard, since her thin voice retorted with: 'You're just saying that! You're just saying that so as to stop me! Keep away, I tell you! Keep away!'

Stolidly, Burns, who was nearest, moved forward again. A gust caught the figure on the parapet, so that it tottered, off balance, and hung dreadfully poised above the drop to the metals below. Burns stopped as if turned to stone; he was still too distant for a sudden rush to be any good. And as Helen watched, her heart throbbing painfully, Penelope recovered, dropped to her hands and knees, dropped further to lie sprawled face down, with her head towards them. For a moment the sour taste of death had been in her mouth; perhaps now she would reconsider. But when Burns strode forward she lifted her eyes, and it was still 'Don't come near! Don't come near or I'll jump!'

And now indeed there was no more time for pleas or reasoning. Already they could hear the rumble of the night express. Helen swung round sharply at the touch of a hand on her arm.

'Give Burns and me just half a minute,' said Mr Datchery. 'Then go and get her – and don't stop whatever she says or does.'

'But –'

'If she should jump, we shall be down below.'

'But she may not really mean to,' said Helen desperately.

152

'We can't rely on that. Somehow the thing's got to be precipit-
ated, one way or the other. Do as you're told – and God help us all
if you don't.' He was gone.

The moon vanished again. Had Helen known it, that was what
Mr Datchery wanted, because otherwise he and Burns would be
too clearly visible to Penelope when they stood beneath the
bridge. Catching Burns by the arm, Mr Datchery hurried him to
the farther side of the bridge – the side away from the parapet
where Penelope crouched – explaining rapidly as they went. On
the face of it, his scheme was insanely risky, but there was no
time for weighing chances. '*A train coming up half does it for
you* ...' Twisting and slithering, Burns and Mr Datchery
scrambled through the wire fence and down the cutting's bank.

There was a platelayer's hut there – small and dingy, with a
tarred roof. Mr Datchery remembered seeing near it, when he
had been on the bridge with Penelope that morning, part of a
tarpaulin such as is used to cover goods wagons. It was still
there – stiff and intractable from long exposure, so that they tore
their nails on it, and grazed their skin, as they toiled to spread it
out – and there were cords attached to it through tarnished brass
rings let into the edges, cords long enough to wind round the
wrists ... But all of that took them a long time to accomplish.
Too long. They were not ready with the tarpaulin until the train
was actually in sight, travelling at perhaps fifty miles an hour
some four hundred yards away along the cutting. With the canvas
stretched between them, they ran along the line towards it, under
the bridge and out at the other side below the place where
Penelope was.

Or rather, below the place where they hoped she was. Of all the
weak points in Mr Datchery's plan, this, the darkness being
almost absolute, was the weakest. They could only station themselves in what seemed the likeliest place and hope for the best. A
poor best, too. The canvas might split under the weight of a falling
body, or the cords break; Burns and Mr Datchery might well lack
sufficient strength to cope with the impact; none of them might be
able to get out from under the wheels of the oncoming engine ...
But it was no use thinking of the scheme in those terms. It was a
gigantic gamble, not a calculated act, in any serious sense, at all.

If Penelope fell, and they happened not to be in the right place to catch her, well, then . . .

The engine was very close now. The ground trembled pre-monitorily beneath their feet, and it needed an extreme effort of will to step directly in the train's path. Its noise, as it came ever closer, shut out most other sounds, but they could just hear Helen shouting, somewhere above their heads, and Penelope shouting back. At the last possible moment, they would jump aside; in the meantime, both waited steadily, feet apart, with hands gripping the edges of the tarpaulin and the cords wound about their wrists.

The noise grew. The tremors of the ground jarred them. The huge weight of hurtling metal was almost on top of them now. Again the engine whistled – a prolonged blast which increased in volume with hideous rapidity as it bore down on them. And then, faint above the uproar, they heard a scream, and in that fraction of a second both of them moved.

They moved by instinct – not farther in under the bridge, but farther out, to meet the train. Had they not done so, it would have been the finish. Even as it was, Penelope's hurtling body landed a great deal nearer the edge of the canvas than the centre, so that they had to twist it in order to prevent her falling out of it. Mr Datchery cried out involuntarily as the cords bit deep into his flesh. Then, a split second later, they had hurled themselves aside, literally scooping Penelope with them, and were lying, all three of them, in a tangled heap with the filthy tarpaulin on the other line, while the train thundered by within inches of them: bruised, pallid and shaken, but in no other way hurt. The long line of lighted windows flashed past; the shrieking whistle diminished in volume, dropped in pitch, ceased. It was over.

Twenty seconds later, and Helen, with Rolt behind her, was creeping down the bank towards them. Seven minutes more, and all five of them had climbed back to the top. 'Thank God,' was all Helen could say. 'Oh, thank God.' Hers had been the easier part, but in all conscience it had been terrifying enough. To her last day she would remember going towards Penelope while the din of the train grew enormous in the cutting below; would remember Penelope, as she came near, scrambling to her feet on the

154

parapet; would remember the high, piercing shriek as, with Helen not three feet from her, she had fallen ... Penelope was whey-faced now, dazed and hysterical. 'I didn't mean to,' she said over and over again. 'It was an accident, I didn't mean to.' And Mr Datchery, who had gone on to the bridge, summoned Burns to join him.

'Look,' he said.

By the moon's wan light they could see that where Penelope had stood a great chunk of stone was broken away. 'That,' Mr Datchery suggested, 'and the wind ...'

'A good thing, sir,' said Burns, 'that that load of rock didn't cosh one of us when we was down below.'

'And as to your report –'

'As to that, sir,' Burns answered steadily, 'an accident's what I shall say. Attempting suicide's a felony, of course, but I don't know of any law to stop you standing on the parapets of bridges, if that's your idea of fun.'

There was a silence while they gazed at the freshly broken surface of stone. 'Nor I shan't be going against my conscience, either,' Burns added. 'She wouldn't have jumped, not if I know anything about it ... Well, so there we are. And we've come pretty well out of it, sir, don't you think?'

Mr Datchery rubbed the weals on his wrists. 'Firemen,' he said with a complacency which for once was not wholly unjustified, 'is what *we* ought to be.'

An hour later, and Helen Downing was alone in the drawing-room of Rolt's house by the mill.

It was one of the oldest houses in Cotten Abbas, and he had bought it along with the land on which the mill was built. The furnishing of the room in which Helen waited was opulent but unfriendly; clearly it was not much used. But Helen, exhausted, both physically and emotionally, as she had never been exhausted before, was in no mood to criticize. She lay back in a chair with her eyes closed, wondering if the day's shocks were ever going to end.

They had driven to the house after dropping Burns and Mr Datchery at the Brankham end of the village street. During the drive, Mr Datchery had spoken only once. 'All this must stop,' he had said quietly, and something in the tone he used had made Helen shiver . . . Penelope, dazed and silent, had been put to bed, had eaten greedily after her day's fast, had fallen, with Helen's nembutal to aid her, into a heavy slumber. Marjory Bonnet, the nurse, had been telephoned, found unengaged; she was upstairs in the bedroom now, would be there all night. And Rolt, whom the evening's events seemed to have aged by ten or twenty years, had gone off to wash, after begging Helen to remain and talk to him . . . The ormolu clock on the mantelpiece showed twenty minutes past ten, and with its drowsy ticking in her ears Helen sat relaxed – relaxed save only for the straining of her eyeballs beneath the closed lids as she strove to stay awake.

Presently Rolt reappeared, carrying a tray of drinks. His eyes were bloodshot and his shoulders bowed; all the aggressiveness had been drained out of him. 'We can do with something,' he said, 'after that. Scotch? Brandy?'

'Brandy, please.'

He poured brandy for them both. They sipped in silence, savouring the fierce warmth it gave. And after a while he said:

'Well?'

'Well what?'

'What's to be done?' He put his glass on a table beside him and folded his thick hands.

'If I tell you,' said Helen, 'you'll only –'

'Only snap your head off? No, lass, there won't be any more o' that. It seems I've managed to make a proper muck of it where Pen's concerned – so now I shall have to do what I'm told.' He stared at the carpet. 'Yes,' he reiterated vehemently, 'a proper muck of it, I've made. Though God knows, I meant it for the best.'

'People always do,' said Helen dully. 'They always do.'

There was a silence. Then, with an effort, he said:

'But you still haven't told me –'

'No, I haven't. I should have thought you could have guessed.'

His face went very white. 'You don't mean a – some sort of a mental home?'

'No!' Helen sat upright, battling against the inertia which was creeping over her. 'Of course not! What I meant –'

'One o' these psychiatrists, then? I've always thought of Pen as being a healthy normal girl like all the others, but now –'

'Of course she's healthy,' said Helen. 'Of course she's normal. And for heaven's sake get it out of your head that she tried to commit suicide. She may have thought of it, but she didn't do it; I saw her fall, and it was definitely an accident.'

'Well,' he said obstinately, 'but she did think of it, didn't she?'

'Precious few people don't, at one time or another in their lives. And God knows, she had reason enough.' Helen leaned forward earnestly. 'Let me just remind you of what she's been through in the past day or two. You told her she wasn't to see her young man. You – you beat her when she did see him. Then she came on his murdered body in a place where – which seems to have had some – some sentimental association for her. And then, eavesdropping, she overheard an interview which convinced her that her father had written a cowardly annonymous letter and caused a suicide by it. All that against a background of loneliness and adolescence, combined, according to you, with physical trouble of a sort which at her age can be horribly worrying ...

'But the worst thing of all, I need hardly tell you, has been your crazy vendetta against everyone else in the village. Oh, she was loyal enough, believe me – but of course *that* was bound to make her doubt you. And if she hadn't secretly doubted you she'd never for a moment have believed that you wrote that letter to Beatrice Keats-Madderly, or any of the other anonymous letters. No, she doesn't need a psychiatrist, because she's not temperamentally in the least abnormal. What she does need is a new father.'

And Rolt winced, screwing up his face as if he were suffering actual physical pain. Then he said: 'I'd have the whole bloody mill pulled down if I thought it'd –'

'That's hardly necessary. In fact, it'd be downright idiotic. A little ordinary civility is all that's required.'

'Well, I dare say I might manage that.' He tried to smile. 'I'm a bit out of practice, but still ... Look, lass, you're sure, aren't you?'

'Sure about what?'

'Sure Pen's mind's all right. This suicide business ...'

'There isn't anything the matter with her,' said Helen, 'that you can't cure.'

Somewhere a telephone was ringing. Rolt hesitated, got to his feet, and lumbered out to answer it. In two minutes he was back.

'Colonel Babington,' he said. 'Wants us both at his house as soon as we can get. Summat in the way of a show-down, I gathered.'

Helen was mortally tired; she had had enough, and more than enough. But she knew it was impossible for her to stay away. Somehow she must see the day through to whatever its end might be. She stood up.

'I don't like leaving the girl,' Rolt was saying, 'but –'

'She'll be all right. She won't even wake.'

They faced one another across the room; and: 'I've been a sight luckier,' he said abruptly, 'than I deserve.' Their eyes met, and for the first time there was sympathy between them.

'Well, Duchess,' said Harry Rolt, 'this is it.'

CHAPTER 16

In the Chief Constable's study the curtains were drawn against darkness. To ward off the late-evening chill a small fire had been lit, and the cat Lavender, asleep in front of it, twitched his whiskers ferociously as he chased mice or Martians through the dim corridors of dreamland. The firelight was reflected in the glass fronts of the bookcases, in the silver necklace-labels of the decanters, in the green-varnished metal of the big filing-cabinet. There were roses, yellow ones, on the roll-top desk; the brass andirons gleamed with a rich butter-colour; the lamps had large, old-fashioned shades. Ever and again an edge of the carpet would stir as the great wind outside crept secretly, through a dozen holes and crannies, into the old house.

Bulking large in his blue uniform, Constable Burns stood on guard just inside the door. His presence there was a reminder, had they needed it, that this was no social occasion. Across the room from him, beside the hearth, sat Inspector Edward Casby, gazing moodily into the clear young flames – Casby who on Helen's arrival, in company with Rolt, had got to his feet along with the other three men, but who had avoided her eye then and was avoiding it still. Mr Datchery, in impenitent possession of the best arm-chair, was reclining comfortably on the small of his back, his lean face tranquil, his ice-blue eyes almost closed, his brown hair standing up, as always, in spikes at the crown of his head. Near him, George Sims fidgeted with a pipe. Helen and Harry Rolt were on the fragile-looking sofa, Colonel Babington in the revolving chair by the desk. And it was Colonel Babington who was speaking now.

'I think you know why you're here,' he was saying brusquely. 'A decision has been reached as to the – the cause of our various troubles. And since all of you have been involved in them, either as witnesses or else in a – a more direct and personal sort of way, I thought it'd be only fair to let you know as soon as possible what that decision is. In the normal way, the police like to get a case thoroughly buttoned up before they say anything to anybody about it. But in view of what's happened already this evening' – his eyes flickered momentarily in Rolt's direction – 'it seemed best to keep you out of your beds an hour or two longer with a view to thrashing the thing out straight away.'

The clock on the mantelpiece chimed the quarter after eleven, like tiny gold droplets falling into a crystal jar. No one moved. With the tempo of her heart-beats quickening momently, Helen glanced at her companions' faces. Rolt's was outwardly blank – but with a native shrewdness lurking somewhere behind the eyes; Casby's, unreadable; Sims's grave, perhaps a little scared; Mr Datchery's very slightly impatient; Burns's, stolid and unmoved. But the wariness which had at first been in Colonel Babington's grey eyes now diminished for a time as he leaned forward to continue speaking.

'However, before we get down to that,' he said, 'there's a sort of – um – introduction I ought to make. You all know Mr Datchery.' The tone of Colonel Babington's voice suggested that he himself considered this fact to be not entirely to their credit. 'You may not have known him before this evening, but you can hardly have avoided *hearing* of him, because there hasn't been so much gabble in the village about a visitor since that wretched Dutchman came here in the first year of the war – the one everyone thought was a German spy ... Well, Mr Datchery is not, as most people seem to have imagined, from Scotland Yard. But on the other hand, his name's not Datchery, either.'

'That,' observed Dr George Sims, 'undoubtedly gets *my* prize for the year's most superfluous remark.'

He grinned uncertainly at Helen – a rueful grin in which she read an apology for his behaviour earlier in the evening. And perforce she smiled back. She was a little afraid of him now – since the unpredictable is always slightly scarifying – but his natural charm of manner still worked.

'It was I' – Colonel Babington had ignored the interruption and was forging determinedly ahead – 'it was I who asked him to come here in the first place. And of course, it's from me that he's been getting his information.' Suddenly the Colonel was aggrieved. 'What I forgot about,' he said irritably, 'was his mania for needless impostures. This "Datchery" business –'

Mr Datchery sat upright abruptly.

'Needless?' he said with much indignation. 'It was *not* needless. You yourself admitted –'

'All I admitted was a remote possibility that someone here might have heard of you.' The Colonel breathed heavily. 'And that if you used your own name, people might realize you were here for a particular purpose. But since, to the best of my knowledge, you've never made the least attempt to disguise the reason for your presence, you might just as well not have bothered.'

'It amused me,' said Mr Datchery more mildly. 'I grant you it hasn't been much practical use, but it's kept me happy, and it's done no harm. What *I* complain of –'

George Sims' brown eyes twinkled; he pressed tobacco into the bowl of his pipe.

'Well, you might put us out of our agony,' he said. 'Everyone in the village has been agreeing that you weren't what you seemed to be, but there've been the devil of a lot of different theories as to what you actually *were*. So do tell us now.'

'I,' said Mr Datchery rather smugly, 'am Gervase Fen.'

As a dramatic disclosure this was not a hundred per cent effective, for Rolt's reaction to it was to say bluntly: 'Never heard of you.' But 'Oh, I have, though,' said George Sims, all at once pensive, and 'And so have I,' breathed Helen, wide-eyed. 'I was talking to Alice Riddick on the phone, and she said –'

'Yes, I'm afraid I overheard that.' Gervase Fen, Professor of English Language and Literature in the University of Oxford, had the grace to look slightly uneasy. 'But look here – didn't you hear me announce myself when *I* was telephoning?'

'No, I told you, I missed the start of that.'

'Well, anyway, that's who he is,' said Colonel Babington, in the voice of a chairman who feels that the meeting is straying too far from the point. 'God help me, I've known him for years. And the thing about him is that on several occasions in the past he's helped the police to clear up one or two criminal matters, with the result –'

'I'll be damned!' said Fen. 'Of all the unscrupulous misstatements –'

'With the result,' the Colonel went on unruffled, 'that it was him I thought of when – when –'

He checked himself, remembering something. 'I say, Casby . . .'

'Go ahead, sir.' Looking up from his contemplation of the fire, Casby still avoided Helen's eye. 'Please go ahead.'

The Colonel did go ahead. But manifestly he was far from comfortable about it.

'Well, it was the letters, d'you see,' he muttered after a short pause. 'A fortnight of them, and they were playing the very devil in the way of suspicion and so forth, and we still hadn't a clue. Of course, one thing I could have done' – the Colonel's discomfort perceptibly grew – 'was to take Casby off the case and substitute someone else out of the county C.I.D. Or alternatively, I could have asked for help from London. But neither of those ideas appealed to me much. As far as London was concerned, the county'd have got a horse-laugh for not being able to cope with anything so – well, so ordinary as a go of anonymous letters. And as far as our own chaps were concerned, there wasn't anyone who was likely to get results where Casby had failed . . .

'Well, we've got our pride, I suppose.' Here the Colonel touched maximum embarrassment. 'Our C.I.D.'s as good as any C.I.D. in the country, and if I could help it I wasn't going to tout around publishing the fact that we'd struck a sticky patch, and couldn't get through it. So I thought I'd try a compromise.'

'Which worked.' This time Casby did not look up, and Helen sensed that he was fighting down the same sort of bitterness she had experienced in being outpassed, professionally, by George Sims. 'Which worked,' he reiterated, suddenly smiling. 'And splendidly.'

'Yes, Gervase has a taste for these problems, the Lord knows why,' said Colonel Babington, 'and perhaps a flair for solving them.' At this grudging testimonial, Fen snorted loudly. 'Anyway, he has, as Casby says, succeeded. Good luck to him, and we're grateful, though mind you, I think that in time we ourselves –'

'Of course you would,' said Fen quietly. 'I've been lucky, that's all . . .

162

'I say, Andrew' – he found and lit a cigarette – 'hadn't we better get on with it now?'

And with that the tension came back. Burns's boots creaked as he shifted his weight from one foot to the other. Helen could see Casby's muscles tighten under the old tweed suit, and beside her, Rolt moved his bulk to a less relaxed position on the sofa's edge. Of the seven people assembled in that room, Fen alone remained motionless. Rising momentarily from his seat, George Sims flung a spent match into the fire.

'Yes, let's have it,' he said.

The Chief Constable nodded. 'Go on, Gervase.'

'I'm afraid,' said Fen, in a certain tone of voice, 'that one of you is not going to like this very much.'

... And in that instant, Helen *knew*. There was a sense, she realized afterwards, in which she had known all along; but the knowledge had been buried deep in her subconscious mind, and until now she had only been very obscurely aware of it ...

'The letter,' she found herself saying, 'the letter which killed Beatrice ...'

From across the room Fen looked at her gravely.

'Yes,' he said. 'You're quite right. It was written, with intent to kill, by Dr George Sims.'

Wind rattled the panes, and the fire flared up suddenly. The cat Lavender stirred uneasily in his sleep. Getting slowly to his feet, George Sims said, in a voice that was not quite his own:

'Are you insane?'

His lips were dry, and he put out the tip of his tongue to lick them. 'Are you insane?' he repeated. 'Or is this some idiotic joke?'

Fen stared back at him dispassionately.

'No,' he said. 'I'm not insane. And you won't find it a very brilliant joke, by the time public opinion, and the law, are through with you. Morally, what you did was murder. The law can't get you for that, unfortunately, but I think we can still guarantee, my fine young gentleman, to make you wish you'd never been born.'

The law can't get you for that ... Helen understood then that what for a moment had seemed to be the end was only a

163

beginning. But the wheels were moving faster now, and there was no time to look ahead ... George Sims said quietly:

'You bloody *fool*.'

'In my time,' Fen answered without perturbation, 'quite a number of people have called me that. Most of them now inhabit prisons, or six foot of earth in a prison yard ...

'But since you apparently still don't believe I'm serious, let's look at the evidence.'

And Sims laughed. He dropped back into his chair.

'All right,' he said. 'If you're quite determined to make an exhibition of yourself, go ahead and do it.'

'Oh yes. Yes, I'm quite determined ... You know, the thing that's worried me most about this whole affair has been an envelope addressed in violet ink.'

Fen paused, drawing thoughtfully at his cigarette. 'Violet ink,' he went on presently. 'When Colonel Babington told me about that violet-ink envelope – as he's told me about everything else that's happened – I remembered vaguely that an acquaintance of mine had always used violet ink. And I worried, in the way one does, because I couldn't at first recall who that acquaintance was. But this evening, at long last, I did remember. A girl I'd known when I was an undergraduate had always used it, and very likely was using it still. That girl's name was Emma Paton; and if you know anything about books at all, you'll recognize it as the name of the best-selling novelist she's developed into.'

'Most impressive,' sneered Dr George Sims. 'You alarm me very much.'

Fen closed his eyes. 'Yes,' he said, 'I think I probably do ...

'Now, it would have been the purest coincidence,' he resumed, 'if Emma Paton's violet ink had had anything to do with the envelope which Beatrice Keats-Madderly received on Friday morning through the post, and in the normal way I probably shouldn't have taken the matter further. But as it happened, I had other reasons for being interested in that envelope. Let me tell you what they were.

'Between the time Beatrice Keats-Madderly looked at her post and the time Inspector Casby examined it, that violet-ink envelope

164

disappeared. It was not burned along with the anonymous letter which (presumably) it had contained – and there was no earthly reason why it should have been. And it was not to be found anywhere in the house.

'Therefore someone had obviously taken it.

'Of the people in Beatrice Keats-Madderly's house at the crucial period, Casby could be ruled out. If *he* had stolen the envelope – for whatever reason – he would scarcely have been wandering round drawing attention to its absence; that absence was a thing he could perfectly well, if he'd chosen, have concealed.

'That left, as suspects in the envelope mystery, Dr Downing, Dr Sims, Burns, Harris the hedger, and Moffatt the gardener. Could any of *them* be ruled out? Probably not, I thought. The thief might – since an envelope's not very difficult to pocket unobserved – have been any one of them. And motive? Well, it seemed obvious at first that the envelope must in some fashion be a tell-tale envelope, capable of giving something or somebody away; and that would mean that the writer of this particular anonymous letter had been careless, and was now covering up – or alternatively, that an accomplice was covering up on his or her behalf.

'Thus far, there was no conclusive evidence. But I did have a theory about that envelope – one of several, I may add – and on Sunday morning I went to Beatrice Keats-Madderly's house with a view to having a look at the house and seeing whether it fitted my theory. It did. It's a very symmetrical house, and the letter-box is in the exact centre of the front door. Which means that a man ostensibly knocking at that door could easily slip a letter in without being observed.

'You see now what my theory was. All the other anonymous letters had come through the post. It was generally assumed that this one had come through the post also. But as it was different from the earlier letters in several other respects, there was no *a priori* reason why it shouldn't have differed from them further in being delivered by hand instead of posted.

'All this – I need hardly point out – was speculation and speculation only; there wasn't as yet a shred of evidence for it. I mention it solely in order to make it clear why, when the name Emma Paton occurred to me in connexion with violet ink, I decided that that lead must be followed up.

'Earlier this evening, then, I went round to Dr Downing's house – she being the person who had known Beatrice Keats-Madderly best – and asked who the dead woman's favourite author had been. "Emma Paton", I was told. All right. No doubt she's lots of people's favourite author. But that, of course wasn't going to stop me telephoning her to find out if by any chance she'd written to Beatrice Keats-Madderly in the last few days.

'And she had. Beatrice Keats-Madderly had sent her a fan-letter. You know the sort of thing. "*Dear Miss Blank, I do not usually write to authors, but I feel I must tell you how much I enjoyed your ... etcetera.*" Authors who get a lot of letters like that tend to have stock typewritten replies in readiness, but Emma, I remembered, was conscientious, and always answered them individually in her own handwriting ... Yes, she said, she had had a letter of that sort from a Miss Keats-Madderly living in Cotten Abbas. Yes, she had replied to it, and the reply had been posted from Manchester – where for some unknown reason Emma elects to live – on Thursday.

'Thursday.

'So it ought to have reached Beatrice Keats-Madderly on Friday morning – the morning of her suicide.

'And according to the postwoman, it did.

'You see, of course, what that means. It means that the whole of Beatrice's post on Friday morning was quite innocent.

'And *that* means – can only mean – that the anonymous letter was delivered at the house by hand.'

Fen paused to stub out his cigarette in an ash-tray. The room was like a sealed globe of silence inside a cocoon of wind. Helen could not trust herself to look at George Sims, but she could hear his rapid, shallow breathing close beside her.

'Delivered by hand,' Fen repeated. 'Well, and by whom?

'Let me be a little inexorable about this, because I don't want any doubt to be left in anyone's mind when I've finished.

'The postwoman could have delivered that letter, but she

166

could not have stolen the violet-ink envelope. She, therefore, is out.

'Moffatt the gardener could have delivered that letter, but it's scarcely credible that, knowing what Harris's evidence would be (they had plenty of time to talk about it), he would then incriminate himself by swearing that no one had approached the house from the back.

'*Mutatis mutandis*, the same argument applies to Harris.

'And that leaves just one person. Dr George Sims.

'He and he alone approached the house that morning – on a professional visit which he intended to combine with a little message-bearing. If you're concerned to defend him you can say, of course, that the letter arrived during the night, or some time in the early morning, before Harris and Moffat took up their positions at the front and back of the house; that Beatrice didn't bother to open it till she got back from Twelford. Perhaps. But in that case, *why was Emma Paton's letter removed?*

'There's only one hypothesis, you know, which will explain that. Summoned, as police-surgeon, to examine the body of the woman he had driven to suicide, George Sims was unexpectedly confronted, when Harris and Moffatt gave their evidence, with a very alarming situation. The anonymous letter had been delivered by hand – a fact which interrogation of the postwoman would soon discover, even if the unstamped envelope in which it came were not found; the house had been watched; and the watchers were ready to swear that only Sims and the postwoman had been anywhere near it during the relevant period. At whatever cost, then, it must be made to seem that that letter had arrived through the post – and three of you may remember what I've only been told, that towards the end of the interview with Moffatt and Harris Sims left the sitting-room, returning a little later to announce the arrival of the postwoman. What, during that interval, was he doing? Plainly he was looking through the morning mail – postmarks would assure him it was that – which lay still unexamined on the hall table, in search of an envelope in which it might colourably be assumed, by the authorities, that the anonymous letter had come. Anything liable to result in further correspondence he would naturally have to reject, since the senders

167

would be only too liable to come forward, when the facts were published, and claim that their letters must have been among the ones Beatrice received that morning. But just as it happened, Emma Paton's letter was perfect for his purpose: it obviously neither expected nor desired a reply. He would take that, then. The envelope would have to be taken as well, since if it were not, if a photograph of it appeared in the papers, if Emma Paton came forward indignantly to claim it as hers, he would only be back where he had started from, in a very equivocal position indeed. And, of course, he would also take the envelope in which the anonymous letter really had been delivered – that's assuming that it was in fact delivered in an envelope, though it needn't have been.

'That's it, then. Unless Emma Paton is lying – which is inconceivable – my explanation is the only possible one. If you can think of another, produce it by all means. But I don't imagine you'll be able to.'

Fen stopped. And Helen saw George Sims's eyes flicker as he glanced first at the curtained window and then at Burns, burly and intensely watchful in front of the door. A great deal of the colour had already gone from George Sims's cheeks, but he was not giving in yet. As Helen stared at him, two pictures recurred to her mind – pictures whose incompatibility ought to have struck her long ago: George Sims white and shaken after inspecting Beatrice's body: and George Sims jaunty and unperturbed after inspecting Rubi's. Yes. He had known Beatrice and he had not known Rubi; Beatrice's body, in death, had been ugly, Rubi's had not. But the discrepancy in George Sims's reactions had still been far too wide. I ought to have guessed just from that, Helen said to herself: I ought to have guessed just from that . . .

'Very pretty,' he was saying now; and he squirmed a little at the unvarying contempt in their faces. 'Very ingenious. And where the hell, may I ask, do you imagine I can have come by the *contents* of that letter?' His head jerked towards Rolt. 'He, I was given to understand, was the only person in the village who knew anything about Beatrice's birth. And he's never told anyone. Not even me.'

Rolt nodded. 'That's right, lad. You may as well take what comfort you can, while you can.'

Fen flicked his fingers impatiently. 'As to that, of course Beatrice told you herself. But without intending to. She'd had measles, shortly before she committed suicide. Her temperature had been very high. She'd been delirious – and I didn't rely on hearsay for that: I questioned the nurse who'd looked after her, and got an answer in spite of all her professional discretion. Well, people when they're delirious rave, and say things they wouldn't dream of saying in their right senses. I think that Beatrice in her delirium talked about her childhood. I think she was coherent enough for you, attending her as her doctor, to be able to put two and two together and investigate further. That, no doubt, was how you knew she was illegitimate. But even if we can't prove that, it won't make any difference. There's quite enough evidence against you without it.'

Sim's colouring was yellowish now and ghastly. His fingers trembled as he pretended to concentrate on the tobacco in his pipe. But he made one last attempt to break out of the net which had tightened round him.

'Well then, why?' he snarled. '*Why* should I send Beatrice a letter like that? What did I have to gain from it, for God's sake?'

'Her death,' said Fen.

'You knew her well enough,' he went on, 'to realize that when she got such a letter she might – just *might* – take it so seriously as to kill herself. If she didn't – well, nothing was lost, even if nothing was gained, either. Of course, you could probably have blackmailed her, but I think you were too cowardly, without even the courage of your disgusting motives, to try that. You've been very, very cautious, haven't you, all along?

'No, you preferred to have her dead. Because you knew who was going to get her money when she did die. And it seemed to you a great pity that that money shouldn't find its way somehow into your pocket.'

Helen half rose from the sofa as understanding came. 'You mean –'

'Oh, yes. The ladies all adore him, you know. In the three days I've been here I've heard that fact retailed often enough to last me

169

a lifetime. He really thought he could have any one of them he chose. He was certain he could have you, together with Beatrice Keats-Madderly's money, for the asking – so certain, that for the sake of being secure from any possible suspicion – he's a great one for looking after his own skin, is Dr George Sims – he felt he could afford to wait, before approaching you with his irresistible proposal, until after Beatrice Keats-Madderly was dead. Yes, he's been very devious, very careful. There's not a great deal we can do to him, in the courts, even now. But we can and shall get him struck off the register. We can and shall make his name stink to high heaven.'

Helen laughed – a bitter laugh, but an antiseptic one too.

'Well, well,' she said. 'No wonder he took it so hard.'

Fen raised his eyebrows. 'Took what so hard?'

'My turning his proposal down, earlier this evening – just before you arrived at my house, in fact. All that trouble to get Beatrice's money into the pocket of a nice malleable little fool, and then he finds she's got herself engaged to someone else.' Helen laughed again – this time with real amusement. 'Yes,' she said, 'he *did* look sick . . .'

And that was when George Sims moved, scrambling out of his chair to run to the windows, thrust the curtains aside, and wrestle frantically with a tight-fitting latch. In three effortless strides Burns had reached him. Sims swung round, panic-stricken, doubled his fist, and drove it straight at Burns's face. He was in fine physical condition, and if the blow had connected, Burns would have been felled. But it did not connect. Burns's training had not all been theoretical. George Sims screamed as his arm was twisted up behind his back, went limp. 'Don't,' he sobbed. 'Don't . . . I'll – let me go and I'll do anything you want. I can't stand pain, can't stand it, I tell you . . .'

The voice diminished to an incomprehensible whisper. Unimpressed, Burns looked inquiringly at Colonel Babington. 'Should I take him away, sir?' he asked.

'No, bring him back to his chair,' said the Colonel with disgust. 'He may as well stay till the finish. And next time, if he tries anything on, you can hurt him a little.'

Cursing under his breath, with tears of self-pity in his eyes –

tears such as Helen had seen once before that evening – George Sims was brought back among them. But Helen had now no attention to spare for him. 'The finish?' she echoed. 'You mean –'

'I mean,' said Colonel Babington, 'that there are still the other anonymous letters, and the death of the schoolmaster, to talk about.'

'Did the same person –'

'Yes, the same person was responsible for both.'

Rolt said suddenly: 'And that – that butchering maniac's here?'

'He's here,' said Gervase Fen.

At Burns's back the study door was flung open. Sybil, the Babingtons' diminutive maidservant, appeared in the doorway, her eyes gleaming with suppressed excitement, and there was another figure behind her in the obscurity of the hall. For a moment, Sybil, in the immensity of her emotion, could do no more than stammer. Then she spoke.

''Ere's the butcher, sir,' she said.

CHAPTER 17

BLACK-GARBED, stooping a little, a fixed smile on his rather
equine face, Amos Weaver stood blinking in the dazzle of the
lights. The lenses of his horn-rimmed glasses glittered as he inclined his head. His sallow complexion was slightly mottled from
the wind. The black hair on his wrists showed below the cuffs.
And when he spoke, they could see muscles move in the long neck
projecting from the stiff white collar.

'I received a message,' he announced after a fractional hesitation, 'asking me to come here.'

Colonel Babington nodded.

'Sit down, Weaver,' he said quietly. 'We've got things to talk
about.'

Weaver's eyes shifted slowly, warily, from face to face. Treading with cat-like softness, he came forward and settled on the edge
of the only unoccupied chair.

'I think,' the Colonel went on, 'that you know everyone here –
oh, except perhaps Professor Fen.'

Weaver stood up immediately, extending a large hand towards
the armchair in which Fen still lay sprawled.

'An honour, sir,' he said, 'and a privilege.' But Fen made no
attempt to take the hand, and after an uncomfortable pause
Weaver withdrew it and sat down again. 'I believe,' he said
presently, 'that I saw you among our congregation this morning.'

'You did.'

'And you will have benefited, if I may be so bold as to suggest
it, from our simple little service.'

'I found it,' said Fen dryly, 'informative.'

With some difficulty, Burns had coaxed a slightly over-
wrought small maidservant out of the room, and was now once
again straddled across the doorway. George Sims, indifferent to
everything except his own plight, sat nursing his wrenched
shoulder, his features blank with terror, the tear-stains on his
cheeks shiny like the tracks of snails. At Helen's side the steady
wheezing of Rolt's breath never quickened, never varied.

'Informative,' Fen repeated, 'though at that time I wasn't, of course, aware of your being a murderer.'

Weaver said nothing. Nor did his expression alter.

'Our problem,' said Fen almost didactically, 'has been this. Time of death, between six and eight this morning. Weapon, quite certainly a butcher's steel, which, equally certainly, was locked up at the moment of the murder in Dr Downing's garage. If you put it as simply as that, and assume Dr Downing's innocence, then there's only one answer you can possibly arrive at: the time of death is wrong.'

Helen stared at him. 'But – but three of us –'

'Just wait a moment. Let's assume – as in fact we've got to assume – that Rubi was killed some twenty-four hours earlier than we've believed so far. Is there any evidence to conflict with that assumption?'

'Yes, there is,' Rolt interposed. 'There's my girl met him some time yesterday. Told me so herself, knowing damned well it'd rile me – so she'd hardly have made it up.'

'But she did make it up, I'm afraid.' Fen smiled. 'A Gesture, she called it, and I can quite see her point of view. If you're firm with anyone that age, and tell them not to do a thing, you can rely absolutely, provided it isn't an immoral thing, on their doing it. The trouble in your daughter's case was that she *couldn't* do it, since Rubi had told her he was going off yesterday on a long hike. But to show her independence she *said* she'd done it – that being the next best thing.'

'Well, I'm –!' said Rolt, using a word which is respectable in the United States and tolerable in the north-country, but which has not so far gained admission to many of the drawing-rooms of the south. 'The little devil! You can't help but admire her for it, though, can you?' Then he reflected, and his brow darkened. 'Look here, Professor Fen, you seem to know the hell of a lot about Pen's goings-on. How –'

But Fen waved this aside. 'People confide in me,' was his only explanation. 'Never mind that now. The point is that our assumption about the time of death still stands. And the more you look at it, the more plausible it seems.

'Just consider.

'Rubi hadn't any duties at school yesterday – that's the first thing. The woman who looked after him didn't go to his house on Saturdays or Sundays – that's the second. He got his milk from tins, so that bottles wouldn't pile up significantly on his doorstep – that's the third. The postwoman hasn't been to his house since Wednesday – that's the fourth. His house is isolated, so that there would be no one to see him come and go, or not come and go – that's the fifth. And no tradesmen deliver there – that's the sixth.

'It's quite *possible*, then, for the time of death to be wrong.'

Helen could contain herself no longer. 'In that sense it's possible, yes,' she said. 'But from the medical point of view it isn't possible at all. *One* doctor might make a mistake over that. But when it comes to *three* . . .

'Listen. Rigor mortis usually starts about three hours after death, in the jaw-muscles. In the two hours following that it spreads down the body to the legs, and in eight to twelve hours after death it's usually complete. In summer weather the rigidity lasts thirty-six hours or so, and then disappears in the order it appeared in, from the jaw downward. Of course, there are certain variable things you've got to allow for, but it's really out of the question that there's been a mistake of as much as twenty-four hours. So –'

'Certain variable factors,' Fen echoed her dreamily. 'Such as what, for instance?'

'Well, heat. That speeds the process up. And cold slows it down.'

'And refrigeration?' Fen enquired blandly.

'Refrigeration? Well, that – that –'

'That,' Fen supplied, 'delays the onset of rigor mortis for just as long as ever you like.'

Helen was staggered. 'Yes!' she whispered. 'Yes! What – what blind idiots we've all been . . .'

'It did seem,' said Fen apologetically, 'to be the only possible answer. Put your corpse into cold-storage immediately after death, and it will stay limp for as long as it's frozen. Then lay it out in the sun to thaw, and as soon as the thawing is complete, rigor mortis will get going in the normal way, thereby causing otherwise reliable doctors to go wildly astray in their estimates of the time of death.

'Once you'd grasped that that was what had happened to Rubi – and if anyone has an alternative explanation to offer, I shall be gratified to hear it – then, of course, it wasn't very difficult to deduce the identity of the murderer, because very few people have cold-storage rooms on their premises sufficiently large to admit a man.

'But now let's leave that for a moment, and go back a bit.

'One of the very first things I heard about your anonymous letters was that they were made up of words and letters cut out of "*lots of different newspapers*". And that interested me considerably, because there are precious few households which buy newspapers in quantity. On the other hand, there are several sorts of businesses which do: newsagents, obviously; and butchers and fishmongers, for wrapping purposes. Those, by the way, are probably the "three kinds of business" Rubi was referring to in his diary. The conjectural fourth that he had in mind was very likely a greengrocery.

'Now, the anonymous letter-writer was clearly an inhabitant of Cotten Abbas: no one but an inhabitant could possibly get to know so much scandal about the other inhabitants. It seemed reasonable, then, to inquire what businesses there were in the village which would involve newspapers. There was no newsagent, I found, nor any fishmonger. But there certainly was a butcher. It was conceivable, I thought, that someone living in the village kept or worked in such a shop elsewhere, so I inquired about that, too. Apparently there was no one.

'All of which was just sufficient to make me mildly interested in Weaver – though as serious evidence it certainly didn't mean much, and I'm not pretending it did. I made a few casual inquiries about Weaver. This morning I went to hear him preach. And as a result of all that, I came to certain conclusions about him.

'There have been two sorts of anonymous letter: the first sort pornographic, the second sort mischievous. Given a certain kind of mental kink – which is to be pitied rather than blamed – anyone might write the first sort of letter. But the second sort suggested a grudge against the community, and the existence of such a grudge – *or at least of good cause for it* – can't easily be concealed. And did Mr Weaver have cause for a grudge against the community? Heavens, yes!

'In working all this out, I naturally wasn't ignoring other people. Mr Rolt, I learned, had a grudge against the village too, since its better-to-do inhabitants had done their damnedest to prevent him putting up his saw-mill. But *he* had a remedy: he could, and did, express his resentment openly and in no uncertain terms. For Weaver, who had suffered in very much the same way, there was no such remedy. Once he started openly expressing resentment, he'd be out of business.'

Colonel Babington stirred uneasily.

'"Suffered in very much the same way"?' he said. 'That's one thing I don't quite see.' Out of the corner of his eye he looked uncertainly at Weaver. But that lean, black-clad figure, balanced with folded hands on the edge of the chair, remained mute, immobile, expressionless as before.

'In very much the same way, yes.' Fen lit a new cigarette. 'You people here seem of recent years to have had two hobbies. One was trying to prevent Rolt's mill being put up. And the other was trying to get Weaver's chapel pulled down. I've no doubt that in both cases your motives were excellent. But you could hardly expect either of the intended victims to appreciate them. In one case, money was at stake. And in the other, something even more important than money.

'I mean religion.

'Now, in my opinion, Weaver isn't, except perhaps in a very superficial sense, a hypocrite. I've listened to a good many preachers in my time, and I think that by now I can distinguish between those who preach for show and those who preach from conviction. Weaver this morning was preaching from conviction. His religion is sincere. And once you realize that, then this gay, aesthetic-minded attempt to raze his chapel begins to appear in a new and less carefree light. To him, the mere threat of it must have been unspeakably dreadful. And the worst of it was that in order to keep his head above water he was obliged, in his everyday business, to be obsequious to precisely those people who were plotting – as it must have seemed to him – against the thing he reverenced. Can you really wonder that that situation should engender hatred?

'Weaver, then, had newspapers – "lots of different newspapers". And he had better reason than anyone else I knew of for using them in the way they were being used. Thus far, conjecture only. But then came the murder of Rubi, and that really did give the game away.

'I needn't go over the evidence again. That point about refrigeration and the onset of rigor mortis seems to me pretty well conclusive in itself. Weaver alone, in this village, has a cold-storage room large enough to contain a man – and it's hardly likely that he'd have put Rubi in it just to oblige a friend. But there's one other thing that's worth considering, and that's the weapon.

'A butcher's steel.

'No one seems to have found the use of a butcher's steel particularly surprising. But I must say, I did – or rather, I would have done if I hadn't suspected Weaver of the murder already. Suppose you're an intending murderer, and you want to stab someone, and you don't possess a weapon. What do you do? Well, I'll tell you one thing you *don't* do: you don't go around *looking* for a *butcher's steel*; you look for something like a dagger. But if, at the moment when the murderous impulse seizes you, there happens to be a butcher's steel ready to hand, then . . .' Fen gestured expressively. 'In other words, the use of that particular weapon suggested convenience, not choice. And that, of course, was yet another pointer in the same direction.

'Here is how I think it must have happened:

'By thinking about newspapers – in much the same way as I thought about them – Rubi became interested in Weaver. As we know, Rubi was an amateur psycho-analyst, and it's obvious from his diary that he was smitten with the idea of enlarging his practical knowledge of that science, in its psychiatrical aspect, by a talk with whoever was writing the anonymous letters. Some time yesterday morning, then (I suspect fairly early), he went to Weaver's shop to do a little probing. And they must of course have been alone there together. As to what was said at that interview, one can only guess. But what *happened* is perfectly clear.

177

What happened was that Weaver, thinking himself discovered in good earnest – in spite of the fact that there was no real evidence against him whatever – lost his head.

'I do not believe that this was a deliberate murder. I believe it was a panic murder. And when I think of the cold-blooded scheming of the other gentleman we've dealt with this evening, the disparity between the penalties they'll get makes me feel slightly sick. But in either case the result was the same: a body. And unlike Dr George Sims, Weaver had somehow to dispose of his. To attempt to remove it from the house in broad daylight would have been impossibly risky. So temporarily he hid it.

'The refrigeration business can't have been design. The explanation of it, quite simply, is that the cold-storage room happened to be the nearest convenient hiding-place – Weaver has no wife and no assistant, remember, so that he was in a position to keep a whole charnel-house in his cold-storage room, if he felt like it, without anyone's being the wiser. Exactly what happened to the *steel*, after the murder, I can't say – and since up to a point I feel a certain sympathy for Weaver, I advise him not to make any statement about that, or about anything else, except in the presence of a solicitor: he may as well take advantage of what few chances he has got ... The steel may in fact have been subsequently stolen by children, as he told Burns. Or he may have felt an irrational impulse to rid himself of it as soon as possible – murderers occasionally do. Whatever the truth about that may be, the steel eventually came by chance into my hands, and from mine into Dr Downing's; and the rest of its history we know.

'I've admitted to feeling a certain sympathy for this man. But now I must qualify that. When he first came in, I refused to shake hands with him, and I had what I consider a good reason for that refusal – a reason I shall remember if ever I should be inclined to fret about his hanging. Because, you see, the thing he did next was gratuitously mean and spiteful. He had to get Rubi's body off the premises; under cover of last night's darkness, with the aid of his delivery-van, that presented no serious difficulties. But you all know where, of the many places he might have chosen, he eventually elected to put it. He elected to put it in a place which,

178

according to the local scandal-mongers – and on the evidence of the letters, Weaver must have had a good deal to do with them; this Mrs Cuddy I've heard of was doubtless a rich source – in a place which according to the scandal-mongers Rubi and Penelope had used as a *rendezvous*; a place where he had reasonable hopes of Penelope's finding the body, as in fact she did. That can't have been just coincidence; it was wilful, and it's largely because of it that I'm stating the case against him with a certain gusto . . . Well, the rest's obvious. The body thawed – its thawing aided, when daylight came, by the fact that the glade in which it lay was open to a hot sun; the normal processes of dissolution set in. And so forth.

'That's my indictment, and there's only one alternative to it – I mean the theory that Helen Downing is guilty. As to that, all I can say is that if she's guilty, she's also quite loopy, because every time she's opened her mouth she's said something to incriminate herself. I personally don't believe murderers do that sort of thing; if any different possibility exists, that possibility is obviously the truth. And as I've shown you, a different possibility very definitely *does* exist.

'There are detectives at Weaver's shop now; they'll stay there till they find the human blood they're looking for in the cold-storage room and the delivery van – and blood-group analysis is such a fine art these days that they'll be able when they find it to be quite certain about whose blood it is. In conjunction with what I've told you, that, I think, will fix him.'

There was a long silence when Fen had finished speaking. Physically and emotionally, they were all exhausted. A log collapsed in a flurry of sparks. The cat Lavender stretched, licked perfunctorily at a paw, began gazing about him with large and speculative eyes. Casby, who of all the people there had spoken the least, remained like a man in a trance.

But none of these things interested them. With the exception of Casby and of Sims, still fathoms deep in his self-pity, they were all looking at Weaver.

His taciturnity, his lack of expression and his immobility had a hypnotic effect, so that you began to wonder if he were conscious of anything that had been said. When at last he got to his feet –

slowly and painfully, so that for a moment they were all off guard – he was like a man drugged.

And then he moved.

He moved not, as they might have expected, in the direction of the door or the windows. Instead, he ran to Colonel Babington's desk, before anyone could hope to stop him, and pulled a drawer open. And in his hand, when it emerged from the drawer, there was a loaded revolver.

They learned later that he must have seen it there more than a month before, when he had visited the study to discuss a possible error in a bill. But however he may have known it was there, he had it now, and that was all that seemed to matter. With the exception of Rolt, they were all of them standing by the time he backed towards the windows. They saw him fumble, still watching them, at a catch, saw him loosen it. Then they saw his eyes change when the window failed to open.

'No use, Weaver,' said Colonel Babington. 'I took the precaution of putting the shutters up. Now, be a sensible fellow, and ...'

But Weaver was not listening. He was looking at Constable Burns, who was between him and the door, and the movement of his head was as plain and as unequivocal as speech.

Burns stayed where he was.

'By the time I've counted three,' said Weaver. 'One.'

Burns's eyes glazed a little, but still he stayed where he was. 'Two.'

'Get away from the door, Burns,' said Colonel Babington quietly. 'That's an order. Even if he escapes from the house, he can't possibly –'

In Burns's powerful body not a muscle stirred. It could have been courage; it could have been simple obstinacy. All Helen knew, through the black mists of her fear for his safety, was that it was somehow splendid.

'Three,' said Weaver. The hammer of the gun jerked back as his finger squeezed the trigger.

'And this,' said Harry Rolt placidly, 'is where I take a hand.'

He heaved himself up out of the sofa. Tank-like, he moved across the room towards where Weaver stood, and the whole

180

magnificent reliability of the great county of Yorkshire was in his unfaltering step. The muzzle of the revolver shifted in his direction.

'Keep your distance,' Weaver said.

'If there's any shooting to be done,' said Rolt without stopping, 'I'm the one to be at the receiving end. Young Burns is sticking to his post, and I admire him for it. But he's no more than a lad – so you can have a go at me instead.'

He was very close now, and still advancing. The gun in Weaver's hand pointed directly at him.

'I'm warning you for the last time,' said Weaver in a high, thin voice. 'Keep away.'

And with that, everything seemed to happen at once.

Looking back on it afterwards, Helen realized that without knowing it she had been aware all the time, in a remote corner of her mind, of what the cat Lavender was doing. To say that she had been in any sense attending to the goings-on of the cat Lavender would be a gross distortion of the truth. But she did (she remembered later) somehow contrive to notice that at the moment when Harry Rolt intervened, the cat Lavender was gazing thoughtfully up at the top of a bookcase against the wall behind Weaver's back. Perhaps two seconds later, it jumped.

So as Harry Rolt moved towards Weaver, the situation was this. On one end of the bookcase-top was the cat Lavender. In the middle of the bookcase-top was a very large and fragile empty porcelain vase. And at the other end of the bookcase-top, invisible to all except the cat Lavender, were a number of Martians.

Simultaneously with Rolt's advance upon Weaver, the cat Lavender began advancing on his interplanetary foes. Reaching the vase, which blocked his path, he paused uncertainly. But at whatever cost, Earth must be guarded from the depredations of her solar neighbours. Head high, the cat Lavender marched on.

The results were immediate.

With an unnerving crash, the porcelain vase fell to the floor. Practically instantaneously, Weaver fired – and the two sounds might almost have been one. Not quite, however. At the violence of that unexpected detonation immediately behind him, Weaver started – and that was just enough to deflect his aim. Certainly

181

the bullet hit Rolt – at so short a range it was scarcely possible to miss. The bullet hit Rolt and he was stopped by it as if by a blow from a hammer. But it only partly disabled him. Recovering his balance, he lunged forward while the echoes of the detonation still rang in their ears, and the acrid powder-smoke was still fresh in their nostrils. He fell on Weaver's gun-arm, twisted it. In the next instant Fen, Burns, and Casby were with him.

The gun-muzzle caught Fen a glancing blow on the temple, so that he collapsed on the floor in an indignant daze. And Rolt, now that his job was done, was down on his knees with his hand pressed hard against his side and the blood spurting out between his fingers. But the loss of two men hardly mattered: against the combination of Burns and Casby, Weaver had no chance whatever. The gun clattered on the bare boards. Handcuffs snapped shut. As she crouched beside Harry Rolt, Helen said:

'Ambulance. With any luck it won't be serious, but we must get him to hospital at once.'

After that, confusion. There were a few images which stood out: George Sims slumped in a chair with his hands covering his face; Weaver, sullen and speechless, being thrust out through the door; the cat Lavender, in a state of high alarm, getting under everybody's feet ...

And last but not least Colonel Babington, saying carefully to nobody in particular: 'I think that in view of all this excitement I might allow myself just *one* cigarette ...'

CHAPTER 18

At the bottom of Helen Downing's garden, on the side away from the churchyard, there was a straggling copse of trees – young beeches and birches, with bracken in drifts and scabious flowering among the bracken. Towards this, at teatime on the Monday, Helen walked out from her house with Inspector Edward Casby beside her. Last night's wind, tamed now to the mildest of mild breezes, blew warm in their faces. They walked preoccupied, aimless, without looking at one another.

To the inquest on Beatrice Keats-Madderly, held that morning in Twelford, Helen had not been, though of necessity Casby had. It had produced no sensations, no surprises. George Sims had given his evidence – medical evidence – with shaky bravado, and had then been returned to custody; he was to face the magistrates to-morrow afternoon. But the question of the authorship of the anonymous letter sent to Beatrice had not arisen, and such rumours of yesterday's happenings as had already leaked out were too vague and contradictory to influence the proceedings to any serious extent. On Wednesday, the same court would be considering the death of Rubi, and at that session Helen, as a witness, definitely would have to be present. In the meantime, she was grateful for a respite, grateful for the chance to refocus and re-examine her own personal problems. Not that it was possible to be in the least dispassionate about them, even now. In a situation like this, you took what came, hoping only that it would be better than you deserved ...

There were still a few late violets along the borders of the narrow gravel path. Afterwards, Helen could remember making some comment on them, though she never remembered what. Then the silence came back. They had been able, up till now, to talk of the inquest, of Weaver's attempted suicide during the night, of this and that detail left out of Fen's exposition the previous evening. But you cannot, in some situations, go on speaking of indifferent things indefinitely, and both of them were conscious, as they strolled constrainedly in the warm sunshine, that the moment had come when certain decisions must be made. It was Casby who spoke first.

'What,' he said abruptly, 'are your plans?'

They had reached the outposts of the trees. Helen halted, sick with apprehension, to stare back pointlessly at the house. In a voice that shook a little, she said:

'I – I'm afraid I was still hoping –'

And then she checked herself. It was not pride which silenced her, but rather the fear that he had not yet forgiven, perhaps never could forgive, her intolerable imputation of yesterday afternoon. 'I don't know,' she went on after a moment in a colourless voice. 'There – there hasn't been time to think about that. I suppose – well, I suppose I shall just carry on as usual.' She tried to smile. 'There's no competition now, is there?'

He did not answer that. But his eyes flickered, and she was suddenly dismayed to realize that he had been oblivious of her faltering – that he had even, it might be, interpreted her words as a dismissal. Panicking, she added:

'I don't mean that's what I most want. It isn't. I – I'd much rather –'

And then, with a supreme effort, she managed to cease this incoherent stammering and to ask the question which had to be asked.

'Are we,' said Helen Downing in the voice of a stranger, 'still engaged?'

They could hear the droning of the saw-mill, and the nearer droning of early bees. But in moments of crisis consciousness shrinks to a pin-point, and those sounds might have been on another planet for all the awareness of them they could show. At the bottom of the garden, close to the trees, they stood facing one another. Their acquaintance was not broad-based; on the plane of everyday communication they had scarcely met. And so they stood hapless for a time, each confronted with an alien being whose reactions he or she did not possess the experience to gauge.

'I haven't,' he said bitterly at last, 'been very bright. Not about anything.'

She waited, and presently, groping for the words, he went on:

'Last night, when Fen was talking, I don't believe I took in a quarter of what he said. Of course, by that time none of it was news to me, but even if ... No, the only thing I could think of was what a bloody fool I'd been. I ought to have thrown up the case the second it began to seem that you were involved in it. I ought to have asked you to marry me the day we first met – when you came to me with that letter. God knows, I wanted to enough. But no, I had to be cool and airy and knowledgeable, while all the time something inside me was screaming at me to grab you and kiss you and never let you go.'

Helen's eyes shone. But he was looking away from her, into the distance, and so failed to see it.

'This puerile shyness!' he breathed, grinding one clenched hand into the palm of the other. 'This shyness! I wanted desperately to see you again, but I was afraid. Afraid of making myself unwelcome, I suppose, and getting hurt ... But what an excuse! Good God, what an excuse for a man in love to have to make! That by itself ought to convince you that I'm not worth your while. And added to the other things –'

'Don't,' said Helen gently. 'Please don't talk like that.'

She put her fingers timidly on his arm.

'If you still want me,' she said, 'here I am.'

He turned his head slowly towards her. 'You mean,' he said incredulously, 'that in spite of everything, you'd still –'

'Provided *you*,' she answered him steadily, 'can forgive *me*.'

'Me forgive you?' He was genuinely startled. 'My dearest girl, what the devil for?'

She told him.

'*That !*' he exclaimed. 'So *that's* all you've been worrying about! Good heavens, girl!'

Helen hardly knew whether to laugh or cry.

'"All"?' she echoed him, deciding to do a little of both. '"All"? Really you are the – the most unspeakable *hypocrite* ... The next thing you'll be saying is that you'd forgotten about it.'

'But damn it, I had!' he protested with obvious truth. 'I remember *now*, of course, and I remember its annoying me at the time. But really ...! I say, do you know what I'm going to tell you?'

'W-why all the Irishry? No, I don't.'

'We *have* been a couple of imbeciles.'

'Yes.'

'Cloth-heads.'

'Yes.'

'Gawps.'

'What are gawps? Darling, what are gawps?'

He took her head in his hands and kissed her lips. 'I'm inclined to think,' he said judicially, 'that this spot is rather too – um – public to be suitable for communicating information of that sort. In among those trees, on the other hand – they being in full leaf –'

'Yes, but we mustn't forget Professor Fen's coming to tea.'

Later, Helen said: 'Darling, we *mustn't* forget Professor Fen's coming to tea.'

'No,' said Inspector Edward Casby with an air of gravity and decision, 'we most certainly must not.'

They then forgot about it immediately.

'Dr Sims!' Mogridge kept saying. 'Dr Sims – just think of it! And Weaver! Not that I ever trusted *him*, mind,' said Mogridge, who as a matter of fact had trusted Weaver implicitly. '"Never rely on fanatics, Mogridge" – that's what the Chairman of our South-eastern Regional Catering Sub-committee said to me once. "Never rely on a fanatic," he said. *And* he's a man who knows what he's talking about. Well, sir, it's all turned out for the best, in my humble opinion. The lark's in his heaven, the slug's on the thorn, as Lord Tennyson somewhere phrases it. And to think,' said Mogridge sycophantically, 'that I myself should have been entertaining an angel unawares!'

The angel unawares regarded him bleakly out of pale blue eyes. 'How you do go on, Mogridge,' it said. 'How you do go on.'

A train was due to leave Twelford for Oxford at 7.5. Fen had elected to catch this train rather than an earlier one in part because of Helen Downing's invitation to tea, in part because he was stiff and bruised from yesterday's adventures, and required time in which to recuperate, and in part because of a congenital incapacity for setting forth on any journey, however trivial, without hours of preparation beforehand. His appearance at the moment was sufficiently remarkable. Feeling a small patch of sticking-plaster on his temple to be an inadequate memorial of his share in the fight with Weaver, he had purchased a large bandage and wound it completely round his head, so that the effect produced was of something carelessly disinterred from an Egyptian tomb. Thus decorated, he left the inn to go and say good-bye to Colonel Babington, and the children emerging from school threw up their hands and shrieked loudly in mock-terror as he passed.

Colonel Babington proved to be in his shirt-sleeves amid a welter of ropes and ladders. The cat Lavender, it transpired, had carried its cosmic war up on the roof, and was now unable to descend again without assistance.

'He's really not much better than half-witted, you know,' said the Colonel sourly as he adjusted a ladder in readiness for the climb. 'But I suppose we can't just leave him there.'

He stubbed out a half-smoked cigarette against the wall of the house and then put it providently in his pocket. 'So you've started again,' said Fen rather coldly.

'Well,' said the Colonel, 'the way I look at it is this. I've proved now that I *can* give it up – and that's really all I set out to do. After all, it's not as if I couldn't afford to smoke, or had a wonky heart or anything. And I'll tell you another thing, giving it up was affecting my behaviour slightly. I wasn't quite my normal self.'

'No doubt,' said Fen even more coldly. 'I admire your moral resilience, I must say.'

Presently, feeling that from the social point of view little was to be gained from the spectacle of Colonel Babington crawling precariously up the tiles, he shouted his farewells – which were returned in a muffled, apprehensive voice from behind a chimney-pot – and set off to visit Helen Downing. There would be lovers' difficulties for him to compose, he suspected, and in addition, he thought he would take the opportunity of explaining the case to them all over again ... At Helen's front door he knocked and waited. From the kitchen of the adjacent house, where Melanie Hogben was talking murders with Mrs Flack, regular,

187

improbable-sounding laughter could be heard. After a pause, Fen knocked again, waited again. Nothing happened.

Prowling exploratorily round the side of the house, he came on a table laid for tea under a beech-tree, with deck-chairs grouped round it. It was laid for three, so apparently he was in fact expected. Not very actively expected, however, it seemed. Having scrutinized the back garden and found it wanting, he sat down in one of the deck-chairs, and after some minutes' uninteresting self-communion ate a cake with pink sugar icing on it. He had just finished this when, Mrs Flack being momentarily quiescent, he heard a laugh from the trees at the bottom of the garden.

It was a woman's laugh, low, unfeignedly happy and also (regrettable to state) slightly wicked. And Fen, enlightened, got to his feet, scowled in the direction from which it had come, and took several strides towards its source in a very grim and determined manner.

Then he stopped.

Well, after all ...

He returned to the table. He poured tea for himself and drank it while consuming a second cake. He appropriated three sandwiches to eat in the train. Then, with a single benevolent glance in the direction of the trees, he left the garden and walked back to 'The Marlborough Head'.

He was packing when Mogridge brought him his bill, and interrupted himself to examine the document in a rather minute and offensive way. 'I ought,' he said severely, 'to make a deduction on account of all these spiders I've had to share the room with. To the best of my knowledge you never made the least attempt to do anything about them.'

Mogridge contemplated the offending creatures with some attention.

'When I was a boy,' he said, 'we used to race them for marbles. It's a thrilling sport.'

Fen thought otherwise, and said so; but he had half an hour to waste before he need leave to catch his train, and he was as prepared to waste it in racing spiders as in anything else. It proved, in the upshot, to be a trying occupation in that the spiders' unreadiness to proceed at their briskest possible pace from starting-

188

point to winning-post required the formulation of a vast network of rules designed to cope with an almost illimitable number of contingencies – contingencies ranging from major mishaps (such as one of the competitors eating another) to the exacting problem of whether a pause in mid-career was to be ascribed to exhaustion, fear, or mere obstinacy. Moreover, Mogridge's propensity for cheating by prodding the runners with the point of a pencil a perceptible interval before shouting the word 'Go!' gave rise to a great deal of altercation and bad blood, as a consequence of which, having lost one pound five shillings and twopence to Fen, he retired from the course in a huff, leaving Fen to dispose of the competitors, single-handed, by putting them out of the window.

He returned almost immediately, however, to announce that Fen had a visitor. And having by now completed his packing, Fen took his bag and went, obedient to this summons, downstairs to the Lounge.

Penelope Rolt got up from the window-seat as he entered. Her narrow, pale, pretty face bore inevitable witness to the events of the day before, and her thin, stained fingers were still tremulous. But she smiled when she saw Fen, and the smile was in her eyes as well as in her mouth.

'I – I had to come,' she said. 'I heard you were leaving, so I had to come ...' Then she became aware of the bandage. 'I say, I never knew you were as badly hurt as *that!*'

Fen was much gratified by this novel reaction to his appearance. 'And how are you?' he asked.

'Oh, I'm all right. The only thing is –'

'Well?'

'I – well, you see, they haven't let me be alone, not since I – not since it happened, I mean. Miss Bonnet's outside now, and I had an awful job to stop her coming in and – and hanging about.'

'It's to be expected, you know,' said Fen gently. 'For a little while, anyway.'

'Oh, but it's absurd!' she burst out. 'Don't they realize that after last night I – I just *couldn't* ...'

'Yes, I think they do realize. But you can't scare us all out of our wits and then expect things to get back to normal again in twenty-four hours ... By the way, did you dream last night?'

She nodded soberly. 'Yes.'

'That too is to be expected. But it will certainly wear off in a week or two, so you're not to fret about it.'

Hesitantly, she said: 'I – I must thank you.'

'Must you?' said Fen cheerfully. 'I shouldn't bother about being grateful, if I were you. You've got quite enough to put up with without the addition of that. I hear your father's going on well.'

Her eyes lit up at that. 'Yes,' she said eagerly. 'He was rather marvellous, wasn't he? Everyone's talking about it, and all sorts of people have been to see him at the hospital, I mean people he hasn't been on speaking terms with, and he hasn't growled at any of them. Sir Charles –'

'Sir Charles?'

'Sir Charles Wain,' said Penelope with reverence; it was evident that in her view this innocuous baronet constituted a sort of one-man accolade. 'He was at the hospital this afternoon. He brought some peaches from his hot-house, and he and Pa stayed gassing for – oh, ages. So there's really only one thing that worries me now.'

'Oh? What's that?'

'Well, it sounds silly, but I'm worried about not being *more worried*, if you see what I mean. About – about Peter, I mean.'

She looked up at Fen in perplexity. And tonically remorseless, he said:

'In that case I should just stop worrying about not being more worried, and worry about something sensible instead.' Then he spoke more earnestly. 'In one sense you're very lucky, you know. It *might* have hurt.'

'Yes,' she admitted with youthful seriousness. 'I s'pose it means I didn't really care for him very much. And it's funny, but in a queer' – she struggled to find the right word – 'in a queer, *sideways* sort of way, I realized that all along.' Then suddenly she laughed, and from what she said next Fen knew that now she was almost grown up. 'Just a pash,' said Penelope lightly. 'So that's that, and as far as Pa's concerned ...'

'Yes?'

'Well, I *think*,' she told him, 'that perhaps things are going to be different, from now on.'

And Fen smiled at her.

'Yes,' he said. 'I think that very likely they are.'

And thus it came about that on the afternoon of Monday 5th June 1950, Gervase Fen (whilom Datchery), having deposited his week-end bag on a bus with the request that it be delivered, at the railway-station, into the hands of a reliable-looking porter, set out to walk the four miles which separate the village of Cotten Abbas from the market town of Twelford. The sun that Monday had risen in a tumult of wind; but at breakfast time the wind had dropped, and by midday the earth had once again begun to absorb and accumulate heat. To an *obbligato* of bird-song Gervase Fen marched beneath a mellow sky towards Twelford. And he carolled lustily, to the distress of all animate nature, as he walked.

'You shall wash your linen,' sang Gervase Fen, 'and keep your body white, in rain-fall at morning and dew-fall at night.' And the cattle, lifting their heads as he passed, lowed a mournful burden to the tune.